Expo City

A Police Story
By Grant Patterson

*Down these mean streets a man must go who is not himself mean,
and who is neither tarnished nor afraid.*

Raymond Chandler

APRIL

HEAD OVER HEELS

In April, 1986, Vancouver, British Columbia was enjoying the last moments of it's invisibility. A medium-sized port, nestled into the shadow of the Coast Mountains, the remnants of the great rainforests all around, it prepared to host a World's Fair.

Like all such events, Expo '86 would bring both wide-eyed visitors, and predatory parasites. One policeman whose specialty is the latter sits in wait, knowing one of the worst parasites is about to go free...

**THE GANDY DANCER
DOWNTOWN VANCOUVER**

**Detective Rick Grohmann
Drug Section
Badge #847**

Rick Grohmann was on duty, but he was actually enjoying his Friday night.

Sure, it was rainy as shit out there. It was April on the Wet Coast. Where Rick Grohmann came from, you'd be shovelling snow for another month before you got a break. Rain was just fine with him. He'd come out from Regina, a freshly minted Mountie, in 1975, and decided there was no way in hell he was ever going back.

Two tours in Cyprus had shown him what the sun looked like. Vancouver was no Cyprus. There were no crazy-assed Turks trying to blow your head off, for starters. But it was as close as you got in Canada.

Tonight, with the drinks comped (they all knew he was a cop), and the new wave tunes going (he'd never admit it, but he loved Tears for Fears), he could almost forget he was in a fruit bar.

Rick Grohmann hated a lot of things and a lot of people. Back in his patrol days, working the Fruit Loop, it was easy to hate the fags. Down there, they did disgusting shit. Like leaving condoms full of spooge on the locks the security guards had to secure every night to block the roads into the park, so the cruisers couldn't fuck each other senseless in there.

Back then, he'd beat the shit out of fruits on the slightest excuse, like his old partner Bevan Wayne, a two-fisted shitkicker of the old school. But here, now, fruits had their own space, which was cool with him. They kept to themselves, like the shines in a ghetto almost, and that was fine with him too. As long as nobody wagged their dick in his face, it was all good. And the bartenders were good about warning off would-be hustlers.

That cop's a psycho. He put Rudy Barnes in the hospital last year. Just let him do his thing and drink our booze. He's here for business.

Rick Grohmann knew his rep. He wasn't stupid. And he knew he was about as "undercover" as the entire 101st Airborne in a Lebanese village. No, what he was doing tonight was called "owning the turf." Another lesson Bevan Wayne had taught him.

Find where they like to frolic and go squat down there like it's your living room. Show them you're the POLICE.

Lately, Rick Grohmann had been spending a lot of time here, drinking watered-down Rye and Cokes. He was sure some assholes back at 312 Main were coming up with all kinds of salacious explanations for that. "Rick Grohmann, closet homo." Let them. If they ever said it to his face, which they never would, he'd calmly challenge them to three rounds in the Police Academy ring.

Nobody ever lasted more than two. Not even Barry Olds, his new Sergeant, who had a wicked right hook.

Rick Grohmann wasn't here for dick. He was here for Blotter.

That is, Neil "Blotter" Boorman. Rick had put him away for eighteen months, a chickenshit sentence considering how much smack and coke he'd been sitting on at the time. If Blotter got out, this was where he'd come first.

Why?

The Gandy was a straight-friendly queer bar. That meant a wide clientele. The queers found the trends, then passed them on like a case of AIDS to the fashionable straights. Plus, it was in Yaletown, a formerly shitty rummy area, newly attractive because of what was going up just two blocks away.

Expo '86. The Vancouver World's Fair. Man in Motion.

The ads said it, the politicians couldn't shut their fucking traps about it. The world was coming here, to the formerly sleepy, Protestant town, where the only fun to be had used to be in Chinatown, under red lanterns and opium haze.

Now, if Blotter Boorman, an LSD dealer who catered to fruits, made his parole like he was supposed to, Rick figured he'd check in here first to see what was trending.

And, since what was trending was a dope shortage so severe you couldn't even score a dime bag of weed on the Strip, that could get interesting. From what his contacts on the Waterfront told him, that was not a supply problem. That was dealers holding on until Expo opened, judging visitors would pay more.

All that dope, in all those dope houses. Prime targets for a ripper like Blotter.

Since Blotter had made biker friends in the early 80s, he'd learned two things: One was how to use violence to increase the size of his operation. The other thing was, how not to get his throat slit for ripping the wrong dope house. A *biker* dope house, that is. All Blotter needed was to get a crew, get some firepower, and put his ear to the street. That process started here.

If Rick Grohmann could stop him, it would earn him Sergeant's stripes, and a chance to get Clarissa off his fucking back about not making enough money.

So, he sat, and he waited, watching twirling shapes in the smoky gloom. Men, women, did it matter? He signalled the waitress for another Rye and Coke, tapping his toes as Roland and Curt sang *Head Over Heels*.

Something happens and I'm head over heels
I never find out till I'm head over heels
Something happens and I'm head over heels
Ah, don't take my heart, don't break my heart
Don't, don't, don't throw it away

A hand clamped down on his shoulder, hard.

"Do I know you?" A thick Scottish brogue came out of a mouth of broken teeth, topped with a mohawk. The face was right in his now, lager stink and smoky exhaust. "Do I fucking know you?"

Rick Grohmann knew that was Haggis Face's attempt at a pain compliance hold. But Rick Grohmann didn't feel any pain. "You're about to know me." He dropped his ass off the chair, grabbed Haggis Face by the lapels, and threw him in a judo toss head over heels.

I made a fire and watching it burn
Thought of your future
With one foot in the past, now, just how long will it last?
No, no, have you no ambition?

Haggis Face sprawled on the floor as the crowd began to part. Rick saw a fruit trying to skirt the fight with a bottle of Corona. He reached up, grabbed the bottle out of the man's hand, and hefted it.

It's hard to be a man when there's a gun in your hand

Oh, I feel so

Rick brought the Corona down hard over the crown of Haggis Face's skull, christening him like a battleship. Then, he bounced onto the heels of his shoes, and snapped fully upright, dragging Haggis Face with him.

Haggis Face's cover, a short, split-faced, red-bearded mick emerged from the shadows with a sap held high. Rick used Haggis Face as a human shield, then reared back with an almighty kick, and drilled the mick in the balls.

And this my four-leaf clover
I'm on the line, one open mind
This is my four-leaf clover

As the mick sagged on the floor like a punctured bagpipe, Rick reefed Haggis Face to his feet, dragged him to the exit, and kicked the door open into the alleyway.

Outside, it was damp and chilly. Two dykes sharing a joint stopped and stared. "As you were, gentlemen. Smoke 'em if you got 'em!"

The dykes huffed and quickly re-entered the bar. Haggis Face lolled in his arms. "Wait a second! I know you, you half-brained, pock-marked deviant! You're Donnie McCrae!"

"So...who's asking?" Haggis Face slurred.

Rick drove a knee into the man's guts. "Detective Grohmann of the Vancouver Drug Section, you ugly piece of kilt-wearing shite. So, who are you working for these days? Who sets you and your papist pal on an honest policeman enjoying a gay night out? Hmm?"

The knee reared again, but Donnie reconsidered. "Wait, wait, calm yerself." Both men's breath evaporated in the chill air. "This is Blotter's turf. He's out now."

"Ah, is he now?" The knee went back into Donnie's ribs. "Then say hello to him. And tell him I'll be here whenever I fucking want to be. I'm a cop. The whole city is my turf."

As Rick Grohmann walked away, leaving Donnie writhing in a mud puddle with the lights of Expo illuminating him, he could faintly hear another one of his favourites come on.

Nothing ever lasts forever
Everybody wants to rule the world

APRIL

JUDGEMENT CALL

Like so many other institutions, the Vancouver Police Department was being forced to change with the times in the mid-1980s. More women, and more minorities were joining the ranks. But the simple fact that the door was now open didn't mean walking through it was suddenly easy. And no edict from on high could change the brutal realities of the street...

GRANVILLE MALL

Constable Balwant Kaur "Bobbi" Sanghera
Badge #903

Bobbi stood in her too big anorak and too short skirt, soaked and freezing, feeling very alone on a street she'd walked so many times before.

She'd walked this street as a little kid, before it all went to hell in the seventies, when her aunt and uncle had a store three blocks west. She'd walked it as a PC, under the watchful eyes of trainers and NCOs. She'd walked it on her days off, an inconspicuous civilian, one among many.

But as she'd learned so many times since taking the oath in '83; she was only one of many shes. She was a different creature holding auntie's hand; walking a beat in full uniform; strolling and shopping as a respectable, and therefor untouchable civilian.

Now, Bobbi Sanghera was a desperate junkie, cruising for smack. And that put her in the very bottom drawer of humanity. Three years of police work had already taught her that.

Of course, she wasn't really what she appeared. Bobbi Sanghera was, tonight, the hidden spear point of a seven-person buy-and-bust team under the command of Barry Olds, the well-respected Sergeant who had hand-picked Bobbi for Drug Section, to the disgust of many more seasoned officers.

Barry had his reasons, reasons that sometimes made the first Indo-Canadian woman on the Vancouver Police Department very nervous. It was enough to be the first, she figured. But to be put on a pedestal? Sometimes she had no idea what Barry was thinking.

A cold, wet wind caught the seam of her skirt and almost lifted it up. Bobbi forced it down. She stood, for effect, in front of a sex shop, a place she dimly recalled her auntie yanking her past in days gone by. She closed her eyes, trying to remember Barry's Rules:

1. *No going off the strip. He has runners who bring the dope. If he wants you in an alley, it's for rape, robbery, or both. STAND YOUR GROUND.*
2. *Don't let them touch you! This wasn't a dealer vs dealer meet; no, this was a member of the public seeking a service. No way do you let them feel you up. You might need that 2-inch Chief in the belly holster, girl.*
3. *If they grab you, fuck the bust: Scream "Backup" at the top of your lungs!*
4. *Relax. We're thirty feet away, at the hotdog place across from the Commodore.*

She opened her eyes. And there he was, in front of her.

Bobbi sized him up, the way she'd learned on Patrol, and came away feeling skeevy. He was white, or maybe Native, hard to tell, with slack black hair, eyes looking two ways, fucked-up teeth. He was only a couple of inches taller than her, so that meant short.

But he had that look. That KFC look, Barry always called it.

Eleven herbs and spices. Yum yum.

The rain began to pound off the awnings again as the creep walked closer.

She decided to beat him to the punch. "You holding?"

He stopped and looked at her askance. Come to think of it, anyway he looked at anything would be askance. "Who's asking? You a pig?"

"You ever seen a brown lady pig?"

"Guess not. Yeah, maybe. But I don't have it here. Around the corner. Come with me." He grabbed her left arm in a tight clench.

"Hey, hey...fuck that! I know how it works. You send a runner."

"My runners are sick. I been busted ten times down here, ain't no fucking way I carry. You wanna stay sick, suit yourself." He let go of her arm and stepped in close. She willed herself to stay calm. He had that smell, that chemical, junkie smell they all had, like he was already dead, and nobody'd told him yet. "I can tell. You're sweatin' hard like it's August out here. You need to fix, momma."

Bobbi looked around as subtly as she could. If her backup team had really been alarmed, they'd have been on top of this shithead already. So, maybe it was time for what Barry always called "The Judgement Call."

"90% of police work is done within the rules, Bobbi." He told her one night when they were still on Patrol. "But 10% skates right on the edge, maybe even crosses it sometimes. That's often where the really good work gets done. I'm not talking about lying, or planting shit, no way. I'm talking about taking risks that might cost you your pips one day. But you'll get busts that make other cops think you walk on water. Especially in Drugs. In Drug Section, risks are what it's all about."

"You getting high, or getting wet, lady?"

"Okay. But hands off." The dealer made an exaggerated show of decorum and walked two steps ahead of her. She followed, nervously, doing a scan for followers. She wished devoutly that she had an earphone, but you couldn't use those on the Strip. That was the first thing dealers looked for, and if they saw one, you were a leper.

Bobbi had to trust herself. They entered the dark-as-a-colon alleyway. Two hypes tried to find a vein 30 feet down from them, in the light of a back entrance. Otherwise, just dumpsters and cats.

How the hell will they find me down here? Goddamnit!

"Over here, lady. Down here, come on, I ain't bringing it to ya." With leaden feet, she followed him past three dumpsters to a solid brick wall. A drainpipe poured a steady stream of water overhead. "Don't get no ideas. I only keep my ready stash here. The big load is a lot harder to find." He felt the wall, and pushed a loose brick, clawing it back towards him with too-long fingernails, crusted with dirt.

Bobbi was peering into the shadowy void left by the brick's absence. Then, the dealer turned, the brick in his right hand, raised to strike.

Victor Rollings. You're Victor Rollings. You did two years in Oakalla for knocking a policewoman's teeth out.

Rollings brought the brick down on her cheekbone, hard. Seeing white, she slumped, her back against a dumpster. She wanted to call for backup but couldn't find the words.

Rollings moved in, lupine, laughing. "Like my place? You're gonna like it just fine when I'm fucking you against that dumpster! You can even have a shower after!"

Bobbi shook her head, clearing her muddled brain, finding the .38 in her belly band, and wrenching it out hard. "Speak into the mike, asshole! Backup! Backup!"

Too late, Victor Rollings realized his victim was a cop. Bobbi was going to shoot him, but he was already halfway to dropping the brick.

She kicked out with her pointed boot, catching him in the ankle. As he was going down, she was pushing herself off the now-rolling dumpster.

Bobbi Sanghera swung the .38 hard, catching Victor Rollings in the temple, and dropping him on top of a massive loaf of shit. She heard running cops behind her.

Victor Rollings lay in a pile of shit, the flashlights of four cops painting him as he breathed shallowly. Barry Olds holstered his .38 and took Bobbi by the shoulders, walking her into the light.

"Ouch. He got you good, Bobbi." He dabbed at her cheekbone with a handkerchief. "Judgement call, huh?"

EMERGENCY ROOM
ST PAUL'S HOSPITAL

Sergeant Barry Olds
Badge# 710

Barry Olds watched the Friday night crowds come and go as the St Paul's Emergency Room filled to, and then past capacity. He idly wondered just how much of a policeman's career was spent in an Emergency Room. If he had to guess, maybe 5-7%?

Time spent getting yourself sewn up. Babysitting your partner, like he was doing now. Taking statements from the beaten, the nearly murdered, the raped. Waiting for the pathologist to slide that drawer open; the orderlies to reposition the body on that metal slab; the sucking sound of the cranial opening.

Cataloguing evidence; the belongings of the family wiped out on their way home from a birthday by a pissed-pants drunk; all hope for the future vanished.

Barry Olds was typically not given to such meditations. But lately, he found himself shaking his head vehemently more often, to drive the dark thoughts away. Pouring two scotches after work, instead of one. Yelling at his kids, instead of hugging them.

Last March had marked twenty years on the force for him. Twenty years of all the above, plus the good and the indifferent. In that time, he'd advanced exactly two ranks, and he was fine with that. A Sergeant's job had always been his dream, and after proving himself on Patrol in the touchy West End, he'd been given the plum job of running a shift on Drug Section.

Ask anybody who'd worked with Barry Olds what they thought of him, and they'd use the same phrase: "A cop's cop." For starters, he looked the part. Six feet one inches, ramrod straight posture courtesy of the Seaforth Highlanders, a thick, bushy moustache, and a preternatural calm born of generations of Irish cops.

When he was growing up, going to John Oliver High, there was no doubt what he would be. The other kids even called him "Constable." In the early 1960s, that was not yet an insult.

He had learned his trade the hard way, walking a beat on the Downtown East Side, as they called it now, "Skid Row," as they called it then. His mentor was the formidable "Whistling" Bernie Smith.

Whistling Smith was as hard on rookies as he was on hypes. Maybe more so. He was never afraid to mark down a man as "unsatisfactory" in his evaluations. The thing was, always, to hold the line. You had to prove back then that you could handle *any-*

thing by yourself. If you called backup for a one-on-one fight: chickenshit. If you pulled a gun for anything less than another gun: chickenshit. If you backed down from a man who needed his clock cleaned: chickenshit.

Barry Olds had proved early on that he was not chickenshit. He had passed both Police Academies; the formal one in Jericho, and the informal one on the corner of Main and Hastings. In later years, the VPD became less rigid, more forgiving. But he was secretly glad he had proven himself in the old ways.

He reminded himself to look up Whistling Smith soon. The blunt-talking old ex-copper was now the Premier's driver. Barry shook his head again. It was hard to picture Bernie biting his tongue around VIPs.

"They say I need to take a couple of days off." Bobbi Sanghera stood in front of him, holding an ice pack to her swollen cheekbone. "Sorry, Sarge."

He stood quickly, always uncertain of how to handle this one. She was so small. And he'd let her go into a dark alley with that degenerate Rollings. "Don't be sorry. You've earned a couple of days off. Let's get you home."

They drove in silence for a while. The streets were deserted, save all the most desperate and depraved. He looked at his watch: 0213. The specialty squads, the hot shots, were all doing shooters or watching their kids sleep by now. It was Patrol's city again.

Bobbi looked out at the rotoscoping streetlights as they drove over the Burrard Street Bridge. "Did I fuck up back there, Sarge?"

"No." He sighed as they drove past the Seaforth Armoury, where he'd been a cadet and a reservist, absorbing the stories of old heroes, men like Smokey Smith, VC, hoping he might one day be tested. Police work was as close as he'd ever get to the Moro River. "You did what I told you to do, remember?"

"Yeah, I guess."

"You took a chance, Bobbi. Next time, you'll do it differently. But you'll still take a chance. That's how good cops get things done."

She dabbed at her pummeled face. "If you say so, Sarge."

"Ah, fuck that shit! The reason I picked you for Drugs isn't just because you don't fit the mold! It's because you've had the whole world telling you you can't do it, and you've gone ahead and done it anyway! Look at me, Bobbi! Come on, look!"

She looked at him. "You look like a cop."

"Exactly. So, how much courage did it take for me to become a cop? None. My uncles were cops. My grandpa was a cop. I look like a recruiting poster. Now look at you. How much courage did it take you?"

She sighed. "A lot, I guess."

"The whole world tells you you shouldn't be here. And here you are. Don't give up. Not yet. Five years, and I'm gone. Somebody's gotta keep the barbarians at bay."

They drove on in silence. One cop wondering if he could last, the other wondering if she should even try.

APRIL
PERFORMANCE REVIEW

In any police department, there are inevitably "Street Kings," men whose performance on the street reveals a preternatural talent for the job. This talent, however, is almost inevitably balanced with a talent for trouble in the office. It takes a special kind of supervisor to manage a Street King like Detective Rick Grohmann, and right now, Sergeant Barry Olds is wondering if he's the man for the job...

VANCOUVER POLICE DEPARTMENT
312 MAIN STREET

Barry Olds was still recovering from his weekend and nursing his third lava-like coffee, chasing it with one of those delicious, orange-slathered Chinese buns from the bakery down the street. Then "Gentleman Paul" Selfridge let the file drop on his desk.

Barry could see the name on it. It was Rick Grohmann's file. "Ah, fuck it, Staff. This is how my Monday starts?"

Selfridge pulled up a chair. He was a tall and wiry grandfather type with a lingering smile, glasses at the end of his nose, and a talent for the bagpipes. He played "The Lament" at every funeral and could usually be persuaded to play "Danny Boy" if you really wanted a good blubber.

"The ferocious Detective Grohmann is your supervisory responsibility. And since Sergeant Kelly was urgently needed by Major Crimes, he didn't have time to get it done himself." Selfridge smiled benevolently. "All bullshit, I know. The heroic Sergeant Kelly never managed to say more than three sentences a year to our prodigal son. Don't worry about the notes he left. If they were really that important, you'd think Kelly would've brought them up himself."

"You'd think." Barry hefted the file. It was a good-sized dumbbell. Cops like Grohmann tended to accumulate files like this. "Where is the prodigal cop this morning?"

"Never in before eleven. A leniency he is granted, owing to the night owl habits that go with the territory. And how is your little bird doing, might I ask?"

"She's good, Staff. Tougher than she looks. I talked to her this morning. She's in with the doctor this morning, figures she'll be cleared for light duties by tomorrow."

"Have we filed on the despicable scum who beat on her?" One thing Barry loved about working for Gentleman Paul was his ruthless attitude towards assaults on his officers, particularly the female ones.

"He had his first appearance this morning. Pleading brutality as usual."

Selfridge looked at him perceptively. "I'm certain a few equalizing shots were doled out, Sergeant. But beware, the tide is turning against the old ways. We've got to be careful."

"All strictly 'heat of battle,' Staff. Anyway, Rollings has a couple of warrants to deal with, he won't be out for a while. Crown filed on him for 267, so he'll be looking at serious time, especially after his last shot at Oakalla."

"Federal time, hopefully now. Good. Well, Barry there's not much going on out there today. The middlemen and big shots are holding on to their supply until the big show starts. Find yourself somewhere quiet and peruse that file. When Grohmann comes in, I want him out there as quickly as possible. If anyone's going to get us out of the doldrums, it's him."

"You got it, Staff." He grabbed a refill and took the file to an interview room. Outside, rain pelted the windows, which quickly steamed up when he entered. He cracked one and inhaled the ozone smell. *Tim's birthday. Got to remember. Not like last year.*

Barry sat and considered for the fiftieth time the wisdom of taking the Drug Section assignment. Patrol was rotating shifts, but it was predictable. Drugs, on the other hand, was technically a dayshift gig, but in reality, the hours were dictated by the targets they were after. That meant strange times for a married man with three kids. *Maybe some flowers for the wife on top of Tim's present wasn't a bad idea either.*

He opened the file. The aggressive, cauliflower-eared ex-paratrooper stared out at him. Oh, the stories he'd heard about Rick Grohmann...

Breaking a leg on a winter exercise after a bad parachute landing, then splinting himself up and *walking* ten kilometres out of the drop zone.

Winning five back-to-back boxing matches in the Academy ring, all against men who outweighed him by at least thirty pounds.

Passing the old, repulsive Drug Section initiation, a Mountie creation banned in disgust by Selfridge. The newbie would, on a night of drunken debauchery, cheep for his "food" like a hungry baby bird. One of the "momma birds" would vomit into his mouth to feed him.

Grohmann went back for seconds.

Kelly's approach to his mercurial man had largely been one of "Hear no evil, see no evil, speak no evil." Even so, a disturbing pattern of very public physical policing revealed itself. Grohmann liked to squat on the enemy's turf, then provoke a reaction.

The tide is turning against the old ways. Selfridge's warning played in his head. But still...

The man had, at least until recently, produced results. Neil "Blotter" Boorman had been incarcerated based on a very patient buy-and-bust chain run by Grohmann and Crown Counsel Mitchell Halperin. Four other high-profile dealers were serving long sentences based on their recent work.

Grohmann's approach was simple and brutish. Consume every minnow on the street until it was the shark's turn.

There was often rough stuff. In five years on Drug Section, he'd spent a year in total recovering from injuries. There were commendations, too.

All in all, Barry did not have a problem with physical policing *per se.* He'd never have survived his time with Whistling Smith on the East Side without it. But it wouldn't be impolitic to suggest a change of approach, he figured.

Besides the bull-in-a-china-shop habits, most of the man's policework seemed solid. He was diligent with exhibits and money; careful to cultivate informants, of whom he had at least fifty on record. If he was smart, he probably had all his best ones on the q/t.

A few notes on the file troubled him. "Call from Clarissa, trouble at home. Speak to R ASAP." Also. "Clarissa talking divorce, alleging cruelty, wants call from S/Sgt." Both in Kelly's handwriting. No indication that anything had been done about them. Typical Kelly. A Deputy Chief's son who'd made a career out of sidestepping the dogshit cops like him had to wade in. And now, he'd be working murders and bank heists while Barry tied up his lose ends.

Barry bit his lip and looked out the window. He'd rationed himself five Export "A"s for the day, and he was finding it hard to put off the first one. Finally, he gave up and lit the smoke, inhaling the rich intake with gratitude. He was half-way to quitting, he figured. So damn hard.

Messing in a man's personal life was a task he viewed with great distaste. But, as Whistling Smith had always said, "They're part of the family, too." If a cop was smacking his wife around, they were honour bound to speak up. Besides, he knew from personal experience that when Patrol, or the Mounties showed up at a wife-beating cop's home, "Go fuck yourself" quickly became "Help me, Sarge."

There was a knock on the door. Rick Grohmann didn't wait to be invited, but simply pulled out a chair and slumped in the seat opposite him.

Barry noticed that Grohmann's knuckles were scraped and bruised. He hoped the target deserved it.

"Interesting reading, Sarge?" Grohmann lit up a smoke. "All full of how great a cop I am, right?"

Barry Olds took a long drag before answering. "Mostly, Rick. Mostly."

"And?"

"And it's your annual performance review, Detective. You know that."

"Shouldn't Kelly have done that?"

"Alas, Sergeant Kelly left me the task. It's not an onerous one, Rick. Mostly."

"How do you mean?"

"You're a physical guy. Nothing wrong with that. But we're entering a new era in policing in this country. The Charter changes everything."

The Charter of Rights and Freedoms, Trudeau's gift to the legal profession, was only four years old. Still too young to have its influence felt on the street. But, back east, the first cases were beginning to get tossed for "Unreasonable search and seizure," a very American-sounding development. Veteran cops were getting uneasy.

"They come at me. All I do is sit down where they don't want me sitting. As for the Charter, as long as the NCA is on the books, that'll be my bible."

The Narcotic Control Act was a godsend to Canadian drug cops, something their American counterparts could only dream about. It allowed warrantless searches of people, vehicles, and premises based on mere suspicion that drugs were there. Sometimes, a mere smell of weed had resulted in a door-kick. Barry had done it himself a few times.

"Nothing wrong with that, Rick. It still lets us get some fine busts, and as long as it's the law, I'm good with that. Just giving you the weather forecast, that's all."

"So, you're good with me being a 'physical guy,' Sarge?" Grohmann smirked.

"As long as they come at you. Fine." Unbeckoned, Grohmann stood to leave. *Oh, really?* "Does Clarissa come at you?"

Grohmann froze and fixed Barry with a savage look. "A man's home life is his own goddamned business, Sergeant."

Barry stubbed out his smoke and stood up. "As long as you remember that when the uniforms show up. Either let me help you now or face the music on your own."

Grohmann squared off with him. "There's always that third round you owe me."

"We'll have to take care of that someday. Well, I suppose you can sign your evaluation later."

"There's not going to be anything about Clarissa in there, will there?"

"Not since you told me it was none of my business. Which means it won't be. Ever. Do you understand, Detective?"

"In Technicolour, Sergeant. May I go now?"

"By all means. After all, we can't have Blotter Boorman thinking he runs the city, can we? This is Expo City, and we own it. Right?"

Grohmann smiled and nodded. "Right."

"Can I ask you a favour, Rick?"

"Yes, Sergeant?"

"Don't destroy yourself, will you? I might need you soon."

Grohmann nodded wordlessly and exited the room. Barry sat down again, took a deep breath, and lit another Export "A."

APRIL

RIDE-ALONG

One of the signs that you're being accepted in cop culture is when you get let in on the joke. But some cops are harder to impress, as Constable Bobbi Sanghera is about to find out...

312 MAIN ST

The next day, Bobbi Sanghera returned to work with a big bandage on her cheek. Dupuis and Connolly, her backup team presented her with a modified shooting trophy.

In this version, the policewoman was holding the pistol backwards, and standing over another kneeling trophy figure. The inscription read:

The Rick Grohmann Pistol-Whipping Trophy

For the Best Pistol-Whipping of 1986

Presented to CST B.K. Sanghera

That Looked Like It Hurt

The assembled cops, even old Selfridge, had a good laugh. Despite her still-tender face, Bobbi felt ten-feet-tall.

That feeling lasted until Sergeant Olds pulled her out into the hallway. "I need you to do me a favour today."

"What's that, Sarge?"

"I need you to go out with Grohmann today. I was going to do it myself, but I've got a sudden re-scheduling from a rape case that never ends. Court all day."

"What about the other guys? Dupuis and Connolly, I mean?"

"Those knuckleheads? They're so in love with Grohmann he'll

have them painting his shed by lunchtime. Nope, it's got to be someone with no male hero-worshiping complex. I'll explain later."

"But I'm on light duties..." He was already headed for the elevators. Exasperated, she turned for the office. Bobbi was fishing her .38 out of her desk drawer when Grohmann appeared.

"Hey. Nice trophy. What happened to you?"

As a woman, you'd have to be dead not to notice Rick Grohmann. Or, as they said in VPD, "A Fan of Comfortable Footwear." Meaning, a lesbian.

Bobbi was neither. She'd certainly noticed the steel blue eyes, the sandy hair and gunfighter's moustache, the strong arms... but she'd heard the stories first. So, she wasn't about to do something idiotic like swoon for the guy.

For starters, he was married. And the rumour was, it wasn't a happy marriage. Also, he was supposed to be a borderline psycho who spent a lot of time in fag bars. So, all in all, the verdict was; nice to look at, but stay away.

Come to think of it, didn't she classify most male cops like that?

Still, he did have an...effect. She stammered out her response, always being too shy around handsome men to avoid embarrassing herself. "Ah...I caught a brick in the face."

"But you pistol-whipped the motherfucker, am I right?"

"Um, yeah. I did."

He nodded, seemingly satisfied. "Well, okay, apparently Grandpa Olds thinks I need an escort now. So, you're it. Strap on your pea-shooter. You got an extra set of cuffs and a flashlight?"

"Um...yeah. But I'm on light..."

Grohmann held up a set of keys. "I'm driving. No offense, but you immigrants drive like shit."

"I was born in Surrey…"

But he was already headed for the elevators.

**WEST HASTINGS STREET
SOUTH OF STANLEY PARK**

The sun was out, and so were the people. From the looks of it on a Tuesday morning, Bobbi was guessing a lot of sudden flu self-diagnoses and calls to the boss. Crowds thronged the seawall, making their way around Stanley Park by foot, bike, or fruit boot.

That was what you did in a city where rain was the default setting. You took advantage of every calorie of heat energy you could find.

"How long you been a cop, Bobbi?"

Bobbi turned to look at him. He drove like a black man, bench seat almost in the back of the car, legs outstretched, head at exaggerated recline. Everything about him screamed "Feral cat at the watering hole." In a universe of alpha males, he stood out.

"Three years, Detective."

"Call me Rick."

"Okay, Rick. How about you?"

"Eleven. I started with the Mounties in '75. As soon as I saw all of this," He waved a hand to take in the park, the mountains, the inlet, "there was no going back to Edmonton. I jumped ship when I got my First Class in '78."

"Ah, that figures. You look like a Mountie."

He smoothed his moustache. "Is it the 'stache?"

"You do look too much like a cop to be undercover, you know."

He flicked a butt out the window. "Except that's not my game. That's what people like you are good at. You're not what they're expecting. I am, so I need to play it differently."

Bobbi shrugged. There was no point in getting offended. Her mother always reminded her she looked nothing like a cop. "And how do you play it, Rick?"

He smiled broadly. "You'll see." They were across from the Bayshore Inn when he pulled the wheel hard left and turned onto Denman. A hippie cyclist wobbled and shot him a finger. Grohmann laughed loudly and picked up the radio mike. "Dispatch from 2337, show us 10-6 at 776 Eihu Lane." He turned hard down a little alley and stopped short of an old brown house, surrounded by high-rises.

"2337 that address is 10-85." The dispatcher must've been new.

"That's the idea, darling. We are Narcs, after all." Grohmann replaced the mike in its cradle and laughed. "Known drug location? I know 'em all."

They sat under the shade of a giant elm, a pleasant enough place to do a stakeout. But Bobbi had an idea that Grohmann was not really patient enough for those. She peered across the street. Scrawny white boys with big new wave hair sat on the big porch, while others who looked just like them came and went. Every second right hand, she noticed even from here, had a clenched fist.

"So, Constable. Observations?"

"Good location for a dope house. Clear view on all sides, close to the park, so it's easy to run. In the summer, a captive clientele from the beaches and the bar scene west of here. Lots of coming and going, but they don't look like hypes. If I had to guess, I'd say weed and hallucinogens."

Grohmann looked at her appreciatively. "Okay, okay, not bad. I guess I can see why Barry brought you along."

"Why did you think he brought me along?"

"Some kind of affirmative action thing. Or he was nailing you."

Bobbi coughed. "It's neither."

"Fair enough." He opened the door. "Let's go."

"That's it? No warrant?"

"I smell weed. Do you smell weed?"

"Uh…uh, maybe. I guess I do."

"*The Narcotic Control Act* is a wonderful thing. Come on."

They were halfway across the street now, when the boys began to disappear from the porch and head, quickly, for the park. "They're getting away."

"Let 'em." Grohmann pushed his trooper shades down the end of his nose. "Small fry." They reached the bottom of the front stairs and started up. Now, kids were bailing off the sides of the balcony. From the sounds of it to Bobbi, some weren't landing so well.

"Fuck!"

"Goddamn it, my ankle!"

"Come on man, I can't get grounded again, grad's coming up!"

A tall, pale, effeminate kid with a giant stalk of black hair, eye makeup, and a *Cabaret Voltaire* shirt tried to push past Bobbi. She grabbed his arm. "Ow! Let go!"

Grohmann laughed. "Not this one, Constable. This one we keep, right, Craiiig?" He imitated the boy's whiny voice when he said the name. "Craiiig here carries the cash, right? Frisk him and cuff him, Bobbi."

His little friend, a beanstalk with stooped shoulders, mustered up an objection. "He's sixteen! That's not right!"

"Fuck off, beanpole. You wanna sit on his lap on the way to jail?"

The kid decided to plead his case to Bobbi instead while she cuffed his boyfriend. "Please, lady, he's not a drug dealer."

Bobbi found a massive wad of cash in the kid's right pants pocket and pulled it out. "Oh yeah? So, where'd he get this? Paper routes must pay a lot more than I remembered."

The kid opened his mouth again.

"Fuck off, string bean. Police business." If Bobbi's mother heard her talk like that, she'd be astonished. *The job changes you.*

The kid glared at her, then looked into the street. Two Patrol units were approaching. His objections forgotten; he ran off towards Lost Lagoon.

She handed off Craig to Colleen Strzok, an Academy classmate of hers. Colleen was more of the stereotypical policewoman, tall, athletic, and mildly butchy. "Hey, Bobbi, how's Drugs? We figured you guys could use a hand when we heard Sergeant Rock on the radio."

"Just looks like a weed house, is all. This one is for juvie."

Colleen whispered in her ear. "Just be careful with him. He's got a bad mojo."

Bobbi handed off her prisoner and entered the house through a stereotypical beaded curtain. There she found Grohmann and Richard Samuels, a veteran black Corporal and Colleen's partner bracing a solid-looking Jamaican who sat in a bean bag chair.

If Grohmann's ceaseless slurs bothered Samuels, it didn't show. "We meet again, Sambo."

The Jamaican looked up at him with bloodshot eyes. "A little ganja for my personal use, Mr Policeman. I don't want no bother with you."

In the background, a stereo played new wave. Something Bobbi figured no self-respecting Jamaican would listen to unless it was to attract clientele.

So I try to laugh about it
Cover it all up with lies
I try to
Laugh about it
Hiding the tears in my eyes
'cause boys don't cry

"Nice music." Grohmann observed. He leaned down. "White Boy music."

"I'm a liberal fellow, you know. I've got an open mind."

"Or, maybe you just like surrounding yourself with little white boys."

"Hey now! You take that back, Mr Policeman!" Sambo made to stand, but Samuels pushed him down, hard.

"This is a very nice house, Sambo. Hardwood floors! You don't see that much. You keep it nice and neat, not like the usual Jake shit shack. But you see, being a policeman and all, I just can't help but wonder. Where is all the dope in this town? Come on now, Sambo! Unless you're going to tell me, your cousin Ridley has gone straight. Because I know for sure, he brings you in five pounds every week, like clockwork, from Montego Bay. That airside pass sure pays off, right?"

He leaned over Sambo again. This time the man's jaw jutted out defiantly, but he said nothing. "Five pounds a week, but still you tell all these little cocksuckers all you got is Mexican shake and seed. So, where's the good stuff?"

Samuels spoke up. "I used to install these floors, before I got on the force. Mmm, expensive."

"Oh yeah, Richard, no lie. Expensive. Too bad that I don't know what I'm doing." Bobbi heard a flicking sound, and a switchblade knife dropped straight into the pristine floor.

"Hey, now, there's no need for that! No need at all! Can't we have a gentlemanly discussion?"

"Nope." He leered at Sambo. "Drug dealers are not gentlemen." Grohmann got to his knees and began roughly prying apart hardwood segments with the switchblade, while Sambo groaned like he was in labour.

"Oh no mon...no mon, no! All my life, I wanted to have nice floors! I grew up walking in the dirt with the chickens!" Bobbi stifled a laugh.

"I'll find that dope somehow, Sambo! I promise!"

"Okay, okay! It's in the drawers in the master bedroom! And the attic too! The dog will show you, right? You got good dogs, right?"

Calmly, Grohmann flicked the blade closed and stood up. "Oh yeah, dogs! I always forget about them."

"Me too." Samuels grinned and hauled Sambo to his feet. "Time to lively yourself up, boy."

Grohmann looked at his pager. "Fuck. Hey, you finish up here. Get Patrol to help, do a final tally of the dope and the money, and write up the Crown. It's your case."

"Where are you off to?"

"Personal business."

And, just like that, Rick Grohmann left Bobbi Sanghera in the middle of her first big drug case.

The dogs didn't hit on Sambo's hardwood floors. They didn't need to. Twenty-eight pounds of weed, 456 doses of LSD, and 47 grams of magic mushrooms were enough.

NORTH VANCOUVER
LYNN VALLEY

Rick Grohmann drove aggressively, more so even than usual. He weaved in and out of two-lane traffic on the Lions' Gate, the fireball on his dash excusing all sins.

He'd called Stubby Perkins right after he got the page, making sure it was what he thought it was. Stubby was an old-timer dope dealer gone straight, now working as a handyman on the North Shore. He'd owed Rick an eternal debt of gratitude for sparing him a five-year sentence after a series of hot shots in the East Side a while back.

Rick had looked into the backgrounds of the dead men and had come to the general conclusion that society was better off. He didn't tell Perkins that, though. He had the poor old bastard perpetually pruning his hedges and watching Clarissa on the mistaken assumption that he owed Rick one.

Actually, it was Mitch Halperin who had said, "Rick, this case is about as watertight as the Titanic when they started playing *Nearer My God to Thee.* Let the old turd retire."

But it had all paid off. Stubby had been unequivocal.

"Yeah. It was that tennis fag, that Lawrence guy. He was over there for an easy 45 minutes, and…well, sorry to say this, Detective, but the sounds they was making was not exactly Christian, if you get my meaning."

"I do." He'd replied through clenched teeth. He looked at his watch as he made the turn off. 1430. Most of his neighbours would be off picking up their own kids. Something he'd never trusted Clarissa to give him. Now he knew he was right.

That movie, what was it…yeah. *Dr Strangelove,* where that crazy General talks about "Denying women my essence…" he was fucking right! Some women just couldn't be trusted!

Rick pulled into his driveway, bailed from the Mustang, and marched up to his door, kicking it open in one go. He pelted up the stairs, finding Clarissa in the shower, eliminating the evidence, no doubt.

Her mouth was agape as he pulled open the curtain. As he reached in and grabbed her by the hair, her smouldering charcoal eyes rolled back in her head, and he dragged her naked, slapping and punching her, into the bedroom.

Had some trouble remembering who your husband was, Clar? Let me remind you.

APRIL

RIP CREW

Like any business, the narcotics trade depends on reading trends in the market for opportunity. A large, well-publicized, international event like Expo '86 will bring an influx of visitors, some of whom enjoy high-quality hard drugs. To cater to their needs, one must have a ready supply on hand, something that has led to a supply shortfall in Vancouver in the months leading up to Expo, as dealers hoarded product in order to demand higher prices when visitors arrived.

For one recently released dealer, there is no time to build up his business again through traditional means. If Blotter Boorman wants to be in on the ground floor come May 2nd, he's going to have to operate more aggressively...

VANCOUVER
LITTLE MOUNTAIN

Also enjoying the unseasonably warm April weather that day were another crew of dealers, these ones more...diversified than the West End crew.

This was important to the man who sat across the street from them, watching their little narrow house and its frequent visitors. This man was not interested in LSD or hashish.

This man was 39 years old today. Old for a dealer. Too old to start at the bottom again after his third prison sentence. Still fit, still handsome, still hip, though. He told himself that every morning. The joint was fabulous for keeping a body to go with the blue eyes and chestnut hair. Hell, he didn't even need to be a rich dealer to get laid.

The problem right now was, he was just a dealer. Not a rich one. He had some money set aside, but what he really needed, he lacked.

Time.

Neil "Blotter" Boorman licked his lips in satisfaction. There were no well-fed college boys shopping here. Only feral junkies, and those rich enough for both drugs *and* food. That indicated that Donnie had found the right address.

Blotter had once serviced the appetites of the UBC crowd, until a particularly unpleasant Mounted Policeman by the name of Mulvaney had put him in hospital. Reborn after a prison stint, he'd decided that if he was going to take the risk of getting curb-stomped by pigs or slit open by his competitors, he ought to be selling something with a fatter profit margin.

Luckily, Blotter's epiphany had corresponded with an explosion in the available selection of hard drugs in the Vancouver area. Asia was opening up, and Asia's gateway was Vancouver. For a few years in the early 80s, it was a license to print money.

And then, he ran into another, even more unpleasant policeman named Grohmann. After the beating, and during the considerably lighter sentence (BC judges were so enlightened), Blotter had made himself a vow.

Never again. Never again would he lick the curb in handcuffs while some pea-brained flatfoot made an example out of him. The next man who tried would spend his last moments trying to stuff his outsides back inside.

Blotter touched the gym bag between his feet for reassurance. It had been ages since he'd fired one, and the bikers he got them from were short on time for lessons. He would just have to fake it till he made it.

He could tell his crew was a little nervous about the gunplay, something Canadians usually were squeamish when it came to. But there was no avoiding it. If he wanted to get back on his feet again in time for Expo, he didn't have time to start from the bottom.

Come May 2nd, False Creek, the formerly polluted haunt of Vancouver's least attractive citizens, would be filled with millions of young, adventurous, and cash-flush explorers. Until October, they'd be flocking here on the flimsy excuse of seeing a World's Fair on transportation and communications.

Yeah, right. The only communicating a lot of these people would be doing was finding out how much Vancouver hookers wanted for a half-and-half and asking where to score dope. Hookers were the best people to ask both questions of.

Rebuilding piece-by-piece wouldn't cut it. By the time he had enough market share, Vancouver would be back asleep, and all of his would-be-customers would be in New York, Sydney, or Singapore. So, he'd done something he should've done last time: he got cozy with the bikers.

Generally speaking, Blotter was not comfortable with partners. He'd learned the hard way in Seattle, where he grew up, dealing weed to high school kids in Ballard with a wetback named Gooter. Gooter was short for "Gutierrez," which nobody could fucking pronounce. Gooter always proclaimed they were *socios*, or partners.

"Nobody gonna make me turn on my *socio*, Neil!"

Yeah, sure. Two weeks after his mom moved him to Vancouver after he got a draft notice in the mail, Gooter stopped answering his calls. So much for the five grand his "socio" owed him. *Sociopath,* more like.

But if you wanted to do pretty much anything in Vancouver these days, you couldn't avoid the bikers. It wasn't like the freewheeling seventies anymore. No, if you wanted to sell dope, run hookers, show strippers, you name it; you needed a nod and a wink from the men in the leather vests. Blotter was no exception.

So, last week, he visited his probation officer, his old biker pal from the Pen, Randy McClarty, had agreed to meet him, way out in fucking Maple Ridge. *Jesus.*

In his day, criminals had lived in the city, not an hour away with the livestock and the Hindus. Still once he'd driven his old Hemi 'Cuda out there on the Number One (nice to open it up), he had to admit; the bikers were on to something.

Wide-open spaces. Back forties where you could fire an AK on full auto without anyone calling the cops. Barns that doubled as sweet grow ops.

Randy had been working on a Harley he was too fat to ride when Blotter had pulled up. He seemed to take an instant dislike to Donnie, as so many people did, so he had his right-hand-man wait in the car like a Rottweiler (or, in Donnie's case, a poodle).

"You just get out?"

"Yeah. Eighteen months."

"Not as bad as your last jolt. What was that? Five years?"

"Yeah. Five years for 2 pounds of grass and 60 tabs of acid. Can you believe it?"

"Hey man, times change. Things are looking up." He'd squinted at Blotter in the weak sunshine. "What you want, Blotter?"

Blotter plowed through the embarrassment he felt. Randy owed him one, and if that story ever came out, the embarrassment wouldn't be all one-sided.

Or, he reasoned, Randy could just kill him. Out here, who would know?

"I need to get re-established, Randy. And I can't do it the low and slow way. Expo is coming."

Randy chewed on his sunglasses and pondered. "Yeah, primo opportunities for sure. But if you can't wait to get back in..."

"I wanna do rips, Randy. I got a crew; I just need some hardware."

Randy sighed. "Rips draw a lot of heat, man. You gotta do them right."

"I got a plan."

"Oh yeah?"

"How many dealers, I mean, well-established house-type dealers, in Vancouver don't give you a cut?"

Randy rubbed his chin. "Aw fuck, I dunno, maybe twenty or twenty-five? Why?"

"Give me a list and some firepower, and I'll make it five."

Randy scoffed. "Ah come on! They ain't afraid of us, what makes you think they'll be afraid of you?"

"Have you done anything to them besides ride by and ruin their beauty sleep, Randy?"

"Careful there, Blotter." Randy's eyes narrowed. "Just because you know...what you know, doesn't mean you can take...ah, whatchacallits. Yeah."

"Liberties, Randy? I'm not taking liberties. I'm just pointing out what all these guys know; that you're all way too busy to deal with them. You've got your fingers in too many pies, Randy. My business is dope. That's all. It ain't hookers, it ain't strippers, and it ain't tow trucks. Let me...*communicate* with these assholes, and in return for a franchise, you get a serious cut, with zero risk."

"Catch?"

"None. I need to get established by May 2nd, and this is the only fucking way I can think of."

"Hmm. Let me make a couple calls."

Randy had returned with two hockey bags full of very heavy shit, and a hastily printed list. "Okay. Just don't fuck up."

As he was walking back to his car, Randy had called out. "You ever tell anyone that story?"

Blotter had turned slowly. "You really have to ask?"

"Good, Blotter. Because if I ever hear anyone else telling it, you're dead, you hear me?"

"If I ever hear anyone else telling it, you'll have their head on a fucking platter."

Randy smiled. "Good answer, Blotter. Get back before it gets shitty, eh?"

Now, it was about to get shitty. "Roach, you got that phoney badge?"

The thick-bodied goon with rolls of neck fat holding up his bald dome nodded. "Yes, Blotter I do."

"Okay, you and Pissy Balls here go clear out those fucking hypes. Be quick about it."

Pissy Balls was another mesomorphic goon Blotter used to "communicate." The origins of his nickname were forgotten, even to him. He hastened to exit the back seat and hurried after his partner. Soon, the street was full of hypes with a bad need to be someplace else. "Let's go." Blotter turned to Donnie.

"Aye." Donnie tucked a twelve-gauge with a folding stock under his leather coat. Blotter reached down and pulled a folding-stock AK-47 out of the duffel bag. He racked the action, then opened the door of the car.

Blotter was halfway up the stairs, Donnie on his heels, when the iron-caged door with the peephole flew open. Behind it, fuming vocally, was Harvey Sam.

Blotter smiled and levelled the AK at Harvey. Pissy Balls had already caught the open steel gate, and now had a Beretta 92 pointed at the dealer's head.

Harvey Sam was the son of a hereditary chief from around Prince George somewhere, one of those dark blots on the map that barely held Blotter's interest. He was a misshapen blob of a man, with an outdated 50s hairdo and crooked teeth. They'd done time in Kent in the 70s.

"Uh-huh. Hiya, Blotter."

"Get your ass back in there, Harvey."

"You got it." Harvey had no pretensions to heroism. Which was why his name was first on Blotter's list. Soon, they were sitting at Harvey's dining room table. Dime bags of smack and coke sat everywhere, interspersed with stacks of cash, US and Canadian.

"Jesus Christ, Harvey. This place is messier than your cell. How the fuck do you stay in business?"

"I dunno. Lucky, I guess." Like so many Indians Blotter knew, under pressure he went quiet and monosyllabic.

"Well, there's going to be a business re-adjustment. Expo is coming, right?"

"Oh yeah. That thing."

"Yes, Harvey, that thing." He slid a letter, on official Expo '86 stationery, across the table. "You need new business partners. And now, you have them."

Blotter walked out of Harvey's place with a signed agreement to go 50/25/25 with Harvey and the bikers. Since Harvey had the good sense not to fight, he got a sweetheart deal.

"That was easy." Donnie keyed the ignition.

"Don't get used to it." Blotter looked out at the house, where the hypes were already back. "It's all uphill from here."

APRIL

HOT SHOTS

In any city, even one as beautiful as Vancouver, there are the places one does not show to visitors. While Downtown, the West End, and False Creek will be on proud display during Expo, the Downtown East Side will remain the city's open sore, best kept hidden from view. A constant reminder of the toxic mixture of poverty and drug addiction, the East Side is where a Vancouver police officer learns his trade. And it's where he learns his ability to make a difference is strictly limited...

**SUNRISE HOTEL
DOWNTOWN EAST SIDE**

The elevator, as always, was not in service in Vancouver's shittiest hotel. As Bobbi trudged up the stairs behind Barry, she thanked her lucky stars it was April and not August.

She'd been a cop for just over three years. How many times had she been here? Hell, she'd never even worked Patrol Northeast, but she still guessed it was fifty or more times.

"Trying to figure out how many times you've been here?" Barry called down.

"How did you know?"

"It's an old VPD game."

"I guess fifty, you?"

"Lightweight. Add a zero. As a rookie, I was here two or three times a shift."

"Ugh." Bobbi stopped to take a breath. "When I see this place in my dreams, a low flying jet dropping napalm is never far behind."

"You and me both. Here we are."

They stepped into the hallway to find two uniforms puzzling over a blood trail. One held on to a handcuffed pisspants who leaned against the wall for support.

"Hey, Ross."

"What's up, Sarge?"

"I thought this was an OD?"

"Nah, this is a homicide. Professor Moriarty here," Ross indicated the pisspants held by his partner, "stabs his next-door neighbour, then takes the dripping knife back to his room to clean it in the sink. A real whodunnit."

Barry chuckled. Bobbi shook her head. If you thought there was a lower limit to the human condition, you'd never worked Patrol Northeast. "Good old Sunrise. Cop traffic jam." Barry chortled.

Ross pointed down the hall. "Ah, there's the Coroner. Must be your OD."

"Thanks Lou. Come on Bobbi, let's see which idiot is killing his customers this week."

In the room, a young PW stood making notes. A tiny girl lay sprawled on the bed, blood-filled rig hanging out of her left arm. Her face was purple and flecked with bloody vomit. Bobbi breathed through her mouth. She already knew what the smells would be and didn't want to smell them.

The Coroner was a legendary fixture on the East Side, a former Mountie with Marxist views and a unique take on the question of drugs and the death they brought. "Hi, Larry." Barry held out his hand. They shook.

The Coroner laughed. The PW glared at him. "Another recruit to the fruitless War on Drugs, Sergeant Olds? It's a crying shame, it is. A man with a brain like yours should be chasing white-collar junk bond traders through the caverns of the VSE! This is beneath you! Now, that troglodyte, Grohmann, on the other hand…"

"Larry, the case?"

The Coroner waved his hand in irritation. "Oh, this is nothing, even the PW here can handle it." Again, the PW, a formidable looking creature, glared. "Just thought you'd like to see the trademark glassine here." He held up a dime bag with a comic rendition of Yoda from Star Wars, railing Princess Leia. "Classy, eh?"

"Hot shot?" Barry peered at the tiny girl's veins. They looked like a dirt bike track, scabby and scarred.

"Oh heavens, yes. The thing is, anyone dealing with this girl should never sell her a full shot. She must weigh 90 pounds, at most."

"I know her. Arrested her for shoplifting at the Bay, remember Sarge? Crystal something. She was from up north. Maybe 21, tops." Bobbi stared down at the girl. "Shitty."

"I'll say, Constable. They should've killed us all as soon as we got off the ships. This is how we reward them for their hospitality?" The PW rolled her eyes.

"Killed us all?" Bobbi glared at the Coroner. "Does that apply to the *Komogatu Maru*, too, Larry?" Bobbi ducked into the hall as Barry stared after her.

"Hmm. I stand by my analysis." The Coroner handed Barry the evidence bag with the envelope inside.

"Give it a fucking rest, will you Larry?" Barry stepped out into the hallway to find Bobbi watching as the homicide victim from down the hall was wheeled out of his final home.

EXPO CITY

"I swear to God, the dicks spent less time at that scene than they did getting coffee this morning." Bobbi wiped her eyes with the back of her hands.

"Life is cheap down here. That's just the fact, Bobbi."

"You'd think I'd get used to that."

"Nobody should ever get used to that. I never have."

She put a hand on his arm. "Thank you."

"For what?"

"For being a good teacher. You could be teaching me cynicism. I get together with some of my Academy girlfriends you know. The stories I hear…"

"I can guess." Barry smiled. "Come on, let's go 10-8."

Bobbi gestured towards the OD room. "Aren't we going to…"

"No, you heard the Red Coroner. His lady friend can handle it. Hell, if we're in luck, body removal will get another call down here. For Larry."

Bobbi laughed so hard she snorted. "Double-death scene, and it's like I'm watching Theatre Sports…what's wrong with us?"

"The whole human race would love to know." Barry opened the door to the stairwell. "Let's go shake down some dealers for shits and giggles."

APRIL

KPBGB

In any conditional release of an inmate in the Canadian justice system, the condition "Keep the Peace and Be of Good Behavior," frequently abbreviated as "KPBGB" is attached. One can forgive a veteran policeman like Rick Grohmann for being skeptical of Blotter Boorman's ability to abide by this condition. In the habits of old-school coppers like Grohmann, it is entirely appropriate to remind a recently released scofflaw of his place in the universe...

PROVINCIAL PROBATION SERVICES
HASTINGS ST

Rick Grohmann leaned against a cold concrete wall, chain-smoking and giving the shit eye to the parade of lowlifes trooping up the stairs to tell their POs what good little boys and girls they'd been.

Keeping the Peace and Being of Good Behaviour. KPBGB for short.

All of it was bullshit of course. Rick had been part of the system for long enough to know it was all theatre. Probation, and its Federal cousin, Parole, were just acts. Criminals pretending they were reforming themselves only long enough for the next arrest. Then the cycle would begin again.

Arrest, charge, convict, sentence, release. Repeat. Meanwhile, on the streets, only the faces changed. The shitty lives of the people, offenders, victims, cops, and the mere bystanders, did not.

He lit a new smoke off the embers of the old. A cold wind started whipping rain into the alcove where he waited for Blotter Boorman.

Rick was overdue for a meeting with his nemesis, and he was

tired of getting misdirected by small fry. This was the one place he knew Boorman legally had to be, at this exact time. So here he was.

He'd made it downtown early after sorting things out with Clarissa. This time was not like the other times; no, this time, he had the upper hand. She hadn't even bothered to deny her affair with Lawrence Dyck. *What a name.*

This time, he had her where he wanted her. Now, she was apologizing to him, a real turn of events. Rick had to admit to himself that the whole thing gave him a sick thrill. The punishment sex, the subservient routine, the begging and pleading. He was feeling ten feet tall this morning, and ready to tip the city over in pursuit of his next case.

It was almost enough for him to want to encourage her to go out and do it again. Maybe now, he understood what swinging was all about. Something to think about.

Another thing to think about; the rumours swirling around Blotter Boorman.

No actual reports, *per se.* But lots of intelligence from his snitches; a four-man car going around, everybody tooled up, ripping dope houses that weren't protected by the bikers.

The first time he'd heard it, he knew it was Boorman. Boorman had made a lot of noise about getting back in the game, but this time doing it smart. If he'd had to guess, Boorman was ripping unaffiliated dope houses with biker sanction. It was the only way to get established in a hurry, before the world's degenerates showed up in town starting May 2nd.

Expo. It was all everyone was talking about now. In general, it was a pain in the fucking ass. The brass were running around like headless chickens, trying to show that they were *doing something.* Like the scum sweep scheduled for this afternoon on Hastings, for instance. A waste of time.

All part of the big act, Rick figured. Another reason why he preferred to work alone; it was easier to keep your eye on the prize.

Speaking of. Boorman was down the stairs and halfway to the street before Rick had grabbed him and spun him around.

Boorman had stepped into a fighting position automatically. For a moment, Rick wondered if he'd gotten the wrong guy.

The last time he'd seen Boorman, the man had been heavier, tanned dark by frequent trips to Mexico, living a slack life. Now, he was muscular and trim, his complexion sallow from prison lighting and shit food. "The fuck you want, Grohmann?" He lowered his fists. "I made my appointment. Go up and see."

"I'll see for myself, asshole. So, you look like you're in a hurry. Got somewhere to be?"

A gust blew more rain into the alcove. Boorman hiked up the collar on his long leather coat. "I tell all that shit to my PO. I don't have to say anything to you, piggy."

Rick laughed. "Yeah, yeah, sure. Like you told him all about you and three friends, cruising the city, putting other hard-working dopers out of work? Tsk tsk, Neil. Sounds like you've made some dangerous friends."

Boorman gave him a poker face in return. "Yeah, sure, Grohmann. Pin every fucking indictable in the city on me. Well this time, I've got a better lawyer. My dangerous friends recommended him. He said to tell you to fuck off."

Rick stepped into the man's space. Boorman stared back, unflinching. "Don't forget. I own you. You're on Probation. Any little slip, like, say, this…" He held up a dime bag of coke to Boorman's nose. "Is enough to get you violated. So easy for it just to fall into your pocket."

"Where'd you get that, Detective? Your own personal supply?

As if you'd violate me on a chickenshit planted possession beef. Fuck off."

Now, Rick was getting annoyed. Clearly, Boorman was operating with more confidence. The bikers had to be involved. "I'm just reminding you, Blotter. Don't forget who the cop is, and who the criminal is."

Boorman smiled coldly. "Maybe somebody should tell you that, too. Excuse me." He turned and walked away. A brown Lincoln pulled up to the curb with that shithead Scotsman Donnie at the wheel. As he made a note of the plate, Rick gritted his teeth.

Five years ago, he would've bounced the fucker off the walls for daring to talk to a policeman like that. But, as Olds had said, the world had changed.

There was nothing for it but to start squeezing his snitches. Boorman was right. There was no way he was going to violate him on a chickenshit beef. No, Boorman was going to give him another major case.

Because that's what cops and criminals did in the big act.

APRIL SWEEPSTAKES

The epicentre of drug-related misery on the Downtown East Side is Library Square, at the corner of Main and Hastings. This open-air drug supermarket is just two blocks south of police headquarters, leading many outside observers to wonder just what the point of it all is. Many a police officer has wondered, too.

In other precincts of the city, narcotics are dealt more subtly, out of private homes, on quiet streets, surrounded by a more placid existence. But that does not mean that the violence at the heart of the drug trade may not visit them on occasion…

LIBRARY SQUARE
MAIN AND HASTINGS

The slow convoy of unmarked police cars drove down Hastings St, with Selfridge and Olds in the lead. In the alleyways on either side of the thoroughfare, Patrol units were waiting to catch the runoff of dopers fleeing the obvious dragnet.

With the opening ceremonies less than a week away, the Chief had decided that a little old-fashioned sweep was in order. Barry Olds wasn't so sure. Like Grohmann, he suspected it was all for show.

"This is bullshit, Staff. All this work for a bunch of charges that won't even hold up."

Selfridge drove slowly and watchfully. On the steps of Library Square, Vancouver's dope ground zero, the first dealers and hypes were already making themselves scarce. "Of course, it is, Sergeant. But we can't have the Prince of Wales see all this, can we?" To their right, a hype had quickly reversed course after running into the alley, pursued by two Constables. "Here's our first customer."

The hype slammed into their hood after Selfridge slammed on the brakes. "What was that speech you're always giving about the old ways, Staff?"

Selfridge shrugged as the uniformed officers cuffed their quarry. "Old habits die hard."

Fifty meters behind them, Connolly and Bobbi Sanghera had pulled up on the curb to chase a dealer known as "Slickfoot" for his running skills.

Gord Connolly was losing steam fast, a rugby player going to fat. Bobbi pulled past him and cursed silently as Slickfoot, a gangly man with a red bush of curly hair and a 1970s wardrobe, ducked into Funky Winker Beans.

Funky Winker Beans was one of those East Hastings shitholes where all the toilet stall doors had long ago been kicked down by cops, and management was sick of replacing them. The lighting was mercifully dark. You didn't really want to see what was on the carpet in Funky Winker Beans.

Sure enough, Slickfoot headed straight for the shitter. Bobbi elbowed a deadhead who was too slow to get out of her way, sending his beer flying. When she entered the john, Slickfoot was already dumping his pockets into a toilet.

"Police, stop!" Slickfoot turned at Bobbi's challenge, a blood-filled syringe in his hand. Momentum was already propelling her into a potential date with AIDS. She had a darkly funny thought about solving mom's marriage fixing dilemma for her before she brought down her portable radio on Slickfoot's wrist and heard a snap.

"Owww! Oh fuck, owww! God that hurts!" Slickfoot began crying. "Why'd you have to do that?"

Bobbi stepped on the dropped syringe and crushed it under a police boot. "Because what you got, I don't want." She grabbed

Slickfoot roughly and yanked him out of the shitter, handing him off to Connolly. "Happy Birthday, Gord."

"Gee thanks." Slickfoot continued to cry as Connolly cuffed him. Connolly nodded towards the toilet bowl. "So, superstar, how badly do you want that evidence?"

Bobbi looked back at the toilet. Twenty dime bags of heroin floated around a massive, corn-flecked turd. "Oh shit."

His pain forgotten, Slickfoot started to laugh. "Oh shit, hahaha, oh shit!"

Connolly grinned. "Ain't policework glamorous?"

MAIN STREET

At that exact moment, Donnie was driving the Lincoln past the epicentre of the police operation, with the two muscle heads in the back seat, and Blotter Boorman riding shotgun. Donnie took in all the uniforms prop-frisking dopers against the old library and began to slow.

Blotter noticed. "Don't do that. You'll draw attention. Just keep driving."

As they left the scene in their rear-view, Pissy Balls looked back. "Wonder what all that was about?"

Blotter cackled. "Dumbass cops keeping up appearances for the politicians. So Prince Charles and Lady Di don't get a hotshot on their royal tour. They haven't got a clue where the real action is."

The real action today was in a house on East 20th, just off Kingsway. In a little over a week and a half, the four-man rip team had acquired ten subject properties for Blotter, Inc. Blotter figured five more ought to do it. The remaining twenty on his list were either too dangerous, too far away, or too small to bother with.

Blotter figured this one ought to be easy. "Tusker" Taakoiennin was a quiet, introspective former safecracker who'd gotten into running a dope house with his old lady. Blotter knew him from Kent, and knew he hated guns and violence. This time, pistols only, therefore. He figured even that would be unnecessary. Tusker would probably smell the wind direction and sign on the dotted line. "Turn here." He ordered Donnie.

"Aye. Not a bad neighbourhood." The area was full of pre-war homes with big yards and hard-working owners. Totally Tusker's style. His house, a lively two-story painted bright Finnish blue, only stood out because of the colour.

"Bah." Roach scoffed. "Too many Chinks here."

"I dunnae mind the Chinkers, Roach. I like tha food. It's the gooks I cannae stand."

"Shut up and pull in here." Blotter ordered Donnie. "You two, go around the back." Roach and Pissy Balls nodded and got out of the car.

Across the street, a teenaged Chinese kid stopped shooting hoops in his driveway and stepped behind a tree to watch. The sun had come out now, and since his mom had taken away his Atari, he had nothing better to do.

Blotter knocked on the door, the house's only concession to being what it was; a drug den. It was painted to look like all the others, but it was clearly made of steel and featured an oversized peephole. "Yes?"

"Tusker? It's Blotter. Open up, you Finnish fuckface."

A moment's hesitation followed. "Okay, buddy. Hang on."

There was a sound of footsteps, hurried, as Tusker unlocked a series of bolts. As the door cracked open, Blotter shouldered his way in, followed closely by Donnie. "Well, well, Tusker. Look at you! What a nice place. Are you teaching piano? Or…selling drugs?"

Tusker had that permanent look of health and well-being that so irked everyone else about the Scandinavians. His runner's body was topped with a sunken-cheeked head with golden-blond hair. His eyes were the colour of a melted glacier. "You know how it is, Blotter. It's tough to go completely straight. But I'm no pusher. I only sell to people who need it. You know, to keep their head."

From a back room, a short blonde woman with deep brown eyes emerged. She looked fearful and couldn't have been older than twenty-five. "And who is this, Tusker? I didn't know you had a daughter."

Tusker laughed nervously. "This is Marianne. She is my wife."

Blotter put out a hand. *"Enchante. Comment ca va?"*

Marianne did not reciprocate. She stood behind her man. "What do you want from us?"

Blotter shrugged and put the Expo stationary on the table. "Okay then. You're working in biker territory, and you're lucky to be alive without cutting them in for half. I'm acting as their agent. You cut me and my red and white pals in for half, you'll never have to worry about protection again."

Marianne made to open her mouth, but Tusker stopped her. Blotter noticed the place was decorated like an Ikea catalogue. "We don't need protection, Blotter, sorry. We keep to ourselves, and don't try to expand. We just serve old junkies who are trying to live their lives. That's all."

Blotter paused. This was not going as planned. Perhaps they didn't understand what was happening, living in their little dreamworld. Perhaps he was the devil, upending these harmless peoples' fantasy life.

He shook his head. *Fuck them.*

"I think what you mean is; you didn't need protection." He motioned to Donnie, who unlocked the front door. Soon, Pissy Balls and Roach were entering. "But now, you clearly do."

"What…what are you going to do?" Tusker was backing up towards a writing table with a drawer in front. Exactly where he'd keep a gun. Maybe he had changed. He was certainly more stubborn that Blotter had remembered.

Blotter drew his Browning and pointed it at Tusker. "No tricks, sunshine." Tusker froze, his hands up.

But Marianne went into overdrive. "Get out! Get out, you fuckers! How dare you come in here with guns? How dare you! We are peaceful people! Get out! Get out before…"

Blotter laughed. "Before what? You call the police? With enough dope in here to get you ten years? Give me a fucking break." He motioned to the two mesomorphs. "Take her into a back room and tune her up. When Tusker's tired of listening to it, he can sign the paper."

Marianne made a pathetic attempt to escape, but Roach and Pissy Balls, smiling with the sick thrill, quickly captured her and bundled her into a bedroom. Now, Blotter stared at his old prison mate. "So?"

"So? I told you. We don't need protection." A tear leaked from Tusker's eye as Marianne's muffled screams came from the back of the house.

"Okay." Blotter flipped the Browning backwards, stepped forward, and hit Tusker over the crown of his skull. The dealer fell on his ass, blood streaming from his wound. "You just gonna sit there, you Finnish faggot? Huh? You just gonna sit there and listen to that little girl get the shit beaten out of her, while you protect your business? Huh? You know what comes next, right?

You know what comes next?"

"Nnnno...please...no." Tusker crawled to embrace Blotter's feet. Blotter smashed him again with the gun, and now he writhed on the floor. The sound of tearing clothing came from the back room.

"Do you know what that sound is? That's the sound of your pretty little bitch getting her dress ripped off! Has she ever had two cocks at once? Hmm? Looks like it, but if she hasn't, today is her lucky day!"

"Okay, okay, I'll sign, I'll sign!"

Blotter slapped the stationary and a ballpoint pen on the desk in front of the writhing Tusker. "Sign here. Make your payments on time, and you'll never see me again." He turned to Donnie. "Tell those two not to rape her. I'll make it up to them."

Tusker wept bitterly as he signed. "What happened to you, Blotter? What happened?"

"Careful, you fuck. You're getting blood on a legal document. What happened to me? Nothing. I was always an asshole. It's just that today, you were on the receiving end."

When the four men left the house, leaving a catatonic and naked Marianne and a bloodied and weeping Tusker, the Chinese boy across the street was still watching.

As Rick Grohmann had earlier in the day, he made a note of the license plate, too.

APRIL

KCD965

Vancouver on the eve of Expo had a burgeoning club scene, already popular with cool kids of the globe. In one such hot spot, Rick Grohmann discovers that lazy policework has potentially obscured a vital incident in Blotter Boorman's return to prominence. As in so many cases, the key to finding things out is a network of well-connected informants...

LUV-A-FAIR
SEYMOUR AND DRAKE

Most detectives had a system when it came to informants.

Technically, all informants were supposed to be registered with the Intelligence Division. Smart detectives registered just enough to keep their supervisors off their cases.

Smart detectives, however, kept their best informants, formally known as CIs, informally as "snitches", to themselves. Therefore, a dried-up old husk like Stubby Perkins, good only for mowing lawns and spying on promiscuous wives, was still on the official CI list.

A plugged-in happener like Jared Cristopolous was not. He belonged to Rick Grohmann, who'd gotten him off an otherwise costly MDMA beef in return for a running report on the bar where they were now meeting.

Ordinarily, there was no way Rick would meet an informant in a club owned by the informant's cousins. But the Greeks who owned Luv-a-Fair were tolerant of their cousin's dalliance with the police. Though it was an open secret that drugs of all kinds were available on the premises, there were certain...limits. The Greeks wanted the truly bad elements pruned, courtesy of the fearsome Detective Grohmann, so people like Bono and Dave

Gahan would feel comfortable partying here.

Rick looked at his watch. Jared was late, as usual. The music was awesome, as always, the DJ playing *Master and Servant* by Depeche Mode, and the drinks were on a permanent police discount of 0%. He was on his third gin and tonic and feeling fine.

There's a new game we like to play, you see
A game with added reality
You treat me like a dog, get me down on my knees

We call it 'Master and Servant'
We call it 'Master and Servant'

"Hey, Detective." Jared sat across from him at the raised table, wiping a long strand of slick black hair off his face. "I hear Skinny Puppy is here tonight."

Rick shook his head. "Fuck that shit. Tell me about what happened in East Van the other day."

Jared looked around dramatically. Rick suppressed an urge to snicker. One good thing about meeting snitches in faggy places like Luv-A-Fair was that most organized crime types wouldn't stop in here to take a piss. "Some of the old fruits who used to come here when it was a gay bar still like to cruise here. One of them has a bad smack habit. He scores from a Finnish guy on East 20th."

"Tusker Taakoiennin."

"Jesus, you do know every dealer in town!"

"Pretty much. So?"

"So, Arnold goes there to score the other day and finds the place swarming with cops. An ambulance is taking Tusker's old lady away, and the cops are arresting Tusker for beating her."

"So?"

"So, that's not what happened at all. Arnold sees this Chinese kid watching from across the street and asks him what happened. He says four guys pulled up in a big Lincoln and went in. Then, the screaming started. They left twenty minutes later."

Rick remembered the Lincoln that picked up Blotter. *Four guys.* "A big, *brown* Lincoln?"

Jared nodded. "Yeah. I think so."

"Kid get a plate?"

"I dunno, maybe. Arnold's not much of a detective, I think."

"That's good, Jared, that's real good." He stuffed a fifty in the kid's breast pocket. Don't spend it all on candy."

Rick was almost out the door when he ran into Chainsaw.

Chainsaw was a massive, usually bloodied, skinhead with a Northern English accent and a terrible fucking attitude. He was usually ready to fight, fighting, or recovering from a fight.

Tonight, Chainsaw was already fighting three bouncers at once. And he looked like he was winning. Rick stepped into the street and looked around for uniforms. Zero, of course. He went back to the coat check girl, as Chainsaw applied a headlock to Freddie, the largest bouncer, and began to drive him into unconsciousness. He flashed his badge. "Call the police."

"Yes sir."

Rick got behind Chainsaw, punched him straight in the right ear, and as the big animal went slack, applied a textbook carotid control. Soon, Chainsaw's grip on Freddie had relaxed, as Chainsaw went limp and rubbery. Rick applied his cuffs and checked the man's pulse.

"Still alive, unfortunately." He slapped Freddie on the shoulder. "Make sure I get those cuffs back from those Patrol fuckers, right

Freddie?"

Freddie was a Sheriff's Deputy who was breaking all the rules by moonlighting here. He assented wordlessly; his face still purple.

As the uniforms jogged down Seymour in the direction of the call, Rick jogged in the other direction.

He had a plate to chase down.

312 MAIN ST

Nobody was in the Drug Section office when he arrived. Just as well. Other cops asked too many questions.

It wasn't that Rick Grohmann didn't like other cops. It was just that there was a time and a place for them. Usually, he preferred to work alone. He had his own ways, and a partner just didn't suit those ways. When he needed other cops, he called them.

He logged into the office PIRS terminal. The Police Information Retrieval System documented all recorded encounters between police and public. He quickly found the file for the report of a domestic assault at 866 E 20th Ave. 86-08990. He tried to find an associated license plate for the file and came up with a very sketchy entry by an obviously switched-off backup unit.

KCD-965. Registered to one Fiona McCrae. Donnie's mother. No subject descriptions, no time of arrival, no witness info. He pushed back from the terminal and sighed.

His first field training officer had always said, "Police work is no province for the lazy."

Then why were there so many lazy pricks in it?

But he had the plate. The first link between Blotter and the rip-offs. If he played his cards right, he had another major case.

He just had to talk Patrol South out of their slam-dunk domestic.

APRIL

FIELD TRIP

Having a witness, or a victim willing to talk, is a great break in a criminal investigation. But, as Rick Grohmann will be reminded, some witnesses and victims are better than others...

FALSE CREEK
EXPO 86 SITE

Bobbi Sanghera had been looking forward to a day off the streets. She still had a stack of exhibits to document from Sambo's dope shack, and the cosmetic pre-Expo sweeps of Hastings and Main hadn't helped.

Thank Christ Connolly had looked the other way when she'd hit "flush" on Slickfoot's stash. She was learning quickly. When she was on Patrol, she'd have gone in heroically, shit or no shit, and scooped 20 grams of smack.

But on Drug Section? Hell, 20 grams was nothing. Vancouver was awash in enough dope to keep her handcuffed to her Smith-Corona 24/7.

Now though, such talk of getting her paperwork done was about as fanciful as booking a trip on the Space Shuttle. No, she, and everybody else on the section, with the unsurprising exception of Grohmann, was on a field trip.

With two days to go till the grand opening, they were taking a field trip of the Expo Site.

When Selfridge had suddenly announced to the room full of very busy cops with lots of open files, there was a palpable lack of enthusiasm. In Bobbi's case, even less so.

It was the first day of her period, and she was cramping like a motherfucker. Of course, outside of the women's locker room, one did not confide such things. And since the only other woman on the squad was the rough-edged Karen Lundquist, a bullish no-bullshit type whose favourite saying was "Sympathy is in the dictionary, between shit and syphilis," Bobbi kept her gripes to herself.

On top of it all, it was raining again. She held up her umbrella in misery and walked against the wind. A tour guide from the security department, a guy she knew from the Police Reserves, spoke futilely to the unengrossed crowd.

"Over here, we've got the Soviet Pavilion." A space station mock-up projected strangely out of a pre-fab building with exposed beams. "Their theme this year is nuclear energy for peace."

Olds spoke up. "Great timing. Didn't one of their reactors just blow up?" The men guffawed.

"Ah, I don't know Sergeant. But over there is the USA pavilion. Their theme is...ah...space travel."

Connolly asked with mock seriousness, "Didn't one of their space shuttles just blow up?"

Now, Bobbi laughed along. She raised her hand. The guide, certain she wouldn't make his life more difficult, pointed to her. "Yes, Bobbi?"

"Can we ride those gondolas?" She pointed to the little cable cars overhead. "My mom never lets me do stuff like that."

Connolly put up his thick arm. "Ooh, and ice cream! Ice cream at the McBarge!"

The guide sighed, gave up, and led them to the gondola station.

PATROL SOUTH
OAKRIDGE SUBSTATION

Rick Grohmann waited in the Patrol bullpen for Constable Krasinski, the investigating officer on file 86-08990. He was missing the gondola, and the ice cream, but he couldn't have cared less.

Pinning a rip on Blotter Boorman was more satisfying than a double-dip by far.

He looked around the cramped old place with its sixties décor and Corrections Canada furniture. When he'd come from Richmond Detachment in '78, they'd stuck him here, until after six months he'd begged for a transfer to the North. The Southland's barking dogs, and neighbour disputes were anathema to an aggressive young cop like him.

Now it seemed like things were picking up. Patrol South's Tac One traffic was evidence of that. Hot calls were coming in this morning, and the uniforms were scurrying in all directions.

But if he had to tackle Pete Krasinski on his way out to his blue and white, he was going to. He needed to talk to that Chinese kid.

Krasinski emerged from the locker room and went for the rack of portables in the bullpen. He was a big, slow-moving kid from the Prairies, like him, a transplanted Mountie and weather refugee.

You could tell all the transplanted Mounties. They all wore RCMP tie clips. "Peter. How's tricks."

"Hey there, Rick. Didn't see ya. What brings you out here?"

"You. You caught a domestic assault last week. Well, it isn't really. It's tied into this doper I'm after. I wanted to ask you a few questions about it."

Krasinski hovered by the radio rack, giving him a suspicious look. "It's just a domestic, man. You're still on Drugs, right?"

"Yeah, I know what it looks like Pete. But I don't think that's what it is."

"You read the PIRS and CPIC?"

"Now you giving me detective lessons, Pete? Come on, of course I did."

Krasinski huffed in frustration and pulled the bulging file folder out of a cubbyhole. "Look, Rick, read the file, okay. I gotta go, the B of M on 41st is getting robbed again. My partner's in the car already, and I gotta pick up a twelve-gauge."

Rick laughed and took the file from Krasinski. "Okay, okay, Serpico. Go get 'em. Probably just another chickenshit Vancouver note robbery, but whatever. This ain't Montreal or LA. But just tell me one thing."

"What's that?"

"Who talked to the witness, the Chinese kid who said he saw four dudes in a car go in before the screaming started?"

Krasinski sighed. "I did."

"Then why is your PIRS entry so shitty, Pete? You're a halfway decent cop."

"Gee, thanks. I didn't think he was a credible witness. He's a frequent flyer, Rick. You read his PIRS file? No? He's got 14 COM files, and he's only seventeen. Kid sees bad guys under the bed. Says he wants to be a cop."

"Did you check out the plate he gave you?"

"Yeah, so what? Registered to some little old lady."

"Whose son is a joeboy for Blotter Boorman. A two-time loser for major dope sales. You find any dope in the house?"

"Did we have a fucking search warrant? No, we didn't look, and there was zero in plain sight. Listen, Rick, I really think you should read the file."

"Why?"

"So, you can read Mr Taakoiennin's confession. Satisfied?"

Rick tried to hide his surprise. *Of course, he'd fucking confess. The truth would land him in prison for longer, wouldn't it?*

"Kid's name in here?" Rick hefted the file.

"Yeah. Now let me go 10-8, will ya?"

"Sure, Pete, sure. Sorry, man." But Krasinski was already racing out the back door for his unit. Rick pulled up his chair to the bullpen desk and opened the file.

Sure enough, Tusker had confessed to beating on his childlike wife, and her flimsy statement, backed up with the excuse of memory loss, seemed to corroborate him.

Of course, he had memory loss! He'd been cracked in the fucking head! Who did that, his five-nothing wife?

But Rick had arrested Tusker Taakoiennin back when he was a safe-cracker. The man was a soft-spoken, almost decorous gentleman. It didn't fit. He searched the file for the kid's statement. Edwin Lo, DOB 68-09-02. Okay, the kid was a bit out there. To make a point to Crown, Krasinski had attached the kid's PIRS history to the file.

83-01-23: Bright lights over the neighbourhood. Aliens looking for naked ladies.

84-08-16: Someone in my room in the middle of the night. Everything moved around.

85-11-23: My penis was erect this morning. Someone must have touched me.

Okay, maybe not the best witness. But his descriptions of the

Blotter crew were dead accurate. And how the hell would he have ever guessed at the plate? Sure, Tusker wasn't known as a dealer, but maybe he'd changed gears? It was known to happen.

Rick Grohmann hadn't gotten as far as he had in policework without trusting his judgement. He shagged the kid's info and stuffed the file back in the cubbyhole. Crazy or not, he had a witness to interview.

853 EAST 20TH AVENUE

Rick pulled his Impala up in front of the witness' house. He watched the long, lanky Chinese kid with the bowl-cut repetitively shooting hoops. He considered his next move.

When he looked across the street at Tusker's house, someone was peering through the blinds. Rick got the creeps, and put his car back into drive, peeling out into the street.

Inside Tusker's house, the man who'd been watching the Detective calmly walked over to the phone and dialled a now-memorized number.

"Yes, is this Blotter? Yes, it's Tusker. I think a cop was across the street just now. Yes, parked in front of the house of the boy, the one who's always watching. When he saw me looking, he peeled out. Yes, I will. I'll let you know."

Tusker replaced the handset carefully. Then, he went over to the couch and put his arm around his battered wife. The one he was determined to confess to beating, for both of their sakes.

MAY

CASUALTIES

Policework is hardly a low-risk profession. There are always casualties...

GF STRONG REHABILITATION CENTRE
WEST 28TH AVE

Police work, Whistling Smith would say, is for the strong. Many fall or are found wanting along the way.

Even those who are judged to be cop's cops, men like Wheels Royer, can fall from their high leather boots, in his case, into a wheelchair.

Barry Olds always took a deep, strong breath before walking into this abode of the damned. It was not that the staff did not ceaselessly fight to keep the preeminent rehabilitation facility in Western Canada clean and sterile; no, but there was simply no way to avoid what this place was.

It had a *smell.* The smell of catheters and bedsores; sweating people deprived of half or more of their bodies in one fell swoop, yet still fighting hard to regain their lives; the smell of despair, from those who had given up.

Wheels Royer, it was sad to say, had given up. In the first sunshine of May, Barry found him parked by a window, his face bathed in light, the rest of him in shadow. It was a fitting metaphor for the man's condition.

Barry walked slowly towards his old friend, not in any particular hurry to do anything in this place of soft voices and light steps. He remembered Wheels Royer, a figure of manliness and authority, six-foot-three in his knee-high boots. Mirrored shades and a perfect moustache, the ideal policeman.

The first time he'd met Wheels, he was just out of the Academy, but powerfully attracted to the Harley Davidson Electra-Glides ridden by Traffic Division. Barry found Traffic work deadly dull. He just wanted to ride one of those bikes.

He'd been out at a disturbance call in the East Side when a giant on a ripping Harley did a flagrant wheelie right past the scene. "Bah, Wheels! He'll never grow up." Whistling Smith had said it with a mixture of irritation and admiration.

It was from men like Whistling Smith and Wheels Royer that Barry had learned the sheer joy, the pure boyish glee of being a policeman. It was serious, sometimes dangerous, and often depressing work, true. But it was also funny, exciting, and deeply satisfying. So, when after five years on Patrol, Barry had put in his transfer request for Traffic on now Sergeant Smith's desk, his first mentor had understood, if only grudgingly.

"Jesus Christ, Olds! You've got twenty years till pension! Haven't you considered suicide?"

"Sarge, I'm just looking for a change."

"Badge bunnies and Harleys, eh?"

"If I have to be honest."

Wheels Royer had shown him, a two-wheeler since he got his first dirt bike at the age of twelve, how to do things on a motorcycle he would never have thought possible. He also showed Barry how to handle a very different clientele than the degraded and the downtrodden of Patrol Northeast.

Traffic dealt with *citizens*. Citizens did not define themselves as scofflaws. They had places to be, rights, connections…great excuses for the idiotic things they did behind the wheel.

Generally speaking, they were supreme pains in the asshole. But where Whistling Smith was an armoured bulldozer with a well-concealed gold-plated engine/heart, Wheels Royer was a diplomat/recruiting poster who could sweet talk a hornet's nest.

As a policeman, Barry Olds was a child of two fathers. But when he looked down at this one, he did not see the man he knew before the crash.

Sixteen months ago, Corporal Royer had been responding to an "Officer Needs Assistance" call at speed on the Number One, when his bike hit a slick patch on a shoulder. He went inverted and landed on his helmet, the back wheel of his Harley bouncing off of him for good measure.

He knew the score right away. Royer had told him more than once that if his spine had been severed lower down, and he'd been able to draw his revolver...

The deep brown eyes clocked his approach. One of the few things Royer could still move. His breathing tube rattled noisily. "No flowers, again, kid? I thought I was specific."

"Sorry, pal. Wouldn't want anyone to think we were going steady."

"Somewhere, someone has a fetish for this." Royer sighed. His formerly sharp jaw was buried under flaccid chins, his once sharp eyes, clouded by things only he could see. All Barry could think of was getting a drink. "What's new, Sarge?"

"Ah, getting ready for Expo. Breaking in the new girl. Keeping tabs on Grohmann. The usual."

"Expo." A laugh rattled in Royer's ventilator. "The greatest show I'll never see."

"Had a field trip yesterday. You're not missing much."

"How's the missus?"

"Oh, she's good, she's good. With the kids all in high school now, she's back at Royal Bank. Soon, she'll be making more than me." Barry paused before asking after Pamela Royer. It was always a soft spot.

"You don't want to ask about Pam, do you?"

Barry shrugged. "I don't want to come down here, without flowers, and piss you off."

"It's okay, Barry. She hasn't been here in weeks. What would I do, really, if the roles were reversed?"

"Fair question, I guess. Still, till death us do part, and all…"

That rattling laugh again. "Aw, come on. That hasn't been the deal since the seventies, partner. Part of me wishes she'd just get it over with, stop pretending."

"Roy…"

"No, it's cool. Fuck it, you got any smokes?"

"Yeah, Roy, but you're not supposed to…"

"Ahahaha…what? It's bad for my health? Could my health get any worse? Do me a favour and walk me outside. Once we're out of range of the Nurse Ratchet brigade, you can share an Export "A" with me."

"Fair enough." Outside, it was one of those brief interregnums between rainstorms, dappled with sunshine. Nurses and family members were out walking other patients, taking full advantage.

Royer drove his electric wheelchair with abandon. He showed off a few tight turns and spins. Barry laughed. "You can take the motorcycle away from the cop…"

Royer gave him a crooked smile. "You can take everything away, Barry. But the only thing that keeps me sane is that time when I had it all. I made the most of it, didn't I?"

"Yeah, partner, you did."

"When I close my eyes at night, it's all I think about. I just…kind of…will the other stuff out of my mind. If I fall asleep thinking of myself on that Harley, I can make it through another night."

They sheltered from a growing wind in the lee of a parks building. Barry helped his partner smoke a cigarette. He pondered asking the question on his mind.

Royer noticed. "You'd have made a shitty detective, Olds. Spit it out."

"What's…what's it like? I mean, what does it feel like, Roy?"

"You mean, when you can't feel anything? Weird. Never get used to it. Like being a severed head on a dinner plate. The only life you have left is between your ears. If you haven't done it already, you won't do it."

"That's not what Rick Hanson would say." The paraplegic athlete was a driving force behind Expo '86.

"Bah. Gimme another drag. Ah, that's good. Hanson wouldn't know. He's a para, I'm a quad. He can do a lot of shit I can't, like drive a car, feel up a chick, feed himself. Fuck." He went silent and glum. Pre-schoolers trooped past them, chattering, with their teachers.

"Doesn't that get to you, Wheels?"

"Fuck off, Barry. You bring any booze?"

"Yeah." Barry pulled a mickey of rye out of his coat pocket, and a can of coke out of the other. "Would sir enjoy a rye and coke?"

"I'd kill you for it, if I still could." Barry mixed the drink, then stuck a straw in it. Royer sucked greedily. "Ah, God bless you, partner. That's the difference between my cop friends and my civilian pals. The cops will all break the rules to keep me happy." Royer paused and looked at him.

"You want another?"

"I'd love to, but I couldn't handle it. I'm not the guy who used to close the Athletic Club bar every night, you know. No...there was something else, Barry."

Barry paused, wishing the moment away. "Wheels..."

"That fucking cunt Pam has access to top-drawer drugs in the ICU, you know that? She just grabs a few sample packs, no sign-out, and I could be done for, okay?" His eyes welled up with tears. "But she fucking won't. Every time I try and convince her, she comes at me with this fucking Jerry Falwell bullshit about how it's not God's will. So, this is? Fuck God's will, Barry. I just want out. You're a supervisor on Drug Section, right? You can get almost pure Asian Heroin. That's what I want, Barry. One smooth shot, and I'll be riding my Harley to the fucking stars, babe!"

Barry twisted uncomfortably. "I...I can't man. Sorry, Wheels. But if an ex-cop keels over from a hotshot in GF Strong, who the fuck do you think they're going to come after, eh?"

Royer went quiet. "Just take me back. Asshole."

They returned to GF Strong in painful silence. When they reached the entrance, Royer wheeled around to face him. "Don't come here anymore, okay? It's hard for you, and if you can't help me die, I've got no use for you. Consider me gone."

Barry watched his friend roll away, back into a life he couldn't imagine, and didn't want to. He lit a smoke and headed off in search of a drink.

COLUMBIA ST
DOWNTOWN EAST SIDE

Rick Grohmann walked the side-street quickly, clocking the

faces, sometimes stopping to move a cardboard box or sweep aside a hood to make sure.

Recognizing him, some of the local denizens with warrants, who were holding, or just plain paranoid, took to their heels. He wasn't chasing them, at least not today.

Today, he was on personal time. Rick stopped in front of a passable lean-to, the sort of shelter a soldier would build, not like the sorry-assed excuses the others hunched under.

"Perry? That you?"

A cadaverous face, framed by the hood of a CF-issue parka, peered out at him. "Grohmann, that you?"

"Sill earning that Leaf of Grief down here, Master Corporal?"

"Ain't nobody messing with me, if that's what you mean. We going for a walk?"

"Of course." At that, Perry scrambled out of his shelter with surprising agility. He was tall, but no longer beefy, hard drugs having consumed his body and a growing part of his mind. Perry pointed a finger at his next-door neighbour.

"You've got the section, Clarke. Don't let anybody fuck with my stuff, or it's pushups till you puke."

The weaselly little junkie next to him, who must have been wearing four lumberjack shirts on top of each other, fired off a salute. "Yes, Master Corporal."

Rick chuckled as they walked towards Sun Yat-Sen Park. "Still got that command presence, eh Andy?"

"Somebody's got to do it, Rick. Without me, those maggots would be selling their asses to anybody, and mugging little old ladies to make dope money. I keep 'em on as straight and narrow as they're ever going to get."

Rick nodded. Andy Perry had been his section leader on his second Cyprus tour, a professional soldier of calm and composure until he'd broken his back in a jeep accident. Then, like so many others down here, pain had driven him into the arms of Lady Heroin.

Stories like Perry's shaped his attitude towards users. Rick Grohmann might have hated a lot of other people he'd met in police work. But he only hated those users who, like Perry had alluded to, lost their humanity in pursuit of drugs.

In his experience, that wasn't all, or even most users. Dealers were another story entirely. Rick Grohmann hated dealers with a flaming passion.

And yet, what was he about to do? They stopped at the gates of the Chinese park and found a secluded copse of trees. In the distance, the new BC Place Stadium sat, awaiting the opening ceremonies. Beyond that, the Plaza of Nations awaited the drug-fuelled visitors Blotter Boorman would supply with other people's dope.

Where some people saw the promise of the future, all Rick Grohmann saw was the same old misery, re-packaged and up-marketed.

Perry intruded on his thoughts, single-minded, like all junkies. A soft rain began to drum on the fresh leaves over their heads. "You, ah...you got what I need, Rick?"

"Sure thing, Master Corporal." He handed over a tight bundle of smack and an envelope with clean rigs. "You get yourself right now." Rick made to walk away.

"That's it? You don't want any info, or nothing?"

"Unless it's about Blotter Boorman, or four assholes ripping off half the dealers in town, not really."

Perry shrugged. "Guess I can't help you. But I'll keep an eye out."

"You do that, Andy. Or just stay alive, whatever." Rick Grohmann walked into the rain, also looking for a drink.

**METROTOWN
BURNABY**

Bobbi Sanghera picked at the noodles on her plate and listened to the litany of grief discharged from her old Academy classmate. Casey Shirlaw had been a superstar in the class of '83, by popular consensus the most likely to succeed, at least among her female compatriots.

She was tall, physically fit, good-looking, and sharp. She'd graduated third in the class. And two years later she was out.

Today, Bobbi had finally given in to her multiple entreaties for a lunch date and was regretting it already. She'd ridden the new Skytrain from Joyce to the swarming mall of Metrotown. Bobbi knew that Casey was a drinker and had no intention of getting an Impaired charge to ruin her career. Casey picked Chinese, which Bobbi found borderline edible thanks to all the MSG. And, to top it all off, since they'd sat down, she'd barely gotten a word in edgewise.

Casey had a lot to say. And Bobbi had the feeling that she was building up to a bombshell.

Other people's problems. Bobbi had impressed her instructors in the Academy as being a particularly good listener. *If they could see me now.*

"What did you hear?" Casey was staring her, chopsticks poised over a gleaming plate of unnaturally coloured pork.

Bobbi stared back. "Sorry, what?"

"Aren't you listening?"

"No, no…it's just real loud in here."

"Oh yeah. Anyway, what did you hear about me leaving the force?"

"Um…I heard you just said it wasn't for me."

"Such bullshit! I told Inspector Franklin that his superstar Corporal was a goddamned rapist. That's what really happened, Bobbi."

"What?"

"Corporal Parkes in Patrol South. Fucking rapo. It's true. His idea of a good time is a back alley, a back seat, and the back door."

Bobbi winced. "Jesus! Did you report him?"

"Well, not officially. But I told Laidlaw and Crippen, and neither of them did a goddamned thing. Fucking locker room, Bobbi."

"Well, I hate to tell you this, but he made Sergeant last month."

"Fucker."

There were others, of course. Bobbi sat and listened politely, not regretting her decision to take transit. More than one beer was required.

She wanted to sympathize; she really did. And it wasn't like there wasn't some pretty rampant macho bullshit on display 24/7 among the former jocks and soldiers of the Vancouver Police Department. She'd been on the receiving end of a lot of it, herself.

Barry Olds had taken over her training after he found out her old FTO had been putting some pretty aggressive moves on her. She was lucky.

But the problem was, she knew some of the guys Casey was badmouthing. Some, like Parkes, it was easy to believe as, if not rapists, then at least handsy jerks who wouldn't take no for an answer. But everybody couldn't have been like that. And if you'd actually been raped, why not report it?

Again, her eyes gave her away. "You...you don't believe me, do you?"

"What? No, Casey...it's not that at all. It's just...a real big shock, that's all. I believe you about Parkes. He's a creep. But Cal Stepanuk...he was always a prince to me."

"Well, maybe you're just not his type, Bobbi." The way she said it, there was no 'maybe' about it.

"I guess. I suppose I'm just confused...if Parkes raped you, why didn't you report it? I would've."

"Really? Really, you're so sure, Bobbi? Like you'd be so ready to take a rape kit and give a statement, if your so-called partner had driven you back to the station to 'clean up,' after he'd screwed you like a hooker in a fucking alleyway? You know what my Sergeant said? He said, 'You had all the gear on, why didn't you shoot him?' Can you imagine that? You think you know what you'd do? You know shit, Bobbi."

Casey stood unsteadily, knocking over her drink, then stormed out, leaving Bobbi with the bill.

Five minutes later, as every eye in the restaurant watched her, Bobbi was walking out to the street, looking for another place to drink.

MAY

VANCOUVER WELCOMES THE WORLD

The drug business attracts a diverse range of characters. Tonight, Rick Grohmann will encounter two of them...

THE GANDYDANCER

Rick Grohmann watched the opening fireworks with mostly gay crowd from the back door of the Gandy. He ignored the kissing and nuzzling men now. You had to, or it would drive you nuts. As he watched the explosions over False Creek, with the blinking lights of the Expo Dome in the distance, he instead puzzled over his dilemma.

He had a witness. But that witness could not counteract a false confession if that witness wouldn't talk.

Clearly, Edwin Lo had been gotten to. But, based on the shitty PIRS entry, how on earth had anyone figured that he'd seen anything? Perhaps the crew had made him?

Or, maybe they'd made *me*, he thought. Panicking and peeling out right across the street from the target, what kind of rookie mistake was that? If Tusker Taakoiennin would confess to a crime he hadn't committed, and get his girlfriend to back it up, what's to say he wouldn't turn informant for his new master, and drop a caribou the second he saw Grohmann hanging out at a witness' house?

Of course, it was Tusker. Fucking had to be. And here he thought the Finns were tough. Fucking pussy.

Whatever the cause, his attempts to talk to Edwin had been a bust. Embarrassingly so. He'd tried calling the kid's house yesterday, only to have momma hang up on him, screaming at him in Chinese. A visit to the kid's high school this noon hour had resulted in the terrified kid bolting like a greyhound, with Rick having to badge his way out of it with uniforms to avoid being collared as a pedo.

Clearly, somebody had gotten to the kid.

And that's what had brought him back here, looking for, if not a past victim of Blotter's, then perhaps a future one. Ray Beuerhoft was a strange cat, a half-black, half-German wannabe Rastafari with dreadlocks and a taste for cock, a regular here.

Ray was not above snitching when it was a matter of pure business interest. If he bumped into Soulschnitzel, as they called him, Rick figured he might have a fighting chance of enlisting his help. From what he was hearing, Ray was one of the few independents left who hadn't gone down over the last three weeks.

Tiring of the 'oohs' and 'ahhs' and the blatant necking, Rick had ducked inside to warm up. Simple Minds were on the stereo. As his eyes readjusted, he scanned the room as the tunes pumped in his eardrums.

Flesh of heart
Heart of steel
So well, so well
I cut my hair
Paint my face
Break a finger
Tell a lie
So well, so well

He found Soulschnitzel in a dark corner, alone. He dropped into the seat opposite as the dealer fussed with his dreads. "Mister Policeman. What do you want?" Ray couldn't sound urban. He was the son of an American GI and a German housewife and had grown up in West Germany. It was all he could do to keep his accent at bay.

"You're an independent. Independents all over the city are getting ripped off by a four-man crew."

"Yeah, yeah. It's Blotter Boorman, of course. Is that what you want to know?"

"I already know that, you sausage-sucking mocha faggot." Ray sucked in his lips like he'd been smacked on the ass. "I just need to prove it."

"Well, you know where I live. Come around after they've tried to rip me, and you can look at the bodies."

"Now now, Raymond. Don't make threats in front of me."

"Does not a man have the right to defend his own property? I have no criminal record, and therefore I legally own guns. The law does not prohibit me from using them in defence, does it?"

"No. No, it doesn't. But be careful, Ray. These guys are working for the bikers."

Ray paused for a second. A shadow fell over his face. "Bikers, eh? Well, whatever. I may be a faggot, but I do not suck dick for just anyone. Not the police, and not the bikers either."

Grohmann set his card on the table in front of Ray. "Call me if you hear anything. I'd rather this didn't end in dead bodies."

Ray sucked in his lips again as if titillated. "Ooh, Mister Policeman, you are becoming fond of me, I think. Why don't you want the dead bodies, mmm? Usually you do not care."

Grohmann stroked Ray's dreads as he got up. "Because if it's dead bodies, it's a Major Crimes case. Now, cut those off before a real Rasta man comes along and does it for you. See you at the shooting range, Ray."

Rick stopped at the bar for another as New Order took over the stereo.

Every time I think of you
I feel shot through with a bolt of blue
It's no problem of mine, but it's a problem I find
Livin' a life that I can't leave behind

He'd just gotten his Tanqueray and Tonic when he turned around to see Ray gone. When he looked back, a kid with long red hair was staring him from the exit into the alley. The kid seemed to be beckoning him. He took a long gulp on his T&T and headed for the exit.

When he stepped out into the alley, the kid was doing a nervous little jig at the corner of the building. The kid made to walk away when he clocked Rick, but Rick was having none of it. "That's enough, asshole. You got me out here. Now talk to me."

The kid's hair was already wet. He looked miserable. He was rail-thin and dressed preppy-style. *So last year.* "You a cop?"

"Yeah." Rick badged him. "Do I know you?"

"No, but I go to Gladstone. I saw you there today. What did you want to talk to Eddie Lo about?"

"Who's asking the fucking questions? You a detective too?"

"Forget it." The kid turned to leave, but Rick grabbed him by the shirt and tossed him up against a dumpster.

"Not so fast. You got me all horny, now you just gonna blue ball me? Edwin Lo. Talk."

The kid swallowed hard. "Um…we just saw him running from you. I maybe figured I could help."

"Why, you a junior detective or something? Hate to break it to you, but VPD doesn't hire fruits."

"I'm not gay! I just like the tunes here. Plus, they never check ID."

"True, sounds like you and I are here for the same reasons. What's your name, kid?"

"Um, Karey. Karey Bezoff."

"You friends with Eddie?"

"Fuck, no. He's a giant fucking Asian science nerd."

"So why do you care if he runs from a cop?"

"See…uh, my friends and I, we deal a little weed at school…"

"You saying I should take you in?"

"No! No…no, I was just thinking, like I heard about you. You don't give a shit about small stuff like that, like you must be more interested in big things. Like maybe Eddie is cooking or something, right?"

"Kid, you think too much. What's your business proposal?"

"Like if we catch Eddie for you and bring him to you, maybe you can put our rivals out of business?"

"Who are your rivals?"

"The Two-Five Devils. We're the Gladstone Ghouls."

Rick guffawed. "Oh shit, that's rich. You guys are only half as scary as the Clark Park Gang, and twice as dumb!"

Karey looked hurt. "Hey, my dad was in the Clark Park Gang."

"What a shocker." *Shit breeds shit, as Bevan always said.* "Now listen, son. I can't go around kidnapping, or soliciting the kidnapping of witnesses, especially not seventeen-year-old ones. And Eddie's a witness, not a suspect. Plus, I'm happy to let low-level dealers feed shit to shitbirds, but you guys are selling dope at a *fucking high school.* Now, if you want me to forget about all the shit you just told me, tell me one thing."

"What?"

"Just tell where I can find Eddie Lo, real soon, without a foot chase?"

"Oh, that's easy. Grad."

"Where and when?"

"Wednesday night. At the Bayshore."

"You sure he's going?"

"Asian kids never miss an opportunity to show off."

"Stop dealing dope. You might make a good cop sometime."

Rick walked out to the street as the last of the fireworks blew their loads. It made him think of Clarissa. She had to be home, as per his orders. Behaving herself.

Or, maybe she wasn't behaving herself.

So much the better.

MAY

TOO SHY SHY

While it is customary to describe drug dealers as parasites feeding on the misery of addicts, there are other parasites this world attracts. Some of these parasites actually make dealers look good by comparison, as Barry Olds and Bobbi Sanghera will be reminded...

LYNN CANYON
NORTH VANCOUVER

Rick Grohmann awoke, thank God, alone. Steady rain poured out of the leaf-clogged eavestroughs he should've cleaned back in November. One more thing for the old Clarissa to nag at him for.

But not anymore. No, like that Stones song said, she was "under his thumb." At first, it was a thrill, if a sick one. But now, like that other song said, "the thrill is gone."

If he wasn't punishing her for being a slut, he had nothing to say to her. So, her being away at work was a blessing. Rick began to visualize what a divorce was going to look like, and quickly thought better of it.

Leave, and have her take half of everything he'd worked for, even if he played the adultery card. She could turn around and play the brutality card. It didn't take much imagination for anyone who knew Rick as a cop to visualize what a hell-on-wheels husband he must be.

Stay, and spend the rest of your life with someone you hated now and couldn't trust anymore. But wasn't that how so many people lived their lives, anyway? Why should they be any different?

He blinked and shook his head, the patter of the rain the only sound in the room, until a foghorn out in Burrard Inlet hooted for attention. Rick sat up, imagining himself at Reveille, and began to search out his pants.

PLAZA OF NATIONS
BY BC PLACE STADIUM

Barry Olds and Bobbi Sanghera slowly walked the grounds of the Plaza of Nations, watching the cleanup crews tackle the sifting dunes of trash left behind by last night's patrons. The rain was dying down now, leaving only a moist sprinkling most Vancouverites considered background radiation, hardly worth commenting on.

"Why are we here, Sarge?" Bobbi Sanghera looked around at the combination of fresh-faced families, relieved that the rain had abated in time to get some mileage out of their day passes; and sweating, toiling, minimum wagers who kept the whole artifice running. "Nothing but labourers busting a hump, and families whining about sore feet."

Barry shrugged. "I dunno. I was getting sick of rousting junkies this week, weren't you? I mean, so far, Princess Di passing out in the ladies' room has been the highlight of the fair."

"Yeah, I heard about that. The Mounties found Scotland Yard trying to slap-start her, from what I heard."

Barry chuckled. "Can you imagine? I wonder if she's pregnant again."

"Nah, I heard she's anorexic."

"Really? Her? If I lived in a palace, I think I'd weigh 400 bucks by now."

"Me too." They both chuckled. Bobbi slowed to watch the hustling teenaged workers. "Now that's work."

"You ever work that hard, Bobbi?"

"You kidding, Sarge? Every summer till I was eighteen, on Sanghera Brothers' Blueberry Farm in Cloverdale. When white kids say, 'summers seemed to last forever,' it's a good thing. When brown kids say it, they really mean it."

"I bet. This reminds me of my first job, too. Summer of '57 at the White Spot on South Granville."

"You're dating yourself." She tittered.

"It was hard, but fun. They always had good music on, like Chubby Checker and Buddy Holly. So, you could work to the rhythm if you were flagging. And you got a cheeseburger with fries and a shake for lunch. Hard work made it taste better."

"You sound like my dad. So, we're here to get nostalgic?"

Barry shrugged again. "Well, since everything's so quiet, I figured we'd take a cruise down here and see if Dirty Dave Poulin is hanging around."

"Sounds like fun. Is he a dealer?"

"Nah, he's a scalper. Sells the real thing, and sometimes, fakes. He likes the area around here. Lions tickets are easier to fake than Canucks tickets, and now, the Plaza is full of his other interest." Barry stopped in front of an ice-cream concession. Three teenaged girls hustled to meet the suddenly swelling crowd's demands.

Bobbi caught on. "Ah. He's a pervo."

"Yeah. Always keeps his shitty little shagging wagon parked close, so he can accept 'alternate payment' from girlies desperate to see Iron Maiden, or Twisted Rabbit, or whatever the hell they call themselves."

"Are we seeing a lot of Expo fakes?"

"There's money in it. They have to be out there. Come on, let's work back to the turnstiles. All the guards know Dirty Dave, there's no way he'll be in here."

As they pushed back through the crowd, fighting the flow, the sun began to paint the throngs, and people started doffing their jackets and sweaters. They stopped just past the turnstiles with a wave to the guard at the bypass. "See anything, Sarge?"

Barry laughed. "You are so damned predictable, Dirty Dave." He pointed to an airbrushed, 70s style disco wagon, diamond-shaped rear windows and all, parked under the Skytrain tracks. "Let's get a little closer and wait."

They stepped down one embankment, and climbed another, as parking patrollers tried to maintain order against a rising tide of people. When they came to the next parking lot, they stopped behind a minivan to watch the action. A diminutive girl in a halter top and mini, with brown hair cut in a bob, was talking outside the shagging wagon with a man wearing a Star Wars t-shirt too small for his protruding gut. The balding slob towered over the little girl.

"That doesn't look promising." Bobbi ventured.

"You said it. That little cutie Dirty Dave is talking to is none other than Wrong Ronnie. I can't believe he doesn't recognize her!" Barry shook his head.

"Wrong Ronnie? So many nicknames on the East Side."

"That's because most people on the West Side aren't interesting enough to give a nickname to. Wrong Ronnie is a tranny hooker."

"Hmm. Convincing."

"Until you look under the hood. Wrong Ronnie has a schlong that makes John Holmes look like a hamster. When the rubber meets the road, he always gets busted. I think he gets off on the rough stuff. Oh no, here he goes." Now, Dirty Dave led his surprise sweetheart into his van. "*Caveat emptor,* Davey."

"What's that mean?"

"Let the buyer beware. Come on, let's get over there. A nice stash of Expo counterfeits oughta make up for the lack of dope lately."

They were almost to the van when it started rocking and heaving. Bobbi snickered. "What's that old expression, 'If the van is a rocking, do come a knocking?'"

"Police officers only, yes." Muffled voices came from inside.

"You fucking creep! You're a dude! Goddamn it!"

"Come on Dave, I can do almost everything! I really need that ticket!"

"Fuck that! Get out!" The back doors opened suddenly, and Dave tossed Wrong Ronnie unceremoniously out with one hand. Then he stepped out to make a speech. "I ain't no homo…"

But Barry Olds grabbed him by the throat before he could finish. "Hi, Dirty Dave!"

"Uggggh…. urrrrgggh…. ack…"

"Remember me? The nice policeman who asked you nicely to stop trolling for fresh meat in exchange for tickets?" Barry turned to Bobbi, who was helping Ronnie to his feet. "Dave's having a hard time adjusting since the Lions moved downtown. You never found a snake when you were hunting for clam at Empire Stadium, did you?"

"Aggggh…. urk…" Barry frog marched his prisoner to the front of the van and handcuffed him. A gaggle of obvious Americans stopped on their way to the turnstiles to film the encounter on a VHS camera. Now that Dave had an audience, and a free airway, he solicited assistance. "Film this people! Look at this brutality! That's how the police treat small businessmen!"

Barry scrutinized a couple of pills he pulled out of Dave's jean pocket. "Phenobarbs? Phenobarbs, Davey? You weren't planning on making your next underage date go to sleep, were you?"

"Uh...I have trouble sleeping!"

"And so you should." Barry tossed the pills into a mud puddle, then handcuffed Dave to a light standard. "Wait right here." He walked back to where Bobbi was taking Ronnie's information. "Ronnie, what have I told you?"

"I know, I know, Sergeant, pick up where it's nice and gay, or you'll get beat up. I know! I just...I just knew he could be had for a quick BJ, and I really wanted those Kajagoogoo tickets!"

Barry looked at Bobbi. She pointed to the interior of the van. Racks of phoney passes and fanned displays of three-dollar bill tickets adorned the inside. "Holy shit!"

"That's my stuff!" Dirty Dave shouted from his light standard, where more curious tourists had arrived to film him.

"Not anymore it's not!" Barry yelled back. "Well, Ronnie, you've been a good girl this year. Let's see what Bad Santa here has for you." He rooted around, finding two Kajagoogoo tickets on display. He stepped out and handed them to Ronnie. "Happy Hanukkah."

"Gee, thanks Sergeant." Bobbi suppressed a laugh as Ronnie's eyes went wide.

"Kajagoogoo, eh?" Bobbi questioned Ronnie. "What songs do they do?"

"Oooh, hang on!" Ronnie posed to start a dance routine.

"Sing it to the guest of honour." Barry pointed at Dirty Dave, slumped dejectedly against the light standard. One tourist, apparently thinking he was performance art, had tossed coins at his feet. "He's earned it. Besides, it'll distract him while we impound his van."

Ronnie began to sing and dance unabashedly.

You're too shy shy, hush-hush, eye to eye
Too shy shy, hush-hush, eye to eye

"Fuck you pigs! Fuck you!" Dirty Dave screamed, as the tourists dumped money at his feet and Ronnie danced like no one was watching.

"Hey, Dave!" Bobbi yelled, "At least you've got bus fare!"

BEACH TOWERS APARTMENTS

Where Blotter Boorman's Probation Officer thought he lived, was not where he actually lived. He'd slipped a half-vacant pensioner two floors down a few bills a month to keep his spare room "lived-in," and say he lived there if anyone asked. The phone number he gave was correct, but Blotter screened his calls through an answering machine, using a brick cell phone to conduct real business. All in all, a pretty easy deal. His PO was too lazy to stay past five to check on his curfew, and he knew Grohmann wouldn't arrest him until he could pin something with serious Federal time on him.

In a few short weeks, he'd taken over the majority of the city's independent drug suppliers, without firing a shot, and with only a little rough stuff. That thing with Marianne had been... regrettable, but it turned out to their advantage anyway.

Men like Tusker knew how to survive in prison. But they couldn't shrug off a green light.

The cash was pouring in, and the experts were saying that Expo wouldn't even really take off until the kids were out of high school in late June. Then, he was on course for riches.

So why was he so fucking paranoid?

Blotter rattled the ice in his glass and looked down at his right hand. A little powder left on his index knuckle. Ah, that was it. He gently sniffed the remnant away.

Blotter had seen so many men go south from getting high on their own supply. How many times had he warned others? But the pace of the last few weeks had been gruelling. He couldn't keep up without a little…freshener. It was the only thing that allowed one four-hour-sleep night after another.

Plus, it had the added bonus of making him a little scarier and more unpredictable when needed. But how long could he control that?

That was a question for the future. His current problem, or, more accurately the man highlighting his current problem, was out on the balcony, admiring his view. Blotter scooped Randy McClarty's rye and coke off the bar and went out to join the fat biker.

Randy was puffing on a Colt and leaning over the balcony. Blotter idly wondered if it would take his weight. He smiled at the thought of 400 pounds of plummeting one-percenter impacting the tourists below.

The sun was setting now over English Bay, the transports riding high at anchor, the beachgoers packing up and heading for the bars. The sky was a brilliant orange, reflected by the sparkling sea.

"This is nice, man. I hate the traffic, and all the cops down here, but man, this fucking view…" McClarty shook his head and took the drink from Blotter. "Hey, thanks Blotter." He took a drink. "Damn, that's good too. Rye and coke, and coke. What a combo."

Blotter forced a laugh. "Sure is, Randy. That view is addictive too, eh?"

"Fuckin' eh rights." McClarty dipped into his drink again before fixing Blotter with a serious look. "The way I see it, you can relax and enjoy it, after you deal with one problem."

"Which is?"

"That loud-mouthed faggot Soulschnitzel. Bad enough he's a queer, who doesn't even bother to hide it. But a nigger, too?"

"I thought we agreed at the start that I was only going to tackle the low risk, high payoff properties. To avoid trouble. Hasn't that worked so far? No shootings, no killings, no witnesses going to the pigs. Just lots of money for both of us. Everybody knows Soulschnitzel is armed to the fucking teeth, and crazy enough to use it. What's the point?"

McClarty held his hands up in appeasement. "I know, Blotter, I know. You got a good point there, and I brought it up at the meeting. But you know how it is. Someone starts talking shit on the street, and it has to be dealt with. See, he's walking around saying you're too chicken to take him on, because he's tooled up, and to some people, that means *we're* too chicken to take him on. Can't have that."

"Why not?"

"Why not? Man, I gotta remind myself you just got out of jail, 'cause you sure don't act like it, Blotter. When one guy is putting you down, saying you're a goof, it encourages everyone else. Maybe they can take a shot, too. And if that happens..."

Blotter nodded bleakly and sat on a patio chair. "Yeah, yeah, I get it. I'm gonna need more men. And guns, too."

"I got some Hangarounds looking for a balls-deep mission, brother. They're yours."

Blotter joined McClarty in a half-hearted cheers. He stared out at the dazzling sunset, thinking of all the things he stood to lose.

MAY

WEST END GIRLS

Police officers know that lots of people don't like talking to them. For members of some immigrant communities, the reluctance runs very deep, as Rick Grohmann will be painfully reminded tonight…

BAYSHORE INN
WEST HASTINGS ST

Rick Grohmann had spent a pointless day squeezing his snitches for information on Blotter and his associates, but all he'd come up with were useless speculations about the bikers behind him and rumours of a coming hit on Ray Beuerhoft.

It seemed that Soulschnitzel's tough talk had been heard by more people than just him. That was possibly very bad news, with a silver lining.

A bloodbath during an international event would wrench the case from his hands and leave him facing questions about why he'd played his cards so close to his vest. But, it would also, finally, put Blotter Boorman at the top of the departmental priority list, demanding a long-time Maximum-Security cell, or a body bag. And as the VPD's resident expert on Blotter Boorman, who better to lead the charge?

Maybe, just maybe, if he played it cool tonight, he could get Eddie Lo on board. That meant Boorman off the streets for now, and a chance for the temperatures to lower.

So, he was hanging out here, like an over-the-hill pervo, watching the six-packs of hopeful teens alight from rented limos, excited for the party of their lives. Rick stood in the shadows outside the lobby, watching the couples troop in, boys fiddling with tuxedos, girls tottering on unfamiliar heels, constrained by too-tight dresses.

Luckily, security knew him here, so they let him be. The supervisor, an ex-West Van cop, had let him in on where the kids would be stepping out for "fresh air." He'd be sure to stake that one out later.

For now, it was enough to clock Edwin Lo, make sure he was here. Sure enough, the twenty-seventh limo to pull up disgorged an all-Asian brigade. Rick pulled back in the shadows and spotted him, escorting an awkward, four-eyed girl who was laughing nervously. His tux was a godawful baby blue retro number.

Later. Later was the time.

Mission accomplished, for now, he hit the bar.

TWO HOURS LATER

The sudden increase in music volume from the banquet hall let Rick know that the grad party had changed gears. Soon, the Security Supervisor had surprised him. "Hey, Rick, listen; the first ones are starting to slip out and light up. Come with me."

He set down his half-finished T&T and followed the portly former cop through the lobby and into a service corridor, before coming out of the edge of a plaza with a view of the sea.

At the sight of two older guys in sport coats, the tokers hurriedly puffed their last and moved on; the illicit drinkers took it somewhere else. Rick hinted to the supervisor that he'd be better off on his own. Then he defused the tension by walking up to an obvious drinker trying to hide a mickey in his tux pocket.

"They're sewn shut, man. Got a light?"

The kid was Asian, too. The colour returned to his face as Rick failed to go all cop on him. "Um, yeah." He produced a Bic and lit Rick up.

The girl standing with him was pale and blonde, with a massive Lady Di cut and a blue chiffon gown. "You a cop?"

Why lie? It's either cop or pervert. "Yup. You know Edwin Lo?"

The Asian kid coughed on his rum. "Holy shit. Is Eddie in trouble? No way!"

Rick took the bottle and confiscated a swig. Out on the harbour, the sailboats of the rich bobbed in the twinkling lights. "Not really. I just wanna talk to him. He still in there?"

"He's such a fucking weirdo." The girl chimed in. "Hey, there he is now."

Rick followed her pointing finger to a tall, stoop-shouldered kid with a terrible haircut and a bad-fitting tux. His date barely came up to his chest. "Excuse me."

Eddie Lo was too engrossed in trying to get to first base when Rick tapped him on the shoulder. "Congratulations."

The kid's eyes went wide at the sight of Rick's badge. "Whoa. My mom said not to talk to you. Hey, Brianna…" The short girl disappeared in a hurry. "What do you want, anyway? I didn't see anything."

"See anything about what, Edwin?"

"Across the street, you know."

"You call the police a lot, Edwin. You sure you got the right incident? You sure that's what I'm here for?" Edwin made to leave, but Rick grabbed his arm. He was aware he was drawing an audience; but how else was he going to get to this kid? "You getting molested in your sleep again?"

Edwin shrugged off the grip. "That was a long time ago. I take my medicine now."

"Good, that's good. So now I know I can trust you when you tell me what really happened across the street at Mr Taakoiennin's place last week. Because it wasn't what the other policemen think, was it?"

Now, the noise had increased. Someone had propped the doors to the banquet room, and the dancefloor was in full swing. Heat followed the teenagers outside, as did their music.

Sometimes you're better off dead
There's a gun in your hand and it's pointing at your head
You think you're mad, too unstable
Kicking in chairs and knocking down tables
In a restaurant in a West End town
Call the police, there's a mad man around

Edwin looked at him suspiciously, already narrow eyes narrowed further still. "No. I guess not."

"If you're afraid, we can protect you."

"That's what I told my mother. But she..."

"What?"

"Look out!" Edwin recoiled as, too late, Rick turned to check behind him. Too slow to avoid the drinking glass that now smashed over his head from behind.

Rick staggered forward, blinking, as blood ran down his neck. A kick found his ribcage from the right side, forcing him into a crouch. The crowd parted as more kicks came.

He felt for the sap in his pocket and went to his knees. Then, he pivoted.

He caught a glimpse of tuxedo-clad, skinny white and native kids, faces twisted with the joy of beating. One of them shouted, "Two-Five Devils!" He remembered the name of Karey Bezoff's ridiculous rivals.

Then, he started swinging for kneecaps. He caught two before a head kick knocked him sideways. The group was about to close in on him in a kicking circle before Bezoff and his crew appeared from inside and attacked them.

Distracted, the Devils let him get to his feet. He slowly pocketed the sap, watching the outnumbered Ghouls fold under punches and kicks. Rick assumed a boxer's stance and moved into the melee.

In a West End town a dead-end world
The East End boys and West End girls
In a West End Town in a dead-end world
The East End boys and West End girls

Rick began sending jabs in, then combos. One-by-one, the Devils, heads snapping back, collapsed on the pavement. The Ghouls, their usefulness ended, simply watched.

One boy, a solid native kid with bad acne, knew a few moves. He swung for the jaw and made a glancing contact. Rick stepped back, skipped to the left, then launched a left jab/right hook combo that knocked him out cold.

He looked around. No more standing Devils. Lots of staring kids, and a few shouting teachers. One running Asian kid, heading for the parking lot.

Rick took off at a sprint, the pain in his scalp and ribs pushed back by adrenaline. He was half-way towards catching the kid when a Toyota swerved in front, hopped the curb, and scooped Edwin up like a pro.

Jesus Christ. Mom was on fucking standby.

As the Toyota peeled out into traffic, making an illegal left onto Hastings, Rick stumbled towards his Caprice. He ignored the shrill shouts of teachers behind him. He reached the car, felt the wound on his head, and with a bloody hand started the ignition. Pulling out through a parting crowd, he drove straight into traffic, blipping the horn.

Two blocks ahead, he saw the Toyota turning right, and then he knew where they were going. If he was wrong, he could always catch them later.

But if he was right, he was about to lose his witness for good.

Rick Grohmann slipped out of pursuit mode, slapped the fireball on the dash, and headed for the airport. With shortcuts, he was sure he'd make it first.

MAY

WITLESS PROTECTION

Imaginative police officers can find unconventional solutions to almost any problem, if they think outside the lines, and trust each other...

VANCOUVER INTERNATIONAL AIRPORT
DEPARTURES LEVEL

True to his predictions, Rick Grohmann beat the Los on their way to the airport with aggressive driving and a cop's city knowledge. He parked his car on the curb with a dash pass and ducked into a bathroom to clean up.

Standing in front of the mirror, ignoring the shocked looks of travelers, he tried to pretty up the damage. Gingerly, he picked glass from his scalp with a paper towel, before dabbing the wound, which had mercifully stopped bleeding, with soap and water.

Probably a four-stitch job. But it can wait.

Then, he cleaned up his neck as best he could, and slipped his coat back over his shirt before tending to his bruised and bloodied knuckles. "Sir."

Rick looked up to see a young, pencil-thin Mountie standing in the doorway, a revolver in his hand. "What?"

"We got a report of a bleeding man with a gun on his hip."

"VPD."

"Got ID?"

"Gimme a second." He finished dabbing at his knuckles. A guy could get a mean infection if you didn't. Teeth were dirty. The Mountie, now joined by another, was getting exasperated.

"You know, I am holding you at gunpoint. Hurry up."

"Give it a rest." With his left hand, he whipped his wallet out of his jacket pocket and tossed it at the startled cop. "Satisfied?"

"I guess so." The Mounties holstered their guns. "But what's going on?"

Rick sighed. "Absconding witness. Gotta intercept them before they fly to Taiwan."

"There's a flight out booking now. Closes in a half-hour."

"Great. Come on." Flustered, the Mounties followed him outside. "Where's check-in?"

"Ah, over there. Have you got a warrant, or a summons at least?"

"Not just this minute. What's your name, sonny?"

"Ah, Chadwick. Alan Chadwick."

"Okay, Constable Chadwick."

"Special Constable Chadwick."

"That's...uh...*special.* If you're not doing anything else, watch the Air China counter for me. If you see a Chinese lady with a gangly kid in a tuxedo, come get me here." Feeling woozy, he leaned against a payphone.

"Those are your targets?" Chadwick was incredulous.

"I said *witnesses,* not *suspects,* didn't I?"

"Er...got it. Detective..."

"Detective Grohmann. Thanks kid. Where'd your partner go?"

"Back to lunch. He says he can't afford to miss a meal."

"I'd beg to differ. Whatever."

Ten minutes later, a breathless Chadwick was reporting back. "I think they're here!"

Rick walked from pillar to pillar, and finally got close enough to scope them out. Sure enough, a woman in a ridiculous floral hat with a broad brim was haggling with a ticket clerk, while a dejected kid with his shirttails hanging out stood behind her, muttering to himself. "Yeah, that's them."

"That's who?" A deep voice demanded.

Rick turned to see a tall, ramrod-straight RCMP Sergeant standing behind him. The man had a waxed Guards' moustache and a nametag that read "MULVANEY."

Chadwick shrugged. "I…er…I had to call it in, right Detective?"

RCMP VANCOUVER AIRPORT DETACHMENT

Rick cooled his heels in Mulvaney's office while a paramedic finished picking the glass out of his scalp. He listened to Mrs Lo giving holy shit to anyone and everyone in hearing range in rapid-fire Mandarin.

"Jesus." The paramedic, a sorry-looking old-timer whispered. "What a cunt. If the kid's trying to run away, I can't say I blame him."

"Is that all?"

"Well, yeah. All the glass. But you need stitches. We can drop you off at RGH."

"Nah. I'll drive."

"Tough fucker, eh? Suit yourself. Have a better one."

He was still listening to Mrs Lo go off across the office, and watching Eddie eat a bag of Doritos, when Mulvaney appeared, shutting the door behind him. "Well?"

"Sergeant?"

"Do I need to elaborate? First you generate a gun run in my terminal building, something my guys are not really that used to, then you saddle me with Miss Screaming Bitch 1986 over here. What's it all about, Grohmann?"

Rick sighed and explained the situation with Tusker's so-called domestic, and how Eddie fit in as a witness.

"Wait." Mulvaney held up a hand. "So, this drug dealing shithead didn't really beat up his old lady? Why exactly do we care?"

"Because we want the people who really did it, who Tusker is too scared to finger. Blotter Boorman and three shitrats who work for him."

A strange look came over Mulvaney's face. Rick had heard the man had a serious rep, having blown away one half of a tag-team rape gang in '81, and taking a couple of bullets for his trouble. From the looks of his posting, the RCMP were not impressed with his work.

"Sarge?"

"Did you say, Blotter Boorman?"

"Yeah. I put him away in '84 for possession with intent. He just made Probation, and so far, he's been watching his Ps and Qs."

"He always does."

"You know him?"

"I'm the guy who got him his five-year jolt in '69. Is he using again?"

"Not the last time I talked to him."

"Watch out, he gets paranoid. So, you gonna tell your bosses now, Grohmann?"

"Guess I'll have to." Across the office, the decibel level had dipped sharply.

"Okay. Ordinarily, I'd be pissed. But I can't put off a chance to fry Blotter Boorman. The time I dealt with him, he'd left a path of dead co-eds all over UBC with a shitty bunch of acid. How he got his name. This time, what's he dealing?"

"He's ripping off smack and coke dealers. Fronting for the bikers. Armed to the teeth."

"Guess he's moving up in the world. Okay, I'll help you. We'll put them up in the Delta, provided VPD takes the bill. I can spare you a Special to guard them 24/7. Don't delay that Crown. If she really pushes, there's nothing we can do to stop her."

"What's to stop her now?"

"Everett Chin."

"Say again?"

"My secret weapon." There was a knock on the door, and Mulvaney admitted a short Asian Customs Inspector with modish hair and movie-star looks. "So? Is Mrs Lo in love yet?"

Everett Chin smiled and shrugged in false modesty. "I said I'd come and bring her some good Taiwanese food in her hotel. She wants a room with a view, and an adjacent room for her kid."

Rick waved a hand absently. "Whatever."

"Kid sure is freaking out." Chin added.

Rick nodded. "There's a reason they were going to pay cash last-minute."

"No shit." Chin continued. "Momma had five grand on her."

Mulvaney chuckled. "Walking around money. Grohmann, get your ass to the ER and get stitched up. Then start pounding the coffee, that Crown ain't gonna write itself. And Chin?"

"Yes Sergeant?"

"Go set up the rooms." He handed the CI a Government credit card. "And do the kid a favour."

"What's that?"

"If you bang her, make sure the kid doesn't hear."

"Sarge!"

MAY

NOBODY EXPECTS THE SPANISH INQUISITION

Television police work omits one central fact of the profession: the paperwork. You can't blame Hollywood for this; it's not very interesting, and it takes hours. Ask any cop what part of the job they hate the most, and, next to dead kids, nine of ten will say "paperwork."

312 MAIN ST
DRUG SECTION

When Selfridge and Olds arrived at the office, they were surprised to find a bleary-eyed Rick Grohmann hunting and pecking at his Crown report. His head was bandaged, and there were flecks of blood on his pants.

"What the hell happened to you?" Barry stood over him.

"I can explain." Selfridge entered his office, peeling a phone message off the door as he did so. "Just as soon as he comes off the roof."

"What do you mean, him? He never gets that pissed."

Rick looked at him miserably. "Today is a new day."

"Grohmann!" Selfridge emerged from his office, his face red. "I just got off the phone with Inspector Kirk! What the flaming Jesus happened at the Bayshore last night?"

"I've got a story to tell."

"It better be a good one." Selfridge warned. "Or you stand to lose your hooks. Maybe even your badge."

THIRTY MINUTES LATER

The three men sat in silence around Selfridge's desk as Rick Grohmann concluded his tale with the Los under guard in the Delta Airport Hotel. "No, I don't know how they got a room."

"Shit." Barry pressed his sinuses. "We'll probably have to eat that one, too."

Selfridge leaned back in his chair. "Let me understand this. Blotter Boorman is doing rips, right? And he and his crew tossed around Tusker's old lady. Now, Tusker is taking the fall to keep Blotter from being breached, and you think they made the Chinese kid across the street as a witness, which is why we're paying for him and his mom to stay, under guard no less, in a hotel that's gotta cost 200 bucks a night? And you haven't even written a damned Crown?"

"Plus," Barry joined in, "You've got another dealer talking war with Blotter. A war, in the middle of Expo?"

"Okay...it looks bad, but there's no need for the Spanish Inquisition here..."

Barry Olds rubbed his hands together in glee. "Oh, I disagree Rick. I disagree one hell of a lot. Matter of fact, I think we should get out the old bellows and tongs. Have a little fun."

Rick glared murder at him and opened his mouth. Selfridge cut him off. "No, Detective, that is quite enough. No more talking. From now on, there are no 'private' snitches. From now on, your every move on this case must be approved, either by myself or Sergeant Olds. And, before you go home today, I will expect a Crown good enough to convince an audience of tots that the Easter Bunny murdered Santa Claus on my desk. Is that clear?"

"Yes, Staff Sergeant. Is that all?"

"For now, yes. I will call Mr Halperin, and ensure he understands the urgency. Dismissed."

When the door had almost closed, Selfridge had a thought. "Oh, and Detective?"

"Yes, Staff?"

"You know what nobody ever expects?"

"No Staff, I don't."

"Nobody ever expects the Spanish Inquisition!"

BEACH TOWERS APARTMENTS

Unaware that he was, once again, a subject of heated discussion in police circles, Blotter Boorman dozed lightly on his leather couch, watching early MLB games. He noted with surprise how tight his Mets were looking this season. Perhaps he'd have to stop everyone who said "Mets" stood for "My Entire Team Sucks."

Yes, he was from Seattle. But his dad refused to cheer for expansion teams. When people pointed out to him that the Mets *were* an expansion team, his dad would always reply in a Brooklyn accent, "New York gotta right to two teams! Two! Since they gonna keep the fucking Dodgers!"

Right now, he could relax. Things were on cruise. There was that thing he had to take care of, like the Sicilians would say, but after that, it was onward and upward.

The phone rang, clicking on the answering machine on the fifth ring. It was a woman's voice, unfamiliar.

"Hey, Neil? It's Tracy! Remember me? I was just wondering what you were up to, me and some of my friends just wanted to party! I hear you look like Aquaman now or something..."

Club music played in the background. He looked at his watch. 5:45 PM. A little early for that kind of call.

Outside, the light was low, but still present. Dinner time.

A good time to serve a warrant. Or do a surprise check.

Suddenly, he bounced off the couch and stepped into his Nikes. He grabbed the Browning from under the couch, and his full wallet and brick phone off the coffee table. Praying they weren't already in the hall, he checked the spy hole, then opened the door with the deepest of breaths.

Blotter took the stairs two at a time, so he was panting like a dog by the time he got to Cecil's floor. He fumbled for the key, only getting it in on the third try as the elevator lights showed an "Up" car in use. Finally, he stumbled through the door, falling to his knees in the entryway.

His brick phone was ringing. It was Cecil. "Is that you, Neil?"

Blotter moved away from the door and spoke in hushed tones, as heavy footsteps came from the floor above. *Typical cops. Get off one floor below, hoof it only one storey. One more was too hard.* "Yes, Cecil? I think I might be having visitors."

"I think so too. There are ever so many police cars in the street. And there is a policeman guarding the lobby door."

"Very observant Cecil. Look, I don't want you coming back right now. Cops are very good at getting you talking." *Especially old senile fuckers like you.* "Just go have a nice dinner at the pub, on me, okay? I'll call you when the coast is clear."

"Sounds grand, old chap! See you soon."

Blotter smiled and set down his stuff on the old man's old coffee table, and turned on the new TV, with cable, that he'd paid for. The Mets had just scored two runs.

Maybe this was their year. Maybe it was his, too.

Blotter lay down on the couch, put his feet up, and listened to cops stomping through the halls impotently. When they stopped stomping and started to talk in low tones outside his door, he muted the game, and started to listen.

MAY

MOST WANTED

Incendiary cops like Rick Grohmann prefer not to dwell on it, for obvious reasons. But in their quiet moments, they may reflect that the criminals who obsess them the most are too much like them for comfort...

BURNABY ST
WEST END

Bobbi Sanghera rubbed her eyes and yawned for the fifteenth time. It was a sunny morning in the West End, a nice contrast to the usual open sores a Drug Section assignment presented the eye. But she was still damned tired.

"You look beat, Bobbi." Connolly looked at her with something approaching concern. "Trouble on the home front?"

Bobbi looked at her sometime partner for a moment. Connolly was one of those people who didn't ask for much from life. He was strictly a "25 and out" kind of cop, and an avowed "CFL" or "Constable for Life."

She trusted him more than most cops with ambition. They had a reason to fuck you over. Connolly didn't, as long as you didn't make his life difficult. "Yeah, I guess, Conn. My mom and dad sometimes forget I have a job. Too much cooking and cleaning."

"You a good cook?"

She looked at him wryly. "If you like Indian food, yes."

Connolly took on a mock-offended look. "*Moi? Mais oui!* You think I exist on hamburgers and pizza, right?"

"Experience suggests that's the case."

"That's because we never have time to sit down in this job. Now, if a certain somebody was to invite a certain other somebody over for some nice curries…"

Bobbi chuckled. "I'll think about it." She peered out the windshield again. "What do you think Grohmann is up to?"

Connolly made a lazy left-hand turn, flipping the bird at a pissed-off granola type on a ten-speed. "I could write a book, Bobbi. Some cops, like him, they just have to be left alone to do what they do. Usually, with him, it works pretty good. The other night, eh, maybe not so much. I wouldn't want to be his Sergeant. But I'll go in a door with him, anytime."

"Think he'll get a jolt for this?"

"Suspended?" Connolly chortled. "Fuck no! They may piss and moan about old Rotten Ricky, but they know they need him. Nobody has snitches like his. I bet he's halfway up Blotter's ass by now."

Bobbi yawned again. "Jesus. Let's get up a cup of coffee's ass."

"Ha ha. If your mother heard you talk like that."

Bobbi rolled down the window as a skinny man in a grey overcoat emerged from an apartment lobby and strolled onto the street. He had a funny, bouncing walk.

But what was most noticeable about him was his mohawk. "Slow down, Conn."

Connolly caught her gaze. "Way to lay low, Donnie." He put the mike to his mouth. "Central from 2339, show us tailing suspect Mike Charlie Charlie Romeo Alpha Echo, given Delta Oscar November Alpha Lima Delta, DOB 58-01-30 in the vicinity 1130 Pendrell."

"10-4 2339, do you require assistance."

"Sure, send us a unit if there's one in the area." He turned to Bobbi. "Dipshit hasn't clocked us yet. Hop out, you're faster. I'll cut him off in the car."

"Okay." Bobbi was out on the curb before the wheels had stopped turning. She felt an old, familiar, queasy thrill in her guts. With the portable in one hand, she picked up her pace.

Then, Donnie turned, looking to cross the street. She didn't even wait for him to make her before she started running at him, full tilt. His eyes went wide, and he belted across the street, narrowly missing Connolly's front fender.

"2339 in pursuit of wanted male, now westbound on Pendrell." She could hear Connolly yelling into the mike as he drove past them. Donnie ran comically, arms and legs flailing like Olive Oyl, cutting between two apartments.

Her fatigue forgotten, Bobbi leapt over a hedge, stumbled, nearly turning her ankle, but recovered and kept going. Her radio crackled demandingly. "Bobbi where the hell are you?"

"In the lane...the lane behind 1160 Pendrell!"

"Copy, I'm 76!" Bobbi could hear the cop V-8 engine going into overdrive. The great thing about being a cop was never being alone. She turned to look for Donnie and caught a boot in the ribs.

"Fuck!" She dropped to her knees, as Donnie took off the way he'd come.

No. No you fucking don't, you little Scotch scab. Bobbi got up and started running again. Ahead, Donnie had gotten ensnarled with two vicious dogs, left the alley, and cut back towards Pendrell. "Conn, he's headed back to Pendrell!" Her breath came in stabs. "Pendrell and Jervis!"

"Right!" The V-8 roared in the background. Ignoring the pain in her ribs, she sprinted hard enough to see the sight that would make her week.

Donnie looked back to clock her at exactly the wrong time. Clearly, like so many people under stress, his auditory senses had switched off, or he would've heard the massive Police Interceptor bearing down on him.

As it was, he only realized that Connolly had stopped short in front of him when his gangly legs crunched against the front wheel well, and the rest of his body shot across the hood like a torpedo.

Bobbi walked around the car, panting, and handcuffed the insensate Scot. "Got you, ya fucker."

Donnie calmly spit out a bloody tooth in her direction, then smiled at her crazily. "Ah need to see a fookin' dentist."

Connolly shook his head. "You're only realizing this now?" He picked up the radio mike. "2339, show us with one in custody, Pendrell and Jervis."

BEACH TOWERS
CECIL'S APARTMENT

Now that he was certain he was not under surveillance; Blotter was becoming more comfortable taking his calls on the balcony. Cecil could be nosy.

Besides which, given what he knew now, the safest bet was to turn himself in. He just needed to tie up a few loose ends, that was all. He wouldn't be in there long, but he would be in for a few days, most likely.

Blotter decided to soak up as much sun as he could. "Hey, Roach?"

"Yeah, Blotter, you okay? I hear they raided your place." A suspicious pause followed. "They didn't get you, did they?"

"Are you asking if I'm a fucking snitch?"

"No...no, no Blotter, it's just..."

"Shut the fuck up. Listen, I already talked to my lawyer. He saw the information that faggot Grohmann laid on me. They only made me, and Donnie because of his car. They don't know you guys, so you're cool, okay?"

"Okay. That's good."

"I bet you think so."

"But, but..."

Blotter laughed. "Relax, you big pussy. I won't be in long. Now listen. I'm calling you cause Donnie's not answering his phone. Maybe they got him already. I'm gonna turn myself in."

"What?"

"Listen, for fuck's sake. When I'm done, all they'll have on me is breaking curfew. And I can just say that was because of all the mean policemen that made me soooo scared! They got a witness. And thanks to their big mouths last night, I know where they're keeping him."

"Uh, I don't know, Blotter..."

"You fucking pop tart. I ain't asking you to kill him. Just go and buy him and his mommy two first-class tickets to Taipei, plus give them some nice walking around money, okay?"

"Oh. That sounds nice."

"I don't want them to testify. Turns out, neither do they. And once they get on that plane..."

"Where's Taipei?"

"Jesus Christ."

Once his calls were done, he poured himself a last Scotch, confident that his lawyer could handle the details, even if it challenged his muscle heads. "You on your way then, Mr Boorman?" Cecil emerged from the kitchen. "Too bad, then, I had some lovely steak and kidney pie on."

"Sounds good, Cecil. But duty calls." He took a thousand out of his jacket pocket and put it in front of Cecil. "For the trouble. You're a stand-up guy, Cecil. Like the wops say."

"Wops." Cecil made a sour face. "They surrendered to us in droves."

"Hey, Cecil? What's got three reverse gears, and one forward?"

"Hmm?"

"An Italian tank."

Cecil chortled. "Grand, Mr Boorman, grand."

TWO FLOORS UP
BLOTTER'S APARTMENT

Usually, when Rick Grohmann was pissing in another man's house, he was careful.

For this man, he'd make an exception. Rick let his spray coat the seat, sprinkle the floor, and soak the toilet roll before zipping up. Then, he washed his hands and dried off, being careful to dunk the hand towel in the toilet bowl.

Nothing but net. Enjoy, you asshole.

Suddenly, Rick heard the sounds of an opening front door. He turned out the lights and waited.

Through a crack between the door and jamb, he watched as Blotter Boorman cautiously entered, sniffing at the air. Then, the dealer started searching each room in turn.

When a hand pressed on the bathroom door, he made himself flat. He saw a Nike slipping past the edge of the door.

So he stepped down on it, hard.

Blotter yelled loudly as Rick followed the stomp with a full body tackle thrown from behind the door, forcing his enemy out into the hallway. All except two fingers, when were caught in the jamb when the door slammed. Another yell, this time higher-pitched.

Now, Rick threw the door open again, and stepped out to methodically box the still-standing Boorman down the hallway, in a flashing combo of body and face shots, until a voice told him: *stop.*

He picked up the sagging, panting, bleeding dealer, and handcuffed him. A search came up empty. Rick whipped Blotter around to face him. "Good morning you fucking cunt."

Blotter spoke with blood bubbling between his lips. "My lawyer's gonna have your ass."

"Why, he tired of yours already? You startled me, is all. Hell, I thought I was under attack."

"Sure. Well, take me in then. Let's see if my lawyer can get me a judge who won't believe your horseshit."

"I pissed on your floor, shitbird."

"Classy."

"You're not even a little curious about how we got you?"

"Don't flatter yourself, Sherlock. My lawyer read me the file. Did your Sergeant have to read it to you?"

"Come on, asshole." Rick pushed Blotter towards the door. In the doorway, the dealer turned to him with a smug smile.

"You know, I don't know which one of us is gonna blow up first. Won't it be fun to find out?"

MAY

CRUSHED

There is one inescapable fact of police work which never ceases to trouble gentle souls like Bobbi Sanghera. Even those with more stolid facades, such as Barry Olds and Rick Grohmann, never completely adjust to it.

This is the death of children, particularly in violent or freakish circumstances. No heart, not even a blue one, is stoic enough not to dwell on these terrible calls...

312 MAIN ST
DRUG SECTION

It was a familiar reprise by now for all three men in the little interview room.

Grohmann sat with his back to the wall, leaning his chair back on two legs. One the other side of the table, Olds and Selfridge watched impassively, waiting for him to Grohmann to finish reading the terms of his suspension.

Rick shook his head. "I get you guys another major case, and for that I get five days on the beach. Bullshit."

Barry fired back. "Yeah, it is bullshit. Bullshit the way you act like you've got nobody to answer to. Like you can hide witnesses without telling us, and shitkick suspects whenever you feel like it. That part is bullshit, I couldn't agree more, Rick."

"Just sign it." Selfridge massaged his sinuses in irritation. "You can always fight it later."

"Don't worry, Staff, I know my rights." Rick planted his chair on the floor with a slam, then signed with a flourish. "Gonna go home and pound the old lady. Maybe somebody else's, while I'm at it."

EXPO SITE (DOWNTOWN)
CANADA PAVILLION

Bobbi Sanghera stood in her raid jacket outside the revolving theatre's entrance. She willed herself not to think of what she'd just seen inside there.

A little girl crushed between moving parts as the theatres rotated. Brought by her family for a fun day out, now turned into a visceral pinata for a procession of cops, first-responders, and forensic types to gawk at.

She'd been summoned to Canada Place to relieve Patrol units for a breath of fresh air, a coffee, and maybe a cry. In doing so, she'd inadvertently wandered inside, not understanding the initial call completely.

Then, the whole picture had hit her. She'd stared for a second, unable to look away from the girl's agonized face for what seemed like an hour, but what must have been mere seconds.

Finally, a sympathetic Corporal had led her outside, posted her on the door, and returned with a coffee. "Don't dwell on it, Sanghera. It's not healthy."

How many times had she been told that? But the kids...the kids were always the hardest part of the job. There was no way to simply not dwell on it.

Two weeks in, a little boy on Denman, cut in half by a trolley bus. A month after that, twin girls, bodies covered in cigarette burns and bleeding from the vaginas. The list went on and on.

She had been raised to believe in the merciful and just God of the Guru Nanak. But increasingly, this God seemed like a foolish abstraction. The reality was, the Devil was in charge. And God was not looking.

Why else would he let a little girl die like that in front of her family? Her final moments turned into a ghoul show to rival any IMAX movie? Bobbi shuddered and finished the horrible coffee, just in time to see body removal wheeling out the girl's remains in a long, misshapen bag.

She closed her eyes. When she opened them, Sergeant Olds was standing there with a young, read-headed Constable. "Constable Fearn will relieve you, Bobbi. I have somewhere else for you to be."

She nodded, wordlessly, and dumped her cup in the nearest trash. The young cop was looking over his shoulder, as if trying to get a view.

"Don't." Bobbi Sanghera warned him. "You don't want to."

NORTH VANCOUVER
LYNN VALLEY

Rick Grohmann's Mustang was a treat to himself. Or a sign of his arrogance. It depended on who you talked to, and he could see both sides.

But as he pushed the forest-green monster across the Lion's Gate Bridge, the feedback of the engine only served to make him madder. Rick stared into the sun with his mirrored shades, effortlessly shifting traffic lanes, intimidating the timid out of his way.

The timid. Like the pussies he worked for. Did they seriously think you could go after someone like Blotter Boorman and come away with clean hands? Of course, they didn't. He knew enough about the histories of his bosses to know that was true. He knew, for instance, that Selfridge had once thrashed a wife-beater so badly he was in the ICU for two weeks. Of course, he was connected, so it was hushed up. And Olds? Hell, when he was a rookie, the dumbass had accidentally fired a shot while going over a fence with his gun out, and just about took off a dog handler's head. Of course, he was connected, and protected, by family ties.

Rick Grohmann had no family ties, and no illusions. He was a hunting dog, useful until that day that he wasn't. A roughneck's son from Edmonton could scarcely expect better treatment. That was the VPD for you.

It was a jock establishment and an old boy's club, had been since the very beginning.

Still, though...he could be stuck in the RCMP. Where sometimes, the reward for being a smart, aggressive cop was a ticket to a shithole posting. Look what they'd done to Mulvaney. The guy was a hero, a couple of times over, and what was his reward? Six years in the same rank and the shittiest detachment in the Lower Mainland. He was going nowhere.

When he pulled into his driveway, still seething, Rick saw the perfect outlet for his aggression.

Lawrence Dyck's white BMW. Sitting there, daring him to make his move.

Rick tapped his fingers on the steering wheel, a beautiful custom job he'd picked up in Arizona. *Lawrence. Fucking rich boy tennis pro poonhound.*

In the back of his mind, he remembered that he had virtually dared Clarissa to keep fucking him. Some twisted part of him was getting off on his wife being a slut, and some twisted part of her was getting off on him punishing her for it.

Still. *A guy named Lawrence Dyck is putting his dyck in my wife. A man needs to do something...*

Rick Grohmann opened his glovebox and pulled out a four-cell

D Maglite and a set of cuffs. Then he marched up to the front door, kicked it in, and charged up the steps.

When he pushed open the door, the two of them were so absorbed they hadn't heard a thing. Lawrence was doggystyle balls deep in Clarissa. He looked over his shoulder like a fighter pilot checking his six.

Fuck, what a hairy ass. Rick brought the Maglite down hard on Lawrence's collarbone, and then the screaming began.

KINGSWAY

Bobbi looked out the window, chewing her lower lip, as Barry negotiated the traffic. "You're awfully quiet."

Bobbi looked back at him. "Sorry. Just…one of those calls."

Barry sighed. "I told you not to go in there, Bobbi."

"Damnit, I know!" She snapped. "Sorry."

"I'm the one that's sorry. It's just…some of the Patrol types there were on the verge of losing it…"

"You don't have to explain. I'm a cop. It's part of my job. I just wish I could stop letting it get to me."

Barry shook his head, lighting his third smoke of the day off the car lighter. *So much for five a day.* "If you do that, you know who you are?"

"No, who?"

"Rick Grohmann, that's who."

"That's a stretch." Bobbi uttered a brief laugh. "I don't see myself fighting six guys at a time."

"Six kids. Guy's rep is exaggerated." Barry scoffed.

"I hear he beat you in two rounds."

"He cheats."

"Sure, he does." Bobbi smiled, and let the sun paint her face. "Thanks, Sarge."

"For what?"

"For getting my mind off of it."

"Ah, I know how it is. Okay, here we are." He pulled up to a curb and parked under a spreading elm tree.

Bobbi looked around. "East 20th. Isn't this Grohmann's rip off?"

"Yes." Barry turned to face her. "Since Grohmann got his very reluctant witness, Mr Taakoiennin is free to come and go as he pleases. And, according to our surveillance team, he went out a half-hour ago. Since he won't talk to us, and nobody's taken a stab at Marianne since Patrol South fucked up the case, I figured it might be time for a little woman-to-woman talk, Bobbi."

"Marianne is the girlfriend, right? The one Blotter's guys were supposed to have done a number on?"

"The wife, that's right. Grohmann has his witness. For now. Parked in a hotel a kilometre from the airport with a mom who's got enough cash to fly us all to Taipei. Forgive me if I'd like a fail-safe."

"Suggestions?"

"Go easy. Don't push. She's unlikely to go for it now, but if you just leave a business card and plant the idea…"

"Got it." She was out on the curb and headed for the front door, determined to distract herself from that kid's agonized stare.

The house was a pleasant, pre-war walk-up, a delicate garden in full bloom taking up the front yard. As she reached the bottom of the stairs, the door opened suddenly. A diminutive woman with bruised cheekbones and long blonde hair stopped and stared at her, half-turning back the way she went. She carried a trowel and a bucket.

"Nice garden." Bobbi smiled. "I try and get those ones to bloom, but I kill what I love."

Marianne Taakoiennin gave a shy, damaged smile. "You're a… a policewoman, right? My lawyer said I wasn't to talk to you. Sorry."

"I'm Constable Sanghera. My friends call me Bobbi."

That shy smile again. "Hi Bobbi. Look…my husband will be home soon."

"I get it. You're Marianne, right?"

"Yes. Look, you seem very nice, but…" She had a curious, high-pitched voice that must've made men want to save her. Look what a job they'd done.

Bobbi stepped forward slowly. Marianne froze as if facing a cobra. Bobbi dropped her business card in the bucket. "I'm here if you need to talk. Just call me. My home number is there, too. That's just for you. I don't want to get you in trouble, so I'll go now." She turned and was halfway to the street when Marianne called out.

"Thanks! Thank you for caring, I mean."

"I always care. Even when I shouldn't. Call me, okay."

"Maybe."

She got back in the car and nodded to Barry. "Seed planted, Sergeant."

Barry smiled. "That's a good thing, Bobbi. Because the judge just denied bail on Blotter and Donnie. But it was close. Without

Marianne, I don't think we'll make it to the finish line."

"If there's one Marianne, I bet there's more."

Barry thought for a second, then keyed the ignition. "Yeah. Yeah, you're right. And I think I know exactly where to start."

MAY

THE PEOPLE WITHOUT TONGUES

The golden rule of any criminal enterprise is: do not snitch. Snitches are the lowest form of life, inside and outside of prison walls. This rule creates some problems for people like Tusker Taakoiennin, when the behaviour of the man he is protecting is indefensible...

**GRANVILLE ISLAND
PUBLIC MARKET**

Rick Grohmann was taking a big chance, and he knew it.

He stood just outside the entrance to the Public Market, watching the hippies and the yuppies come and go in the rain, which drummed a staccato pattern on the awnings. The smoke rising from his mouth mingled with the giant raindrops, which fell to earth like heavy artillery.

He felt, alternatively, like sleeping, or screaming. Almost a full week off duty had done his head in.

Rick Grohmann was never much for vacations or idle time. Two weeks a year at his dad's time share in Arizona was the yearly routine, something Clarissa found so mind-numbingly boring that she had stopped going there years ago. Rick basically only went there for car and motorcycle parts. Things lasted longer in the dry air.

He was here today, amongst the people who didn't give a shit about Expo 86 and were just as happy for it to have never happened at all. Right across the inlet from the fairgrounds, Granville Island was a hideout for artists, craftsmen, and people who preferred to pay twice as much for broccoli as their neighbours.

People like Tusker Taakoiennin. Rick knew his case was on very thin ice. Since it had already cost him a suspension, he felt he had a lot invested. So maybe more risk was required.

To think, a month ago, he'd actually been deluded enough to think he might make Sergeant. He didn't know anybody who'd been suspended *and* promoted for the same case.

He flicked a butt into a deep puddle, sending a seagull scrambling. To be honest, Rick was surprised he'd made it this far, what with uncooperative victims and a witness with one foot out the door. Still the pressure of Expo and Mulvaney's rep had helped convince Justice Moore to stretch things a bit and keep Blotter and Donnie on ice. But he knew he needed more.

How the hell to get it? Blotter had run things so tight until Eddie Lo came along that he didn't have a single fucking witness. And why not? Dope rips were, in a lot of ways, the perfect crime. The victims, such as they were, were already criminals who stood to lose everything if they opened their mouths. Only a chance witness with nothing to lose, or a lucky traffic stop, could blow a rip team.

So far, his weak case was leading a charmed life. He had Eddie Lo, and some delirious statements made by Marianne on the way to the hospital. Easily challenged at *voir dire.* He needed more. And that was why he was here, shivering in the chill rain. Because he'd established one mundane detail of Tusker's life.

Tusker was a European, used to a higher quality of food than North Americans, and, since he was a drug dealer, he could afford the ridiculous prices here. Being a creature of habit, an extremely stupid thing for a dealer to be, he tended to show up twice a week here, right about…now.

Sure enough, the lithe, wiry form of Tusker, his too-big head topped with silver-blond hair, emerged from the crowd. Rick scooped him before he could make the entrance. "Welcome to Granville Island. Enjoying your shopping experience?"

Tusker planted his feet and stopped cold. "No, I'm protected.

Protected by Blotter. Check and see."

"Fuck your protection. I'm a cop." Tusker's eyes went wide, as Rick dragged him around the corner of a little arts studio. Rick found a dry bench under an awning and pushed Tusker onto it. "Now, you're going to sit for a minute and listen, before you head off to spend a hundred dollars on fucking mushrooms and cheese."

"Hey now…I didn't get your name, man."

"Detective Rick Grohmann. If you're looking for references, just ask Blotter. We go back a long ways."

"Oh yeah. You."

"If by that you mean, 'Thank you officer for exonerating me from false charges of domestic violence,' why then, you're welcome! Jesus, Blotter really has your balls in a vise, doesn't he?" Rick leaned down and got close. "They dragged your little sweetheart into a back room and were going to fucking spit roast her, Tusker. After they used her as a goddamned punching bag. Doesn't that make you mad, Tusker? Doesn't that make you wanna get even?"

Tusker tried to avoid his gaze, but it was obvious to Rick that he was picking at the right scab. He kept at it. "Blotter protects you, you said. Really? He was gonna stand right there and listen to his goons tag team Marianne. Some protector."

"You don't know that! You're making it up!"

"Ah, is that why it's got you so worked up? Because I'm pointing out that you're a little pussy who'd rather stay in business than defend his old lady?

"Fuck you man!" Tusker spat the words at him. "I testify, Marianne testifies, and what can you do for us, eh? Witness relocation, living straight in Winnipeg or some other shithole. So I can what? Work as a fucking locksmith? You've got nothing. As long as I don't go against him, Blotter protects us."

"He can't do much from that fucking cell, now can he? I hear some of his recent 'partners' are already rebelling. So how can he protect you? Testify against him, and he can't do shit."

Tusker sneered. "You are as dumb as you look, cop. It's not him I am afraid of, it's who is behind him! The bikers, man, the bikers. They don't forget. So fuck off, you've got nothing for us." He made to stand, and Rick pushed him down.

"Nah. Fucking off doesn't work for me right now. Give me a name, and I'll leave."

"Are you fucking serious? Now you want me to snitch? In exchange for what?"

"In exchange for leaving you alone, dipshit. Give me a name. One guy who's walking away from Blotter."

"Why?"

"So I can fuck with him, instead of you."

Tusker shrugged. "Harvey Sam. He's a dick, anyway. And that's all you get." He stood again, and this time Rick did not stop him. "Oh, and Detective?"

"What?"

"You were wrong about my shopping. I am not spending a hundred bucks on cheese and mushrooms. I am spending it on tongue. Because I no longer have one, understand?"

"Cute."

LITTLE MOUNTAIN

Bobbi Sanghera crept towards the little house with the iron bars on the windows, trying to keep her breath still.

It wasn't the exertion. It was the nerves. Though she'd watched her fair share of drug raids from the perimeter as a uniformed officer, this was her first chance to go right through the door.

Behind Barry Olds, of course. Sergeant Olds always went first. One of her old trainers had warned her about that.

"Being a cop means having the guts to be first through the door sometimes. It also means having the brains to not be first *every time.*"

Though she would never accuse Barry of being short on brains, perhaps he was a bit too long on guts. Some of her Academy classmates had almost swooned at the mention of his name.

"Ooh, Sweet Barry. He's the nicest man, always holding the door open, or kicking it in for you."

Barry took a knee behind a giant oak tree. The target was in the adjoining yard. He carried a heavy metal ram; she carried a ballistic shield almost as tall as she was. Behind them, Connolly and Dupuis hefted 12-gauge shotguns. Bobbi could see two more cops on each side of the house from Sergeant Bartels' team making their way down the sides of the house to cover the exits.

The rain had died down, but the earth was sodden, and the chill permeated Bobbi's bones. "Okay, we wait for Bartels to call in place, then we charge that door and hit it. Conn, you come up the stairs with us, Larry, stay at the base and cover the windows, okay?" Barry searched out each officer in turn. *Are you with me?*

Bobbi nodded quickly as Barry looked at her. Her guts were rolling. Her radio crackled. "Team 2 in position."

Selfridge came on the air. "Team 1, hit it."

Barry picked up the ram and ran for the stairs, Bobbi hefting the shield behind him, hearing Connolly panting behind her.

Barry took the steps two at a time, then, without even pausing, swung the heavy ram with both hands, smashing in the outer door lock. Bobbi reached out from behind her shield and pulled the mangled screen far enough back to reveal an ordinary-looking wooden door. Barry dropped the ram on the porch and gave the door a hellacious kick at the jam.

Connolly pushed past Bobbi and shouldered the door, the last part of which had now fallen inside the house. Someone, maybe her, was shouting "Police! Search warrant! Police!"

They found Harvey Sam sitting on the couch with his hands in his lap. "For fuck's sake, you could've knocked."

A HALF-HOUR LATER

Bobbi was photographing evidence *in situ*, then handing it off to Connolly, who weighed it and noted the result on an evidence bag. She looked up from her work when she heard yelling outside.

On the sidewalk, Barry Olds and Rick Grohmann were going toe-to-toe.

"What the fuck are you doing here, Detective?"

"I got a call. I thought I'd take a stroll."

"Oh yeah?" Barry sneered. "Who called you?"

"They're called 'Confidential Informants' for a reason."

"I thought we straightened that out last week. There's no such thing for you. So fuck off, before Selfridge finds you here, and you're doing school bike rodeos till you eat your gun."

"Can I ask you just one question, Sergeant?"

"Can I stop you?"

"How'd you twig to Harvey? I heard he was ready to go against Blotter, now that Blotter was inside. You sure you ain't being set up?"

"Rick, I have informants, too. Some pretty damn good ones. And when they give me the info they did yesterday, I go and get a search warrant. Remember those, Rick? Now, you may have forgotten, because maybe you've been on Drugs too long. But dealers are not our clients. The people of Vancouver are our clients. Dealers are the problem. And from now on, we are going to get at Blotter by folding up his branch offices. Starting with Harvey."

"He say anything? About Blotter, I mean?"

"No. Cat got his tongue. A lot of that going around."

"Who's next?"

"Who is asking, Rick? You, or your snitches? See you on Monday. 0800 hours."

Bobbi watched as Rick Grohmann, the air let out of his tires, turned away.

MAY

COURTESY SHUTTLE

Contrary to popular depictions, most criminals like Blotter Boorman prefer to fix problems like testifying witnesses with honey instead of vinegar. Bloodshed is expensive and attracts police and media attention. So, the solutions, provided the solver is not too deep into a cocaine habit, can sometimes seem very reasonable indeed...

VANCOUVER PRE-TRIAL

Donnie was talking big about his Glasgow days with a bunch of cons in the breakfast line when Blotter surprised him. "Hey ho, Donnie." Donnie almost dropped his tray. "Nervous?"

"Oh no, Blotter. No. Why would I be?"

Blotter leaned in close. "I'm asking the fucking questions, Donnie. How'd they grab you?"

"I...ah...I went for a walk. It was a lovely day and all..."

"You fucking pop tart. I told you to lie low until I could fix this. I'm the one on Probation, not you, right?"

"Right. Ah...sorry Blotter." An edgy native inmate pushed past them both. Blotter grabbed his arm.

"I'm sorry, are we in your way?"

The native con looked Blotter up and down. "Yeah. I'm hungry. And take your fucking..."

He didn't get to finish his sentence. Blotter had rammed a knee between his legs, and now he writhed on the floor amongst the contents of his upended tray. Blotter carried on as if nothing had happened. "Roach and Pissy Balls have it in hand. We'll be out this time tomorrow. Till then, stay away from these fucking morons, and keep close to me."

Donnie was staring at the native con, who only now began to sit up.

"Donnie? Wake up, ya Weegie shit."

"Ah...yeah, okay man. Okay, top notch."

"Jesus. It's like talking to a pack of gum. Just keep your mouth shut."

**THAT MORNING
DELTA AIRPORT INN
RICHMOND**

"Housekeeping."

Eveline Lo opened the door cautiously, relaxing when she saw the Mountie on the other side. "It's okay, Mrs Lo, he checks out."

"Okay, beds need changing, come in."

The housekeeper was a middle-aged Chinese man, who surveyed the room as he entered. Eddie Lo sat on the far bed, watching cartoons. Despite the fact that it was a gorgeous morning, the curtains were drawn tight. He turned to see Mrs Lo watching him closely. "Okay now, get to work, guy."

"Wo shuo ni de yuyan."

"Suoyi ne?"

"Kan kan maojin. Hen zhongyao."

Mrs Lo's eyes went wide. She reached into the stack of towels the housekeeper had set on the first bed and pulled out a small envelope. Inside, there was a letter in Mandarin script. The housekeeper went about his duties as if nothing had happened.

Mrs Lo
Greetings

Tonight, we will send a driver for you. He is carrying cash and two tickets to Taipei out of Seattle, along with new passports in other names. He will be waiting in the parkade for you after 6 PM.

We know that the policeman guarding you sometimes takes bathroom breaks, and nobody is watching for a little while. Have your son check the peephole. If he sees no cop, you both go into the hall. If you are caught, say "We were worried something happened to you." If not, keep going for the stairwell, and don't stop till you get to the parkade. Our driver's name is Mr Chen. He will be waiting in a black Corolla. Do not try to bring anything larger than your purse.

We are an organization dedicated to helping Taiwanese people having trouble with injustice. Please do not speak of us, now, or after. It will jeopardize our vital work.

The Taiwanese Benevolent and Fortunate Assistance Society

Mrs Lo folded up the note, looked at her son, and wondered what to do.

Soon, when he had made the beds, the housekeeper left. He never saw the Los again. But he did enjoy the 500 dollars he made. All for passing a note.

TWELVE HOURS LATER

Special Constable Chadwick was fighting a losing battle against the expanding contents of his own bladder. *Shouldn't have had a large coke with that Whopper meal.*

Ordinarily, their guard shifts here were four hours at a time. Even he could handle that. But two hours ago, there'd been a bomb threat at the Canadian cargo warehouse. Everyone was tied up, since, after the Air India bombings in '85, that stuff was taken very seriously.

Now, his shift was stretching into six hours. He had the key to the janitor's room. Nobody would know.

MAY

STAY OF PROCEEDINGS

In the Canadian justice system, the Stay of Proceedings is the legal equivalent of smothering an old lady with a pillow. It's a low-profile way to kill a case that has lost something very essential. Like a star witness...

**312 MAIN ST
DRUG SECTION**

Barry Olds sat at the head of the conference table, already on his second Export "A", and quietly deciding to fuck the whole quitting smoking thing. This case was not conducive to changing bad habits. He looked at his watch. 0809 hours. No sign of Grohmann yet.

He raised the blinds, staring into the strong sun. Three weeks till vacation. If he could ram the Criminal Code up Blotter Boorman's ass before then, it would be all the sweeter.

But that was looking increasingly unlikely. A door opened behind him. Rick Grohmann entered, wearing a wrinkled suit and a sour expression, to desultory applause. "Fuck off, all of you."

"Well, welcome handsome. Isn't the morning sun glorious?"

Grohmann slumped into a chair. "Fuck the sun."

"Great." Barry smiled at Bobbi, who shrugged. "Because if you were in a great mood before, you're gonna love this. I just got off the phone with Mitch Halperin. He's going into court this morning to enter a Stay of Proceedings in the matter of R v Boorman et al."

Grohmann buried his head in his hands. "Fuck." Connolly and Dupuis joined in the grumbling. Barry suspected a round of anti-

Crown Counsel bitching was about to follow, as it usually did.

Bobbi raised her hand. "May I ask why, Sergeant. I mean, granted, it was kind of weak, but…"

"Well, Bobbi, it's gone from 'weak' to 'non-existent' this morning. Our star witness and his mommy have flown the coop."

"What? Goddamn horsemen!" Grohmann gripped the edge of the table. "They said they'd watch him."

"They've got the same problems we do, Rick. Too many jobs, not enough bodies. Somebody, maybe our pals, called in a bomb threat last night, meaning the kid watching the Los went six hours without relief. When you gotta go, you gotta go. He slipped away for two minutes to drain the lizard, and when he came back, he didn't notice a thing. Security cameras in the parkade picked up a black Toyota with an Asian male driver entering at 1802, and driving away, with the Los, at 2305. Video wasn't good enough to shag a plate, and the entry card was swiped from a cabbie that night. Mounties were watching the Air China desk before the flight and didn't spot the Los. Since their Taiwanese passports were being held, it's no surprise to see their names not on the manifest."

"Seattle?" Bobbi mused.

Barry nodded. "Quite possibly. There is an Air China flight to Taipei nightly from SeaTac. But we would have no way of knowing if they were on it."

"I could call down there, see if there were two people boarding together with similar ages, travelling as mother and son? I'm guessing, cash-paid, last-minute tickets." Bobbi offered.

"Do that, please. I'm pretty sure Blotter didn't have them whacked. But it would be nice to be sure."

"Back to the drawing board." Grohmann mumbled.

"And here I was hoping you'd have more." Barry teased him. "Ideas, Detective?"

"Okay. You want my ideas? I say, watch Soulschnitzel."

"Ray Beuerhoft? That little fruit?" Dupuis scoffed. "Why him?"

"Hey, dumbass. That little fruit is the only independent to have the guts to tell Blotter to go fuck himself. And, he's armed to the teeth. Legally. He's smart enough to stay off our radar, and to take advantage of Blotter being out of circulation for a week. My sources tell me he's already got three dealers Blotter turned in his back pocket now."

"The bikers will kill him." Connolly added.

"Yeah, they'll try." Grohmann agreed. "But they'll use Blotter to do it. That's part of the deal."

"Jesus, Grohmann, where'd you go on your vacation? Angel Acres?" Dupuis prodded. "I didn't know you owned a Harley."

"Fuck off, all of you." Grohmann glowered at the room.

"There is one other witness we can still connect with." Bobbi offered.

Barry shrugged. "She's got your card. But is she likely to use it?"

"I don't know, Sarge. Marianne's scared, but she's not cowed. I get the feeling she'll use it if she feels the situation changing." Bobbi was painfully aware that Rick Grohmann was glowering at her. He was like a jealous toddler, the case, his personal toy.

Maybe Marianne was too? A random thought batted away quickly.

Barry closed that line of inquiry. "For now, we wait for her to change her mind. Rick's avenue seems to promise more immediate results. And dangers, if we don't act quickly. Imagine how pissed the Chief will be, rival gangs shooting it out in Expo

City?"

"But we've got time, right? I mean, Blotter's PO has got to violate him over his curfew breach, right?" Rick reached for reassurance.

Barry was blunt. "Nope. PO says he believes Blotter was 'intimidated by an overbearing police presence.' SFU grad, of course. Blotter walks this afternoon. With Donnie."

"Fuck that!" Rick objected.

"Detective, I swear to God, I am setting up a swear jar for this office."

"But Sarge! He kicked me in the ribs!" Bobbi objected.

Barry commiserated. "Sorry, Bobbi. On the Crown Counsel scale of concern, 'Assault PO' comes in right around 'Failure to Signal a Turn.' Nobody gives a shit."

"Welcome to your dream job, sister." Rick smirked at her.

"Okay, let's break this up. We're gonna press hard on the Beuerhoft angle. Rick, you've got the sources. You and Bobbi go press them."

Rick squirmed in his chair. Bobbi smiled demurely at him. "Ahhh, Sarge, that's..."

"You heard me. You and Bobbi. Dupuis and Connolly, park it and wait outside Pre-Trial. Let them see you. Send a message."

"You got it, Sarge."

222 MAIN ST

OUTSIDE VANCOUVER PRE-TRIAL

Blotter let his eyes adjust to the light as he stepped onto the curb, followed by Donnie, and Paul "The Pitbull" Romans, his lawyer.

The first thing he saw was an obvious DT car across the street, with two dipshit plainclothes cops in it. They waved at him. He answered with a middle finger.

"Aha. A little obvious intimidation." Romans noticed the car, too. "How subtle. How VPD."

"Fuck them." Blotter smiled and shook his lawyer's hand. "Sweet fuck all they can do."

Romans frowned. "Shall we try and keep it that way?" He was a tall, slick-looking dude with expensive suits and greased-back hair, who looked like exactly what he was. What the Sicilians would call a *consigliere*. Here, there being no Mafia to speak of, he belonged to the bikers.

"I've gotta take care of some business. That faggot Soulschnitzel is fucking me in the ass all over town. I can't let that slide."

Romans straightened his tie. "I don't want to know. Call me if you need me."

"Yeah, with my luck it'll be soon. Hey, can you do like, an injunction or something on these cocksuckers, Pitbull?" Over in the DT car, one of the cops was slowly drawing a finger across his throat.

Romans sighed. "That all depends on you, Neil. Keep the peace, and be of good behaviour, and the police's attentions will seem wasted. Be a bad boy, and the judge will seem to be endangering the community. Understand?"

Blotter answered the lawyer through gritted teeth. He so hated being spoken down to. "Fine. I'll be a good little boy. I'll even send flowers to that faggot's mother."

Romans frowned again. "Haven't you got a party to go to? Your PO must love you."

Blotter laughed. By now, he'd figured out that his PO was a swish, but he had closed his eyes and played the angle like a good boy. It wasn't like he didn't know how to suck cock, now was it? "Yes, he was very concerned about the stresses I was under, thanks to those mean policemen." He pointed at the cops across the street. "He got the judge to relax my curfew, too."

"Have a good time."

"Oh, you bet I will."

LUV-A-FAIR
SEYMOUR AND DRAKE

It was early yet on the nightclub beat, but Rick and Bobbi were already sliding past the bouncer on the door, letting their eyes adjust to the light. The DJ was trying out the night's playlist on the first trickle of visitors, who bopped around listlessly on the dance floor.

Come 'round cause I want the one I can't have
And it's driving me mad
It's all over, all over, all over my face

"Little early for the nightclub crowd, isn't it?" Bobbi yelled in Rick's ear.

Rick grunted. "Not for Jared. He's probably been doing speed all day anyway."

"What's so special about Jared?"

"He's a party kid. He's the cousin of the owners here. He knows everyone, and everyone writes him off as a waste-case. But he hears, and remembers, everything. That's the kind of snitch you want, Sanghera. The kind who just kind of folds into the wallpaper." He waved a waitress over. "What are you having?"

"Oh…ah, just a coke. I'm on duty."

"Not with me you don't. This scene runs on dope and booze. Now we can't do dope, but if they don't even see us drinking, it's like they're talking to Patrol. They clam up."

"But they know we're cops anyway."

Rick Grohmann rolled his eyes. "Jesus. What has Olds been teaching you?" The waitress, a bob-haired, curvy new-wave creature, sidled up to Rick.

"Hi sexy. Haven't seen you around in a while."

"Been busy with work, Leonore. How's it been here?"

"Lots of Eurotrash in here from Expo. Bono was here last night. Big tipper. The Edge just sits in the corner like a potted plant."

"U2 was here?" Bobbi couldn't help herself. "Wow."

Leonore looked her up and down. "This your new partner?"

Rick rested his chin on his fist. "Yup. I need minding."

Leonore chuckled. "That's for damn sure. What are you having?"

"Two T&Ts, honey. You seen Jared around?"

"Every night. Same time, which is…right about…now."

They both followed Leonore's gaze to where a nimble young new-waver with a shock of big black hair was negotiating a couple of tables of too-young girls. The kid took his time getting over to them.

"Aren't you gonna go after him?" Bobbi quizzed.

"Why? He likes talking to me."

"He does?"

"Bobbi, you can't get all of your snitches to love you. But everybody wants to tell their story, some more than others. Jared is one of those kids who can't keep a secret, and he always knows I'll listen." Now, Jared was making a beeline for them. "See?"

"Isn't he worried people will see he's a snitch?"

"Nope. Most of the people here are not that dirty. Some of them, like Jared, move in other circles. His cousins like seeing me here, because it warns off those dirtier elements. If the cost is a wastecase cousin with a snitch jacket, that's acceptable to them."

"Hey Detective. How's life?"

"Jared, this is Bobbi. My new partner. Bobbi, this is Jared."

"You never work with a partner."

"I'm in the sin bin, Jared. Now, give me something good to get me out."

Jared licked his lips when the Tanqueray and Tonics showed up. "Another one for Jared, Leonore."

Leonore tut-tutted. "I believe this young man is underage."

"Can't be worse than any of the other shit he puts in his body."

"Well, only if you promise to speak up for me to the Liquor Board."

"You got it." Rick sipped at his drink and watched Jared. "Well?"

"Yeah, yeah, okay. I just, I don't like outing people, okay?"

"You know we don't give a shit about that. Who is he, and why should I be interested in who he's fucking?"

"My friend Greg. He's a total jock, but…he's gay. And he's fucking Ray Beuerhoft."

"He can't be that bright."

"He needs money. And Soulschnitzel's got it."

"Not for long. Blotter is out."

"What?" Jared's face fell. "I have to warn him."

"Do what you like, but after you tell me a few things. How deep is Soulschnitzel in? How many of Blotter's houses has he ripped?"

"Three. I think. But you guys raided one the other day."

"Is Ray still looking for trouble?"

"He says Blotter is a pussy. He laughs at him."

"Then he's fucking stupid. Anything else?"

"Greg says when he was over the other night, they woke up at 3 AM. Harleys driving by. Lots of them."

Rick nodded at Bobbi. "Tell Olds that the hit on Soulschnitzel is either tonight or tomorrow. He can't fuck around."

Bobbi nodded and went outside. Rick waited until she was gone to talk again. "Jared, listen to me."

"I'm listening."

"Tell your friend Greg two things: One, tell Soulschnitzel to call me. He's pushing his luck. And two, tell Greg to find a new sugar daddy. Okay?"

"Do you really think there'll be shooting? Here?"

"Jared, I'll practically fucking guarantee it."

MAY

PUSH THE BUTTON, OR THE BUTTON PUSHES YOU

No matter how much a dealer like Blotter Boorman may prefer a businesslike approach to his affairs, there comes a time in every career when a problem must be dealt with, violently and ruthlessly.

Violence is the true currency of the narcotics world. And Ray Beuerhoft, AKA "Soulschnitzel," has invited Blotter Boorman to push the button on him. As with any battle, what happens after the first shot is unpredictable, except to say that chaos is guaranteed. And when a dealer has started using his own product again, that guarantee is ironclad...

**UBC ENDOWMENT LANDS
POINT GREY**

Blotter snorted a line off the bar, then sat back, swirled his cognac, and looked around.

Out past the wide balcony of Doug Harris' mansion, the rolling artificial hills of an 18-hole PGA course swelled. The pot lights bathed his backyard in alternating blue, orange, red, and white tones. Women, outnumbering the men two-to-one, some paid for, some not, chatted and flirted with guys on the balcony.

The bikers shot pool and played darts. Someone had started warming up the hot tub, and he smelled roasted meat smoke welling up from the balcony.

He wasn't hungry. The coke made sure of that. But he was sure horny. Doug was sure to have ordered exactly what he liked for the occasion.

Doug Harris was that rarity in the drug world. A man who'd made a fortune and had walked away. Now, he lived the dream so many of them shared, but so few ever got to enjoy. A life of leisure lived without fear.

Doug had been so very smart. Always staying in the background, keeping potential trouble at arm's length. He had been an import/export specialist, spending twenty years getting dope across borders, serving all manner of masters, and coming out respected by people who could agree on precious little else.

Because he had fucked nobody who hadn't tried to fuck him first, he slept with both eyes closed. And those who had tried to fuck him were long dead and mourned by no one.

Blotter snorted another line off the bar. Doug Harris appeared beside him, shaking his head. "That shit will be the end of you, Blotter. Makes you paranoid. Trust me, there's always enough to worry about for real."

Blotter chuckled and wiped his nose. He looked at Doug, who, with his stout frame, wire glasses, and bushy beard, his golf shirt and chinos, looked more like a professor than a drug dealer. "I gotta keep an edge on, Doug. Competition trying to fuck me."

"They always are, Blotter. Always. Three things in this business never go away; customers, competitors, and cops. The three c's. Never kill customers, or cops. But competitors? Kill them fast, and clean."

Blotter looked over at the bikers. "That's the plan."

"Except you like to do things yourself. Risky."

Blotter shrugged. "That way, I know it gets done right."

Doug waved a hairy arm in annoyance. "Fuck that! You'll never get all this by thinking like that. I mean, what are you doing with turds like Donnie? I wouldn't trust that smash-toothed sheep fucker to change a light bulb."

Blotter sagged over his cognac. "He needs me. I promised his dad

I'd look after him."

Doug shook his head vehemently. He lifted the mirror full of coke away from the bar. "Two things right there that'll get you killed. Coke, and sentimentality. At least I can take one away. Now, I'm gonna lock you in here with Randy and the boys. Help you get rid of that scrawny little over tanned kraut for good, okay? Just nod and say yes to everything. Trust me. When it's done, there'll be two Mexican girls waiting for you in the hot tub. I promise." Doug patted him on the back.

"Why do you do all this for me, Doug?"

"Easy. I promised your mom I'd look after you."

"Huh. Sentimentality." Blotter looked over at the bikers. "I really wish there was another way, you know that, Doug?"

Doug whispered in his ear. "It's the way things are done. Push the button, or the button pushes you."

CORNWALL AVE
KITSILANO
THE NEXT DAY

Barry Olds' strategy for pre-empting Blotter's assault on Ray Beuerhoft's empire was a predictable one, even though Rick Grohmann had to concede, it was smart.

Shut him down with raids before he could be hit. But that required a successful buy from each one of his three properties before a warrant would be approved. And at this point, Rick Grohmann was observing, it wasn't looking like that was going to happen.

Well, anyway, it was a day at the beach. And it was pensionable time. Beachgoers came and went around them, too preoccupied with pleasure to pay them any mind. Families with blow-up toys and fold-up chairs. Teens with coolers full of beers and joints behind their ears.

Keller had returned to the OP, empty handed, like the rest. They were using up an entire Academy class this way. "Well? You get anything?" Rick quizzed the big-eared baby cop.

"No sir. He said they were closed. Jewish holiday."

"Fuck me! Wait a second, Keller. Aren't you Jewish? What holiday is it?"

"All I know is Hanukkah and Yom Kippur. And this isn't either."

"Shit!" Bobbi was laughing next to him. "What's so funny?"

"Looks like your little warning backfired."

"Fuck off. Okay, Keller, piss off. I think we're calling this one." The sun was getting low over the beaches of Kitsilano when Rick put the portable to his mouth. "2337 to 2335."

"Go ahead."

"This op is a bust. He's closed up tight."

"10-4. Bring it home." If Olds was disappointed, he wasn't letting it show.

As he turned over the ignition, a thought occurred.

What if Soulschnitzel had decided to hit first? Maybe they were watching the wrong houses.

FOUR HOURS LATER

WEST 1ST AVE

One of Blotter's recently acquired properties was two blocks away from Soulschnitzel's flagship. Now, with the regular occupants cleared out, and the scouts reporting no cops around, the property was transformed into a military base.

Blotter was high again. In fact, he'd never really stopped snorting rails since last night at Doug's. It didn't really matter, anyway. He was only ostensibly in command. The bikers had seen to that.

He sat in an old armchair, nursing a warm Canadian, watching Turgeon, the mysterious new arrival, a thick-necked, heavily muscled Quebecois who looked like he could bench-press a VW. Turgeon was only a prospect, but he moved with the authority of a patch holder, directing the two Hangarounds, Mullen and Hecht, who had arrived with him.

Pissy Balls, Roach, and Donnie stood nervously against the wall and awaited orders. Through the haze of an almost 24-hour coke binge, Blotter could read the signs. *They're elbowing me out. The bikers want it all.*

Like a patient under general anesthetic, there was fuck all he could do about it. Doug had warned him, and he'd just kept doing rails, fucking, and drinking. Now he was a mummy, ready to be lowered into his own tomb.

Turgeon and his guys, also muscular men with "Don't fuck with me" hardwired into their auras, spread a long, thick chain out on the hardwood floor. Turgeon affixed a giant hook to each end. Then, Mullen and Hecht hefted it out to the GMC pickup in the back drive.

He would've thought that was a job for four men. *Jesus.* Soon, Mullen and Hecht returned with two duffel bags, and set them down on the floor. Three 12-gauge shotguns with folding stocks and three Sterling sub-machine guns were placed carefully on the floor. Turgeon took six curved magazines out of one of the bags and handed them to Pissy Balls. Mullen took four boxes of 9MM ammunition and handed them to Roach.

"Start loading." Turgeon commanded. He turned to Blotter, eyes searching him out for some sign of awareness. "That little cocksucker is finished."

Blotter nodded and drained the last of his beer. He felt a sudden, strange sense of kinship with Soulschnitzel.

Tonight, you are finished. Tomorrow, it's me.

KITS BEACH

Barry Olds had fished a six-pack out of his trunk, and now he sat on a log, smoking and drinking. While others in his position would be staring out to sea, he was looking across the broad avenue, to the house on Cornwall Ave.

His unique orientation had caught the eye of a Patrol unit, which had slowed twenty minutes before and painted him with an alley light. He'd held up a badge and waved, and the unit drove away. Save for the gentle waves behind him, it was quiet now.

"Got a spare?" Barry's heart skipped a beat. He turned and saw Grohmann, dressed down for once in Levis and a short-sleeved shirt.

"Fuck. You're quiet when you want to be."

Rick plopped down on the log and unhooked an Old Stock from the pack, cracking it open. "Airborne, baby. Silent killers." He hoisted the beer and looked across the street. "Anything going on?"

"No. Lights are on, blinds are down. Nobody coming or going."

"So why are you still here?"

"Same reason you are, Rick."

Rick nodded. He lit smokes for them both and passed one over. "You can feel something coming."

"Cop instinct. Or whatever."

"You're right. It's got to happen now. If it doesn't, he's done. Listen, I just got a call from one of my snitches. She's a high-end hooker, and she says last night, she was working a party. You'll never guess where."

"The Mayor's house?"

Rick snorted. "As if Harcourt would know what to do with a hooker. Probably teach her how to read." The Mayor was a notorious square. "No, she was at Doug Harris' place."

"There's a name I haven't heard in a while."

"Yeah, smart guy, right? Made it out with 20 million in the bank, a house in Point Grey, and not a single fucking conviction. Blotter should be so lucky."

"Maybe he will be. We can't seem to make anything stick." Barry took a long pull. "He's fucking Teflon."

Rick shook his head. "Gotti, he's not. For one thing, according to my girl, he was higher than Stevie Wonder all fucking night. The bikers were there in force. She ID'd that fat pig, Randy McClarty. Toots Hellenberger, too."

"Nomads Toots Hellenberger?"

"The very same. If the Nomads are involved..."

"Somebody's going to die." Barry puffed thoughtfully and sipped at his beer. The Nomads were an enforcement unit within the one percenters, an elite brought in to solve problems with finality.

"According to her, they kicked everyone out of the den, then Harris and the bikers went into a confab with Blotter. Looked more like they were dictating than they were discussing."

"He's losing it."

"And the bikers are picking it up."

"I don't know." Barry shook his head. "He's survived a lot of shit. I wouldn't count him out just yet. Right now, I'd rather sell him life insurance than Soulschnitzel."

"No argument there." Rick hesitated for a moment. "Your wife okay with this?"

Barry laughed nervously. "What, the sudden change from shift-work, me being away at strange times; to Drug Section hours, me being away all the time? No, she's not okay. How about Clarissa?"

Rick looked away. "If you don't ask, it's better. For both of us."

Barry Olds knew there was something he should say, or do, to help his man from going over the rails. But maybe what he was worrying about had happened already. Maybe there was no Ideal Sergeant solution to this manpower issue.

What would the cops of the future be like to manage, he wondered? For sure, there would be more women, more educated types. Fewer rough-edged killers like Grohmann.

Which one could he handle better? Which type made the better cop? The sound of a low, growling, big-block engine brought his attention back to the house.

While they'd been chatting, they'd missed a Pontiac GTO parking right in front of their target. Now, the trunk opened, and three men manhandled a chain with a hook up the stairs of Ray

Beuerhoft's house. While they were hooking it to the grill of the front door, an even louder vehicle, a GMC pickup, turned onto Cornwall, then began backing up onto the front lawn.

"What the fuck?" Rick Grohmann's smoke fell out of his mouth. "What the actual fuck?"

"It's going down!" Barry Olds grabbed his portable from between his feet. "Station 2335, 2335, 10-33 at 2330 Cornwall. Robbery in progress at known drug location, five to six suspects. Officers need assistance."

Rick was already sprinting for his Mustang. He popped his trunk and grabbed a 12-gauge shotgun and a box of shells. He ran back to rejoin Barry, who had his .38 out, and was taking cover behind the logs.

Rick belched. "Fuck. Not sure those beers were a good idea."

Barry smiled at him. "You really want to die sober?"

The sound of the waves was replaced by the sounds of sirens, as Patrol units all over the division responded to the assistance call.

2330 CORNWALL

Mullen had just finished hooking the chain to the grill on the front door. He turned to the pickup truck, raised a hand to give a thumbs up, and disappeared in the pink mist of a shotgun slug blast at medium-close range. He looked down at his guts, now replaced by a large, mangled hole, before the GMC pulled the grill off the frame with the power of 325 horsepower, taking his body with it.

Roach looked up from the balustrade where he'd taken cover, to a side window, to see a man with wild blonde hair and a long beard working another round into the shotgun's action. He raised his SMG and let a long burst go, ripping apart glass and gunman at the same time, sending the longhair sprawling. Now, Turgeon was taking the stairs twice at a time, almost slipping in the gore that remained of Mullen. His SMG was slung across his back, and he hefted a crowbar.

Now, to Roach, it all seemed to slow down. *Way* down. He heard nothing but sirens, and that could not be a good thing. He saw Pissy Balls, frozen, a dark stain spreading on the front of his jeans. *Have I pissed myself?* He wondered.

I killed a guy. I just killed a guy. He looked down the stairs, seeing the folded-up body of Mullen lying underneath the metal cage, as Donnie fought frantically to unhook it all from the truck. The other Hangaround revved the truck's engine, sending an unmistakeable signal. *We're fucked, let's leave.*

But then, Turgeon reefed the heavy old wooden door of the house off of its hinges with the crowbar, tossing the tool down the stairs, and racking the action of his shotgun. He went in the door, screaming something aggressive. Roach turned to Pissy Balls and said something like "Let's go!" but he never remembered for sure. Just as they both stood up from behind the balustrade, he saw Turgeon somersaulting back down the stairs in a blue cloud, his left arm spraying blood.

Pissy Balls awoke, firing his shotgun twice at the shadow in the doorway, who staggered but did not fall. His return fire came in the form of a steady blink of muzzle flashes, which punched four neat little holes in Pissy Balls' enormous guts.

Pissy Balls dropped to his knees. He turned to Roach, a look of tremendous disappointment on his face, and then he rolled down the stairs on his leaking gut.

When Roach looked back at the doorway, the shadow was there again, and now he felt a burning pain in his left shoulder and chest. He fired the Sterling one-handed, forcing the shadow to duck back, but then he heard a "click."

Forgetting he had a spare magazine, he dropped the gun and stumbled down the stairs in a panic. He ran now, faster than he would've thought possible just a few minutes ago.

He ran past Donnie, who was throwing himself into the truck bed, screaming something at him, dragging a pale and leaking Turgeon. He ran across the street, seeing the bright red and blue lights of the cops on either side, not knowing where to go.

So, Matthew, what's it to be? A swim to Japan? He stumbled over a log, in time to see the GMC peeling into the road, a tall man with a revolver firing three shots at it, cop cars careening off the road in its wake.

"You one fat, dead motherfucker!" A curiously accented voice came from the darkness. He rolled over and saw a naked Soulschnitzel standing over him with an M-16. Blood dripped from his scalp, all the way down his sweating, gleaming body.

Roach had no breath left to plead for his life. He heard, "Police, drop the gun!" Coming from the sidewalk. He saw Soulschnitzel turn, intentionally or not, pointing the barrel of the M-16 at the source of the voice.

From the voice, now came a shower of sparks, and a boom. Soulschnitzel flew backwards, just like in the movies, his M-16 flipping end over end like a majorette's baton.

Roach looked up at the stars. Then, he closed his eyes.

BURRARD ST BRIDGE

Blotter drove the Corvette aggressively, judging from the red and blue lights congregating in Kits that the VPD had bigger things on its plate tonight.

Besides, as soon as he'd heard the shots and the sirens, he'd figured it was time to go home to address of record. Someone would soon be knocking.

Yes, it had been a disaster. But it hadn't been *his* disaster, had it?

If nobody talked, and that was a big if, he was back in control of his own destiny. Let the bikers sweat this one. It hadn't been his idea, and he'd spoken against it.

Blotter Boorman cranked the Bad Company and raced home under the starlight.

MAY

POST-MORTEM

Another thing television gets wrong about policing: shootouts are a rarity. However, they do occur. Afterward, those around the officers involved are often at a loss as to what to say. Reactions amongst friends and family range from silence and avoiding the subject, to an unseemly celebration of the taking of human life...

BURNABY
MORLEY ST

Barry Olds opened one eye tentatively. From the feeling in his long-suffering back, he hadn't slept well.

A commitment to opening both eyes resolved the issue. Coming home after daybreak, exhausted and emotionally drained beyond all prior experience, he'd crashed on the foldout couch in the basement. He blinked three times and sat up, wanting both a long piss and a large glass of water.

In search of his needs, he staggered up the stairs to find Tina washing the breakfast dishes in the kitchen. Barry was painfully aware of the smells of spilled beer, tobacco, and cordite on him.

She turned, a little package of red curls and sarcasm. "Fun night?"

He held up a hand as he headed for the bathroom. "Gimme a minute." When he emerged and plodded to the sink, she was leaning against the counter, arms folded, waiting for her answer.

"Well? Is this the way this new assignment's going to be? You roll in at 6 AM smelling like Mardi Gras, and I'm not supposed to ask questions?"

He held up a hand as he drained two tall glasses of water in one go. Finally, he answered. "There was a shootout last night."

Now, her face was uncertain. "Oh. Are you okay?"

"Yes."

"Any of your guys hurt?"

"No. It was just me and Rick Grohmann. I fired a few shots at a fleeing vehicle. Rick killed a suspect."

"Oh. Sorry." She looked uncertain of where to go with it next. Like him, she came from a cop family. But this was something outside her experience, as it was his. "Are you in trouble?"

"No, I don't think so. We just had to stay late to give our statements and talk to Major Crimes. Turn in our guns, all that. I'm going in today to finish up the paperwork."

"Okay. Glad you're alright." She hugged him, awkwardly. When he released her, she looked up at him with gleaming green eyes. "Barry?"

"Yes, honey?"

"When you come home, can you fix the dishwasher? It's not draining right again."

Hail the conquering hero.

VANCOUVER GENERAL HOSPITAL
PATHOLOGY

Bobbi Sanghera walked into the chilled corridor and shuddered. Selfridge had told her on the phone to "dress like a detective today," and so now she tottered on high heels and chafed against an unfamiliar jacket/dress combo. She relaxed a little bit when she saw the familiar face of Phil LeBretton.

The always nattily dressed detective had interviewed her when she applied for the Department, doing a stint in Recruiting, and now, as a Major Crimes investigator, he flipped through his notes, awaiting the arrival of the pathologist. Phil LeBretton looked more like a banker than a cop, a permanent half-smile on his face hiding some truly dark experiences. He looked up and brightened when he saw Bobbi.

"Constable Sanghera! I hear you're making an impression on Drug Section." He gave her a decorous peck on the cheek. "It's about time you dragged that bunch into the 20th Century."

Bobbi smiled nervously. "Is this your case, Phil?"

"Yes, unfortunately. What a bloody mess. Four dead bodies and one mute survivor. At least no actual humans were hurt." He took a folded *Province* newspaper out from under his arm and handed it to her. "From an internal investigation standpoint, it always helps when the reporters pick our side."

Bobbi stared at the picture. A black foot peeped out from under a crime-scene sheet on the sand of Kits Beach. "Hero Cops Battle Drug Traffickers in Wild Shootout."

The nearest door opened. A little man with glasses peered out. "Dr Bloor is ready for you, detectives."

"They're playing our song." Phil entered with his customary aplomb, causing the pathologist and his assistant to look up from their work.

Dr Bloor was a grizzled old veteran of the basement world of autopsies and cadavers. He squinted at them through thick glasses. "Ah, the debonair detective arrives. I see you brought a secretary."

Ray corrected her. "Constable Sanghera is a police officer, Doc."

"Oh, really? Good for you. Well, let me put some music on, and we'll get started." Bloor signaled to the little man with glasses, and suddenly Bach suffused the chilly background.

"Nice choice." Phil beamed. He opened his notebook and began to write. Bobbi got out hers and followed suit. The little man paused for effect, then whipped back the white sheet covering the guest of honour.

A thin, mocha-coloured man with high cheekbones and long braided hair occupied the slab. A patch of pink, tangled flesh took up more than half of his torso. Single-ink tattoos covered a large percentage of the skin below the neck. "Identified by relatives as Raymond Beuerhoft, AKA 'Soulschnitzel', DOB 56-09-22. No prints on file." Bloor announced into his Dictaphone. "Subject is a male of mixed Caucasian and Negroid ancestry. Special barrier precautions due to HIV positivity."

Bobbi raised an eyebrow. Phil LeBretton took a face shield from the counter and handed it to her. She didn't argue but put it on. AIDS terrified her.

Bloor continued his monologue. "Subject is an apparently healthy individual for his age, small in stature and with an athletic build. Toxicology screen reveals alcohol in moderate amounts, plus some cocaine and THC. Surface examination reveals one site of serious trauma, a large hole in the mid-torso consistent with a shotgun blast at close range." Bloor looked at Bobbi over his glasses and gave her a creepy smile. "Let's begin with the Y-cut, shall we?"

Bobbi supressed a shudder. She smelled formaldehyde and meat. It was not her first autopsy. But she was sure it was something she would never get used to. Phil LeBretton whispered in her ear as they both watched Bloor open Soulschnitzel's insides.

"Think of a beach somewhere. It works for me."

312 MAIN ST
DRUG SECTION

Rick Grohmann nursed a sore head and a throbbing pain in his shoulder, where the night before he'd steadied his shotgun before blowing Soulschnitzel into the next world.

VPD was the last place he wanted to be. But if he was going to be off for a few days, he'd need those Canadians tickets in his desk drawer. Beer and hotdogs could be enjoyed at home, but they went better with baseball.

What did he feel? Clarissa had wanted to know. *What did he feel?*

He killed a guy. He had to. The barrel of an M-16 was pointing in his direction. But the irony was, the guy he killed wasn't anyone he particularly disliked. In fact, it was someone who he'd tried to save, in his own way.

But he was sure some of the people writing letters to the editor would have other ideas, of that he was sure. Black body, white cop behind the trigger. To some people, that was all that mattered.

Walking through the halls was luridly weird. "Good shoot, Rick!" and "Nice job on that fucking monkey." Backslaps from people he barely knew.

Even in the world of policing, shootings were rare. Most cops never experienced it, and since they lacked experience, they got the reactions wrong. They thought what the man involved needed was reinforcement and encouragement, when what he really wanted was to be left alone.

As a matter of fact, Rick Grohmann felt little about shooting Ray Beuerhoft, except maybe disappointment that it wasn't Blotter Boorman.

Maybe it could give him some inroads with Roach Lehmann. The big fat fuck was showing his gratitude by saying exactly nothing. Maybe if he met the man who saved his life, he'd feel obligated to say *something.*

Or maybe not. Anyway, until he was cleared to come back on duty, it was all academic. Beer and baseball were a more immediate concern. Drug Section was deserted when he got in. He unlocked his desk drawer and retrieved the tickets, then turned to stare at a large whiteboard dominated by pictures of Blotter and his gang.

It hit Rick Grohmann then that, without intending to, he'd turned Blotter's Waterloo into an Austerlitz. He'd done the fucker a favour. Now, he was more determined than ever to end the little piece of shit.

But that would have to wait. He walked over to the whiteboard, and drew a big black X over Pissy Balls' picture. "Nice job there, Detective."

The voice startled him. He turned to see the Chief Constable staring at him. "Sir. I was just picking up some personal items."

The Chief cleared his throat. "Holding up well, I hope?"

"Yes sir. Thank you for asking."

The Chief sat on Connolly's desk and admired his "Sitting Duck" coffee cup. "Listen, Detective. This use of force investigation will be a ground ball, understand. LeBretton knows the score. I want this son-of-a-bitch Boorman off the streets ASAP. And that means you back out there."

Rick smiled. "That suits me fine, Chief."

"Good." The Chief stood and smoothed his uniform. "In the meantime, take in some early season ball, take it easy, and don't go too far from a phone. Oh, and by the way Detective…"

"Yes sir?"

"What were you and Olds doing down there anyway?"

"Having a beer, sir."

The Chief smiled. "Well, damn good thing then. See you next

week."

"Yes sir."

MAY

MARKET SHARE

In the years leading up to Expo 86, the inhabitants of the Downtown East Side had to contend with mass evictions, as landlords cleared out low-income tenants in anticipation of lucrative new development. Now, with the fair in full swing, they were subjected to flagrant drug supermarkets, dealing new varieties of cocaine and heroin, often stronger than addicts and dealers were used to. Some populations never catch a break...

**THE SYLVIA HOTEL
BEACH AVENUE**

Blotter Boorman loosened his collar and got into his second martini, the booze finally taming the cocaine rush.

Damn it, he was feeling good. With his principal rival dead (courtesy of the police...how ironic), he could focus on expanding and enhancing his market share. With Roach staying quiet in hospital, and Tusker behaving himself, his legal worries appeared to be at an end.

And now, the bikers were opening up the floodgates of supply. Better quality cocaine and heroin was flowing in, with a ready audience waiting to experience a higher high. Some of his street dealers had taken over 24-hour grocery stores in the East End, and were now moving shitloads of product at lightning speed.

Which was not to say there were no problems. Foreign accents had been heard in Library Square, spics and shines moving in on his street trade, following their clientele north to Expo. Some examples would need to be made.

Also, his dealers, while keen to meet audience demand, were not always skilled enough to do it safely. Speedballs, in particular, were a problem.

Speedballs mixed cocaine and heroin for a potent, up-and-down rollercoaster high. They took skill to mix, though, and too many overdoses might bring the hammer down. As it was, the cops were so busy with Expo that their aggressive expansion was practically flying under the radar.

And the money? *Jesus fucking Christ, the money.* It was stacking up in every place he could park it, his laundering efforts hampered by a lack of personnel. He had Donnie working on that angle. Speaking of...

Donnie plopped into the booth next to him, his typically out-of-date Ska clubwear now replaced by Don Johnson chic. There was still the matter of those teeth, though.

"You want a drink, Donnie?"

"I could murder one, aye. That looks good."

"It is." Blotter signalled for two more. "How were your rounds?"

Donnie grinned wolfishly. "Productive. No bumps. And every operation in the black. No pleading fucking poverty for once."

Blotter grinned. "That's what spilling a little blood gets you. How's your talent search going?"

"Sanjay says he's got two accountants lined up for me. The three of them together can chew through a million a day."

"Vetted?"

"Aye, fresh off the fucking boat they are. And Sanjay's got cousins at B of M, and the Royal. No bothers, mate!"

"And Roach?"

"Mr Romans says they may not even be able to charge him. They didn't catch him with a gun, and there's no living witnesses."

"Good. Tusker behaving himself?"

"Alright, I suppose, though as a performer he's a wee bit weak. We can always put the squeeze on him, if ye want…"

"No. No, that's fine. Well, Donnie, since you've got all that sorted, how about taking a stroll down to Library Square? See if there's anybody you don't recognize."

"Aye, alright. Newcomers, then?"

"Right. I don't recall asking for their help."

"I get the picture." Donnie began to slide out of the booth. Blotter stopped him.

"Finish your drink, Donnie. And eat something for once. You're wasting away, man."

Donnie smiled and picked up a menu.

LIBRARY SQUARE

While Blotter and Donnie downed martinis behind the ivy-enwrapped walls of the venerable old Sylvia, to their east, a decidedly more downbeat crowd sought out less approved pleasures.

The sun was out, and like iguanas stirring on Galapogean rocks, the drug seekers and drug sellers awoke and sought each other.

One of the drug seekers had only recently started coming here. To the extent that the experience was still new and scary. He was a tall, thin kid in preppie style, with an untamed Jew-fro hanging over his face.

His parents had kicked him out after the chaos at Grad. And that flinty fucking Finn Tusker Taakoiennin wouldn't sell him what he really wanted, only weed. So here he was. If only his parents had known he'd move in with his cousin Seth. Seth liked harder pleasures.

For Kary Bezoff, like Seth, weed would no longer cut it. Library Square was scary, but at least here, dealers didn't have scruples. They would sell, if you had the money. And of all the problems in Kary Bezoff's life, money was not one of them.

A tall African, taller and blacker than anyone he'd ever seen, sold him an eightball, no questions asked. Desperate to score, Kary ran two alleys over and sat on a milk crate, going through the little ritual his cousin had taught him.

Dilute, cook, load up, tie off, shoot.

Soon, the wave came over him. Again, and again. But this time, he couldn't quite get his head above water.

Now, Kary Bezoff stared out at the world with open eyes as he died painlessly.

EAST 20ᵀᴴ AVENUE

Marianne Taakoiennin walked quietly into the living room to find Tusker hunched over "The Table," where all transactions of import took place. It was also where the money was counted, and that was what Tusker was doing now.

In all of her wildest dreams or worst nightmares, never could she have imagined she would be married to a drug dealer. Let alone, a Finnish one. Before she met Tusker, she didn't even know they had drugs there.

Fair enough, he'd started off as a safe cracker, something she had a lot more respect for, for whatever reason. After all, he was still a thief.

But dope made her skin crawl, given her own experiences as a hype, especially when kids came looking to score, if she had to be frank. And she had been very frank with Tusker lately, especially since his "friends" had almost gang-raped her. She touched the tender spot under her eye. Still soft and swollen but dying down gradually.

As she watched him count the big bills from the morning's take with robot-like speed, Marianne repeated to herself a truth she had only just learned to accept: if it's me or the money, I'm fucked. He won't choose me over Blotter, no matter what his sweet words. And that made her think of escape hatches, and friendly policewomen.

"What did that kid want this morning, Tusker?"

Tusker set down the cash in frustration. "Fuck, Marianne! You made me lose count." He ran a hand through his thinning hair and paused before answering. "Heroin, Marianne. He wanted heroin."

"I hope you didn't…"

"Of course, I fucking didn't!" He seethed for a minute before conceding. "Why do you think he walked out of here swearing? I don't sell hard shit to anyone under 21. But there's lots of scum in this city who will."

"What do you think will happen to him?" In a world of pain, why did she care about this skinny little rich boy, she asked herself.

If not him, then who? If not now, then when? It was the sixties' radical voice of her mother, the ever-present conscience.

"He's dead." Tusker said simply, without knowing how right he was. "Too much high purity smack and coke floating around because the people coming to Expo know their dope and expect a kick in the ass high. But there's too few people around who know how to cut it properly before selling. The bodies are going to stack up this summer."

Marianne drifted off, not wanting to hear more. She walked upstairs to her room, opening a dresser drawer, and peeling off a layer of wallpaper inside to reveal a dog-eared business card.

B.K. "BOBBI" SANGHERA
CONSTABLE # 903
VANCOUVER POLICE DEPARTMENT
DRUG SECTION TEAM 1

She had a pocket full of quarters, and an overdue trip to the grocery store to cover her tracks. All she needed was the guts to make the call.

Hearing feet on the steps, she hurriedly tucked the card back in its place and shut the drawer.

All she needed was the guts to make the call. But she wasn't there. Not yet.

MAY

PROFESSIONAL COURTESY

In the days before independent investigation units, when cops were still trusted to police themselves, the receipt of a criminal complaint against a serving officer initiated a delicate dance. The concept of "professional courtesy" meant that, often, a police officer assumed to be a valuable member of the team would be extended considerations often denied to mere civilians. Still, decorum demanded at least the appearance of an investigation.

Interviewing a hardened criminal such as Blotter Boorman, on the other hand, was often a futile exercise, particularly if he had retained the services of an attorney such as Paul "The Pitbull" Romans...

NORTH VANCOUVER
LYNN VALLEY

Rick Grohmann squinted up at the sun as it slipped behind a cloudbank. He'd better get his ass in gear on the lawn. Two weeks without a cut in a wet spring was not a good idea. Soon, his house was going to look like it belonged on a reservation. Resentfully, he pushed the old Toro up the hill that backed his property, noticing the Goggins were out on their patio, watching and sniping, no doubt.

A smoke hanging off his lower lip, ash drifting into his chest hairs, Rick cursed under his breath. If he had it to do over, he'd fuck getting married, and settle for a high-rise with a sea view. All the tail a single cop could handle, and no more mowing lawns.

The Toro sputtered at the crest of the hill. Rick cursed and revved it up again, his shoulder still feeling the pain from shotgun recoil. When the mower started, he scalped the top of the tall grass, then circled in a haphazard pattern that drove Clarissa nuts. She seemed to think he ought to be some kind of Zen-gardening Jap. He would've told her to hire one, but he was pretty sure she'd just wind up fucking him, too.

That was how the whole Lawrence Dyck fiasco had started. Tennis lessons. "I'm bored," she's said. When he suggested she get a fucking job, she'd pulled out the old charm, and convinced him to rent her a Dyck instead.

Rick glanced back at the house. She washed dishes and watched him carefully. What was she looking for? He had no idea.

"Detective Grohmann? Detective Grohmann! DETECTIVE GROHMANN!" Finally, Rick caught on that someone was yelling at him. He saw two dudes in badly dated suits with wide lapels and too-short ties standing next to the garbage cans at the side of the house. He shut off the mower.

"It's not Saturday. I thought you Jehovahs only came out on Saturdays." He walked deliberately towards them.

The taller of the two men held up a badge. "I'm Corporal Poincare. This here is Constable Fratelli. North Van GIS. You are Detective Grohmann, right?"

"Yeah." He finished the last of the cigarette and dropped it in front of them. "What are you doing on my property?"

The shorter of the two, who otherwise would have been moustachioed Mountie clones, spoke up. "If you'd rather talk to us at the Detachment, it can be arranged."

Rick took another two steps. "Is that so, woparoonie? What if I don't want to talk to you at all?" He knew what this was about, and the only surprise was it had taken so long. He'd even talked to his lawyer about a defense.

Fratelli opened his mouth to respond, but Poincare held him back. "Come on, Rick. We're all cops here. My OIC took a look at this complaint and asked me to come down and talk it over with you first. Off the record. Professional courtesy, eh?"

Rick forced a laugh. "How many cops have been screwed by those words? 'Off the record?' Pardon me if I'm cautious."

"I get it, Rick. But our OIC is a good guy. He doesn't like frying cops, especially not for slime balls like Lawrence Dyck. We know he was fucking your wife, Rick."

"Oh yeah?" Rick grimaced. "That common knowledge around the detachment?"

Fratelli stepped around his Corporal. "Hey, asshole! I heard you were supposed to be some kind of super cop? You just seem like another dipshit who doesn't know a break when he sees one."

Rick cracked his knuckles. "That's funny. I was thinking of breaks, too."

The back window screeched open, and Clarissa yelled at him. "For fuck's sake, Rick, you are not fighting two cops in our yard. Sit down and talk it over!"

He stared up at her. "Did you call them?"

"No, I fucking did not call them! If I was going to call them, *sweetheart*, I'd have done it a long time ago." Rick caught Fratelli raising an eyebrow at Poincare.

"Then it was..."

"Of course, it was. Talk to them. Please, Rick."

"Fine." He looked at the Mounties. "You guys want a beer?"

Poincare held up a hand, "Rick, we're on..."

Fratelli cut him off. "Sounds good to me." Rick signalled to Clarissa to bring out three beers. They sat down at the old picnic table under the cedars. When Clarissa walked away after bringing the beers, Rick noticed Poincare's stare lingering a bit too long on her ass.

You just had to marry a cheerleader, right? No marketable skills but Queen Bee pheromones that would make Freddie Mercury want to hump her. Now here you are.

"I can guess why you're here." He said, finally. "That fucking wife-stealing prick, Lawrence Dyck."

Poincare nodded. "Yes. He says you did quite a number on him."

"Did he tell you he was 'doing a number' on my wife at the time?"

"Only reluctantly. He left a lot out, I think."

Cynthia went back to the kitchen after dropping off the beers. She watched for a moment, then walked into the living room and dialled Larry.

"Who is this?"

"Me. Why are there two fucking Mounties here, Larry?"

"I've got rights, Clar. He shouldn't have done that to me."

"Wow. Practice saying that in court, idiot. You think a jury is going to sympathize with you? I think you'll have twelve people wondering why he didn't pull his .38 and blow your nuts off."

"Well, I can see whose side you're on."

"Think, for Christ's sakes, Larry! Every time I brought up commitment, you shrugged it off. 'Let's just enjoy the moment' you said. Okay, so now, my husband stands to lose his job because you were 'enjoying the moment'…"

"As if you weren't!"

"I won't pretend I wasn't, Larry. I miss you. But a big dick is no substitute for a roof over my head, and what you're doing is putting that in danger. Think about it. I'll call you when it's safe."

"What are you going to do?"

"How the fuck should I know?" She slammed down the receiver hard. She was angry for his dramatic wounded feelings. As if the police would sacrifice one of their own for the likes of him.

But she was also conflicted. He represented freedom, a chance to escape Rick's domineering, insecure, macho prison. But how freedom could she have with someone who couldn't even commit? She wandered back into the kitchen. Outside, the three men were exchanging handshakes.

Cops. She shook her head.

"Let me talk to my lawyer. I'll come in and give you a statement."

Fratelli interjected. "And your bosses need to be in the loop. Or my OIC has to call them."

Rick nodded. "I get it. Give me a couple of days. I'm working on something big."

Poincare grinned. "We heard, trust me. We don't want to fuck that up. All we need is what we think really happened anyway. We already gave Crown a sneak preview. They think the case is a bag of dogshit."

"It is." Rick smiled, finally a little more relaxed. He walked them to their car, then looked back at the house. Clarissa watched from the picture window, then disappeared. He opened the front door and walked inside. He heard sounds from the bedroom, but he paused next to the phone.

Rick lifted the receiver, then hit "redial" on the touch-tone. He knew exactly whose voice he was going to hear.

"Who is this? Hey...Clar?"

He dropped the receiver and took off his belt. Then he walked towards the bedroom.

**312 MAIN ST
MAJOR CRIMES**

Phil LeBretton looked across the table at Blotter Boorman and realized immediately that today would be nothing but a formality.

The guy had shown up at 10 AM on the dot, arriving like Elvis in a big black Mercedes, accompanied by asshole for hire Paul Romans. Boorman had obviously dressed on the assumption that his next stop would not be processing at Vancouver Pre-Trial.

It would be filet mignon, not baloney sandwiches, for dinner tonight. Blotter Boorman had the best lawyer the bikers could afford, and, from all accounts, an airtight alibi. Even his PO was vouching for him.

LeBretton supressed a laugh. Blotter's PO was a notorious cockhound who excelled in harvesting favours from his clients in return for glowing reports. One day, he'd be able to prove it, and bust his ass. But until then, he just had to accept the fact that Blotter would never get rolled on a probation violation. It was make a major case, or watch the man do donuts around law enforcement.

If you looked close enough, though, there were cracks in the façade. The darting eyes and continual sniffing were telltale signs of a serious coke habit. LeBretton figured that, given the number of serious enemies Blotter had made, the temptation to get high on his own product wasn't going to go away.

Romans pointedly looked at his Rolex. In a case he'd worked many years ago with the Mounties, Sergeant Gerry Mulvaney had pointedly humiliated Romans, forcing him into hiding for six months and sticking him with the sobriquet "Paul the

Poodle." LeBretton cherished that memory every time the giant douchebag put on airs. "We're here on time, Detective. As a show of good faith, one would think you'd endeavour to be so too."

LeBretton shrugged. "No doubt Sergeant Morely is on his way. But we do appreciate your coming in at such an early hour. I mean, after all, your business is a nocturnal one."

Blotter shrugged carelessly. He let Romans get agitated for him. "We do not appreciate your casting aspersions."

LeBretton held up a CPIC printout. "I must be reading this record wrong, then."

Romans smirked. "People change, Detective. How many years have I been trying to convince policemen of that?"

LeBretton smiled. "I have no doubt that if Charlie Callaghan were still alive, you'd be arguing that on his behalf."

The mere mention of the Callaghan case shut Romans up. A deep red tone overcame his tanned complexion. The door to the interview room opened, and an overweight, balding cop with meaty hands and a disheveled suit entered. "Sorry I'm late, gentlemen." Sergeant Mickey Morely sat next to LeBretton. He smiled at Romans. "Did I miss your 'the good in everyone' speech?"

Romans shifted in his seat. "Let's get to the point."

Morely smiled broadly. He was known in the Detective Division as "Machine Gun Mickey" for his rapid-fire interrogation technique.

"Okay." Morely folded his hands on the desk. "Your number one rival and his boyfriend wind up shot to shit, and the next day all of his business folds into yours, Blotter. Convince me that you're just the luckiest little FPS'er in the universe. Go."

Blotter yawned. "You prove things. I don't. I think you got that mixed up."

Now, it was LeBretton's turn to look at his Rolex.

NORTH VANCOUVER
LYNN VALLEY

Clarissa Grohmann clawed at the belt wrapped around her neck as her husband thrusted the last few stabs he had left into her. Choking and sweating, she crossed the frontier into orgasm at the same time he did. Then, he pulled out of her, and unceremoniously pushed her down onto the bed.

He stood over her, relishing the moment. "I oughta call somebody else over her to finish you."

She rolled over and pulled the belt off her neck. "Would that turn you on? Why not?"

He licked his lips. "Maybe. Maybe it would."

"Then stop getting mad at me for fucking around. You want me to be a slut, admit it."

"Maybe I do. But not with him."

"I already told you. I called him to tell him to back off on you. You think I want you to lose your job?"

The phone rang in the living room. He walked out to grab it. Clarissa sharpened her ears to get every word.

"Grohmann. Who?" Rick sat down heavily in the wingback. *Must be bad news.* "When?"

He listened for a long while, shaking his head. "Okay. I'm sorry... I know he called; I was just very busy. Look, I'm sorry for your loss. I know. I know I should have. Listen, I'm back on duty next

Monday. Can I talk to you then? It's Linda? Okay, I will talk to you on Monday Linda." He set down the receiver. Rick stared out the window for a long time.

She drifted out of the bedroom, still naked. "Problems?"

"One of my informants…just a kid, really…died of an overdose. Mom found my card in his dresser."

"Sorry to hear that."

Rick shrugged. "Drugs kill people. It's what they do."

Clarissa looked at him, wondering if she wanted him to be one of those people or not. Then, something overtook her, and she straddled him, kissing aggressively.

Soon, they were back where they had started.

MAY

CONFESSIONS

Veteran police investigators collect information the way squirrels collect nuts. Sometimes, they need to be reminded to share...

VANCOUVER
OAK PARK

Bobbi Sanghera mixed a pitcher of iced tea for her parents and looked out the back window. Her mother was on her knees, vigorously rooting out weeds from a flower bed. She wore a floppy hat to keep the suddenly urgent sun off of her head.

Her dad dug savagely with a hoe at a row to overturn the soil for fertilizing and watering. He wore an old singlet and a kerchief over his head, in place of the usual *dastar*. Bobbi smiled. Her parents were so unfashionable, it was amazing. She cautiously made her way down the two-steep stairs with the iced tea.

Bobbi dreaded the thought of either one of her parents doing a header down the rickety old stairs and was constantly on Sat's case about it. His perennial answer: "I'll get on it."

Ah, Sat. The successful one. He'd presented the little house on West 61st as a retirement present for their parents, after they'd sold the place in Surrey. Sat owned a very successful trucking company, and he, unlike his unmarried, civil servant sister, could afford it. Something he never shut up about.

"Take a break, you two. It's too hot, and you're tending a garden, not trying to stay alive in the Punjab."

Bobbi's dad shook a finger and head together, the way only Indian people could do. "Hard work is good for you, daughter."

"Yes, and I've worked very hard to make you this tea, so drink it." She handed them both glasses and took one herself. Then she set down the platter and hoisted an umbrella over the little table.

"Oh good. She sits with us." Her dad carried on. "Finally, we can talk about Devesh."

Bobbi raised en eyebrow. "That fat guy? My second cousin?"

Her mother shushed her. "Don't talk like this. Devesh is a lawyer now."

"Even worse."

"He makes good money." Her mother persisted, stopping only to sip her tea. "I hear that Rupi is interested in him also, so you'd better move fast."

"Let Rupi have him, then." Her cousin Rupi was a gold digger, better suited to the seedy business of arranged marriage.

"Such insolence." Her father huffed.

Bobbi set down her glass. "Father, I have much respect for both of you. You know that. I am grateful for all the sacrifices you made for Sat and I. But I am my own person, not a commodity to be traded for cash and appliances. I am a policewoman. Someone important. When I get married, it will be a love match. And nothing you say can change this."

"My God." Her father got dramatic. "This would not be happening in India! Think about what your poor mother, with her weak heart, thinks when she sees the news, with the police shooting it out with bandits! Police from your unit, Balwant! This could be you! Don't you have any regrets about this?"

"Yes." Bobbi replied evenly. "I regret that I wasn't there. Excuse me."

She walked back into the house and grabbed her purse, hearing her mother start to cry. *Emotional terrorism. I'm not going back.*

When she pulled her Honda out of the driveway, she felt a weight lift off her shoulders. The weight of two parents and two thousand years of tradition and expectations. She needed to talk to someone. She needed to talk to a cop.

BURNABY
MORLEY ST

It was a beautiful day outside, but Barry Olds was too preoccupied to notice.

He sat on his couch in boxers and a wife-beater, engaged in a death struggle with a video game. *Defender* had become his nemesis, and he would not quit until he'd out-levelled Tim.

But the phone rang, and resignedly he hit the "pause" button. Barry took a last hit of Old Stock, forgetting too late that he'd started to use the can as an ashtray. "Fuck! Gack!"

He finally made it to the phone, on the ninth ring. "Olds."

"Sarge? It's Bobbi Sanghera. What are you up to today?"

"Saving the universe, why?"

"Oh. Don't you need beer for that?"

"I'm listening."

"I figured we might meet up for some drinks. I've got a lot on my mind, and I could really use an update on the case."

"Sounds good. Hope you don't mind North Vancouver. You know where Lonsdale Quay is?"

"Other end of the Seabus line, right?"

"Yes, that's it. I've got to stop off at the office and pick up something. Meet me there, we'll go together."

LONSDALE QUAY
NORTH VANCOUVER

Rick Grohmann was nursing his second pint and feeling pretty damned good. The freighters sat at anchor in Burrard Inlet, and the little boats darted amongst them on a sparkling blue sea.

Then he looked up and saw that Olds had brought a guest. "What the fuck is she doing here?"

Bobbi froze in her tracks. Barry sat in front of Rick, his body language challenging and aggressive. He plunked a heavy package on the table. "She's your partner. From now on, the fucking prima donna show is over. I'm sick of it. And before you empty your purse all over the table, with excuses and woe is me, you ought to know that I called North Van RCMP right after I got off the phone with you this morning. I spoke to Inspector Bloomfield. He laid it all out for me. Once again, Rick, you're lucky. But that luck can't last forever. A drug squad is a team. Not a supporting cast for one man who plays Serpico. Until you learn that, Detective, you'll be on a very, very short leash. And if you don't like that, Patrol Northeast has an opening for a Corporal. I can always put your name in."

Rick looked around the almost empty pub. Then he drained his pint in one go. The two men stared in silence at each other. Bobbi looked at her hands, unsure of what to do or say. Finally, Rick spoke.

"He was fucking my wife, Barry. What would you do?"

"You already knew that. Part of you gets off on it. That's a fact. As of now, you are getting a hotel room. No more domestic drama, that is, if you want to be the guy who puts the cuffs on Blotter Boorman."

Rick nodded, resigned. "Alright. What else?"

"Spill everything you've learned since the shootout. No secrets."

"Okay. First: Blotter is insulated from the Kits Beach hit. It was a biker job, 100%. Donnie and the twin fatties were there, but the bikers know how much blow Blotter is doing, and they're starting to worry."

"How deep is he in?"

"My sources say, he's hitting the mirror three or four times a day. Getting real fucking paranoid. Beginning to wonder if Roach can keep his mouth shut."

"So far, he has. And Blotter kept it together well enough to feed Major Crimes a big nothing burger with fries yesterday."

"Not surprising." Rick nodded. "He's a tough one. But his paranoia is going to unravel him."

"Yes, but at what cost?" Bobbi interjected, relieved that the subject had shifted away from Rick's quirky sex life. "If he snaps, he could waste a lot of people."

"And that blood winds up on us." Barry agreed. "My sources tell me Blotter is behind the two grocery stores in the East Side selling coke and smack 24/7. Two story operations with a secure second floor. He's quickly moving from middle-class dope to the underclass, where the real money is."

"Yes, but his new employees aren't very good at dealing with dope that strong. Good stuff is flowing into town, stuff that meets New York and Miami standards. His street dealers are fucking up."

"Six ODs this week." Barry agreed. "Three fatal. Even the media is pulling away from Expo for a few minutes a night to cover it."

Rick went quiet for a second. "A kid I talked to about Edwin Lo, he was one of the OD victims. A kid named Kary Bezoff. His mother found my business card and called me yesterday. Apparently, he tried to score off of Tusker and got nowhere. So, he went downtown."

Barry nodded. "Tusker, eh? Could be an opening there. Make him think we like him for the sale?"

Bobbi was alarmed. "But if Blotter's as paranoid as you guys say, and he thinks they're talking to us…"

"Risk worth taking." Rick popped some beer nuts in his mouth.

She looked at him sternly. "Says you. Not everyone in that house might see it like that."

Barry interrupted. "I asked Bobbi to try a woman-to-woman approach with Marianne. She's got Bobbi's business card."

"And?" Rick challenged. "Is your phone ringing off the hook, Sanghera?"

"No." Bobbi admitted. "She's scared. But making her more scared won't make things any better."

Barry shook his head. "We're at an impasse, Bobbi. We have to free up the jam." He turned to Rick. "Take a run at Tusker tomorrow. Tell him you hear the kid scored from him. Let it dangle, and we'll see what he does. Then meet me downtown."

"What's going on downtown?" Bobbi asked.

"The Chief is pissed with those smackmarts operating in plain view. He wants them squished. All hands on deck, both teams, plus Mounties and Major Crimes. We hit them, whether or not our informants score, at noon."

"I guess that's what this is, then?" Rick toyed with the package.

"Yeah, we're both cleared. Told you the Chief wanted you back out there. Not riding the pine, and definitely not in a cell. Forget about going in with your lawyer. Crown has already passed on it. The price is, you deliver Blotter trussed up like a pig with an apple in his mouth by the end of June. Or it's back to Patrol. And the next time you smack Lawrence Dyck around, you're on your own. His words, not mine."

Bobbi spoke up softly. "What about me, Sarge?"

Barry smiled. "You keep an eye on your partner. And get Marianne alone if you can."

"Okay." She nodded. "Now what?"

"Now?" Barry put up a hand for the waitress. "Now, we see how much beer you can drink."

MAY

BLUE MONDAY

Prolonged use of cocaine produces both physiological and psychological symptoms in the user. The physiological symptoms include jittery movements, dilated pupils, increased heart rate, a running nose, and bleeding from the nose. Psychological symptoms include mood swings and paranoia.

Blotter Boorman's prolonged use of his own product is starting to affect his business decisions...

EAST VANCOUVER
KINGSWAY

Bobbi squinted into the morning sun and massaged her temples. The beers last night were causing a sympathetic thumping in her head, matched perfectly by the bass line on the New Wave tune Rick was playing on the car radio.

How does it feel
When you treat me like you do
And you've laid your hands upon me
And told me who you are?

I thought I was mistaken
And I thought I heard your words
Tell me, how do I feel?
Tell me now, how do I feel?

Like shit, answered Bobbi silently.

"Feeling all fresh this morning?" Rick teased her. Rebounding from near disaster, his spirits seemed to be up for once.

"Ugh. Never get trashed the night before a major operation."

"Hmm, I can't remember the last major operation I didn't get trashed for. Anyway, you can stay in the car if you like. This won't take long."

"No. I need to talk to Marianne."

"She'll never talk to you, Bobbi. You'll just be disappointed."

"Maybe. But I have to try."

PAYPHONE
CORNER OF BIDWELL AND BURNABY

The payphone rang at 9 AM on the dot. Blotter picked up the receiver. "Do you accept a call from Robert Lehmann? If so, press one." He pressed the button and waited for the rest of the ridiculous ritual to play out. Down the sidewalk, Donnie watched out for cops.

Blotter wiped his nose with the back of his hand. *Blood. Shit. Time to cut back.* Roach came on the line as he fumbled for a tissue. "Hi cousin." It seemed like the time in hospital hadn't erased his memory of the agreed-upon script.

"How are you, Roachman? Is the food good there?" *Are you feeling pressure?*

"Oh no, it's shitty, but I'll live." *Nothing I can't handle.*

"You got your own cell? You like your cellmate?" *Have they stuck you with a rat?*

"No, so I just keep to myself." *Probably, but I don't say anything.*

"Are you going to be in there long?" *Should I kill you now, or later?*

"No. My lawyer says they'll probably just drop it. Not enough evidence." Blotter's eyes narrowed. He got caught, armed and full of lead, at the scene of a multiple homicide. *Not enough evidence? Or somebody's ready to talk?*

"That's super. Really great." *You're dead, cocksucker.*

When he had hung up the phone, he walked over to Donnie. "How was Roach, then?"

"There is no fucking Roach. Roach is dead."

EAST 20TH AVE
TAAKOIENNIN RESIDENCE

Rick pummeled on the door while Bobbi snooped around the garden. "Police! Open up, asshole!"

Tusker's reedy voice came from inside. "Get a warrant!"

"Okay!" Rick replied. "When I tell the judge you sold smack to a high school kid and killed him, should be a slam dunk."

"That's fucking bullshit, Grohmann!"

"Then come on out and convince me, you Finnish fuckface."

A moment's hesitation, and then: "Back up to the sidewalk. I'll talk to you there."

"Thought you'd see it my way." Rick and Bobbi dutifully retreated to the sidewalk and waited. A series of bolts opened. Tusker emerged, wearing a moth-bitten Canucks t-shirt and a pair of baggy shorts. He cautiously edged towards them, leaving Marianne to guard the door.

"What is this crap?" The weathered old Finn demanded. "You know I don't sell hard shit, if, hypothetically, I sell anything at all, to kids."

"Mother Theresa of the pushers, you are." Rick scoffed. While the two men spoke, Bobbi caught Marianne's eye and edged towards the door.

"You come here to insult me?"

"No, I came here to tell you that one of your neighbours, a sixteen-year old named Kary Bezoff, died of a smack overdose the other day. His mother says he used to buy weed here. So, you are the only proven link to a dead kid. What a bummer."

Tusker scoffed. "Fucking bullshit, even for a cement-head cop like you. That kid died in an alley by Library Square. How many hypes you know hold their dope so they can drive across down and shoot it?"

Rick stepped in close. "Ah. So, you do know something?"

"I read it in the paper."

"Horseshit, Tusker. They didn't release his name to the papers! Let me explain this to you, okay? You work for Blotter. I want to crush Blotter. Blotter was going to have his two goons spit roast your wife, you giant pussy. I am on your side, believe it or not. So, either I can go to a judge with mommy's half-assed information, or you can give me a hint. Who sold the kid the dope?"

"Ah, fuck." Tusker shook his head. While he decided what, if anything, he was going to tell Rick Grohmann, Bobbi Sanghera was coming face-to-face with his wife.

Bobbi gave Marianne a shy wave. "Your face has healed."

Marianne shrugged. "Good as new, I guess." She was so small, so fragile. Eyes, impossibly big, like a doll. "What's all the trouble?"

Bobbi sighed. "Some kid died of an overdose."

"Tusker doesn't..."

"We know. But he did come here just before he died, so we have to check it out. Listen, Marianne..."

"Bobbi, I'm sorry. But I just can't tell you anything..."

"If you can't tell me anything yet, I understand. But please, you have to listen!" Bobbi's intensity seemed to have grabbed Marianne's attention.

"I'm listening." She replied, softly.

"I hear Blotter is doing a lot of coke. Shitloads of it, Marianne. And you've been around people on drugs long enough to know what that means. He's getting paranoid. Pretty soon, it may not matter that you and Tusker didn't talk to us. He may assume you did, anyway. Understand? Please think about that. You still have my card?"

"Yes."

"Anytime, day or night." When Bobbi returned to the sidewalk, Rick and Tusker were just concluding. The Finn gave her a suspicious look as he walked by, then re-entered the house, arguing with Marianne.

"You get anywhere?" Rick quizzed her.

"Baby steps. You?"

"Yeah. I got a name. Supposed to be some big African dude who kills more junkies than Hep B. Looks like we're not going to the party empty-handed."

"I go after the soft target, and you're the one who scores?"

"Stick with me kid, you'll learn."

Learn how to make divorce lawyers rich, you mean. Bobbi's headache had returned as she sat on the passenger seat, and her partner peeled out, headed for Main and Hastings.

LIBRARY SQUARE

The Downtown East Side's drug supermarket functioned 24/7, rain or shine, in all temperatures, police action only having an occasional and incremental effect on its business.

Here, the constant, slow-motion, welfare-fuelled misery of addiction was propelled. Junkies came hungry, cash in hand from a government cheque or pawned stolen goods, or a blowjob, and left with a glassine envelope in pocket, promising relief of a pain that never went away.

The only problem was, the relief lasted only fleetingly. Soon, the junkies came back, and the cycle repeated itself.

Today, the people who fed the cycle of misery had miscalculated somewhat, killing some of their customers with relief that was altogether too *permanent.* They had also become too bold, for a city showcasing itself to the world. And so it was that, on this sunny day, a convoy of police officers were planning a somewhat more lasting disruption.

But when it was all over, the dealers would be back, as long as there were junkies. And there would always be junkies.

Rick Grohmann mounted the curb and walked right into the middle of it, watching the dealers ditch whatever they had on hand, with those that couldn't afford to ditch, running instead.

One man who ran caught his attention. He was the only man who looked anything like Tusker's description. Already, he was all the way across Main and headed south. Rick ran after him.

Bobbi cursed and jumped back in the driver's seat of the car. For Rick, catching the long-legged African would be nearly impossible. For her, it required four wheels and a big engine. She put the PC into gear and reefed the wheel around, blooping the siren for a few deadheads who were too slow in the intersection.

Four unmarked vans drove past the commotion without stopping. Barry Olds peered out the passenger side of the lead van, watching the dealers and hypes scatter like ants from a kicked-over hill. "I'll say this for him, he's one hell of a distraction."

Paul Selfridge laughed as he turned onto Main St. "Should be an education for young Bobbi." He peered down the street at the pursuit, as the African pulled a hard left onto Keefer, a surprisingly fleet Grohmann hard on his heels, Bobbi swerving into the oncoming lane to keep up. "He might even get us an entrée. If I had to guess, Mandingo here is running right for our target."

"Allah be praised."

KEEFER ST

Rick Grohmann came to the same conclusion as Gentleman Paul, at exactly the same time. The African had ducked into a doorway beside what looked like a grocery store, thinly populated with people who didn't look like they ate much, with a few Chinese clerks as window dressing.

Above, the black clouds had moved in and now dumped their load with a vengeance. Over the sounds of pelting rain and distant thunder, Rick could hear the African yelling.

"Let me in! Let me in!"

"Who are you? What you want?"

"Theo! It's Theo, let me in!"

"You being chased by police? Go away!"

"You let me in! Let me in! I kill you!"

"Hey! Hey, you drug man! No go downstairs! No! Is crazy guy there!"

Rick skidded into the doorway just as a befuddled hype walked out, clutching his treasure, which Theo knocked into the sodden street as he pushed past. Rick elbowed him out of the way and followed up the steep stairs as Bobbi screeched to a halt in a long, wet skid.

The African was taking two or even three steps at a time, his long legs pumping gleaming white Adidas up the rickety stairway. But when he got to the top, he stumbled, falling flat on his face.

Rick Grohmann landed on top of him and punched him hard in the head. The African threw an elbow and connected, solidly, catching Rick in the jaw and sending him rolling, six steps down.

The African was on his feet now, trying to push past two small Chinese women, who were making a comical effort to lock a never-used door at the top of the stairs. He pushed them aside in a shower of Mandarin curses, but now Bobbi had leapt over her tumbling and swearing partner, and arrived, swinging a four-cell D Maglite and hitting him right behind the shoulder blades.

The African tumbled forward, a winded Bobbi following him, into a hype's wet dream of open drug sales. A wrap-around counter offered all manner of enticements, with scales, baggies, and even paraphernalia laid out like the jewellery counter at Eaton's. The staff were busy opening chutes in the floor and dumping dope, those who were not already heading out the back door for the fire exit.

The African turned, picked up a scale off the counter, and hurled it at Bobbi's head. She caught a glancing blow on the temple, and went to her knees, hearing the African chuckle. Then, he kicked her, hard, in her already damaged ribs. Her vision went white with pure pain. Bobbi rolled on her back, kicking out desperately at the African's long shins, catching him just under the knee.

He gasped, but did not stop, and now, as she shimmied on her back to get away, he chased her around the counter, kicking her repeatedly, laughing hysterically now.

He was still laughing when Rick Grohmann punched him in the kidneys, laying him low. Bobbi watched as Rick put a carotid control around the man's long neck, then jerked him off his feet with a grunt as he closed the blood supply to the brain.

A stampeding herd of drug cops followed them up the stairs,

hefting baseball bats and prybars. They stopped to watch Rick. "You guys remember Rick Grohmann?" Barry asked a group of bearded Mounties in jean jackets.

"Hasn't changed a bit." One of them offered.

"Goodnight, asshole." Rick whispered in Theo's ear as he nodded out and sank to the floor. Bobbi was standing, painfully, breathing in raggedly through re-broken ribs. "You okay, partner?"

She winced. "No. I think I gotta go back to the ER."

"Well, thanks for nailing that prick for me. Sorry I took so long." Now, the two Chinese ladies were yelling and pleading with a bemused Selfridge, who finally gave up and started handcuffing the more obnoxious of the two.

Rick looked around as his fellow drug cops began to ransack the place. He caught the attention of the now arrested madam of the establishment. "Ma'am? Ma'am, please?"

The woman looked at him in disgust. "What you want?"

Rick picked up the flashlight from the floor and hefted it. "Before I take my partner to the hospital, I wanted you to see this." He lifted the Maglite, and began to methodically smash in the countertops, and everything in range he could find.

The woman looked at Selfridge. "You stop him! He wreck everything!"

Selfridge laughed. "Lady, I don't know where his off switch is."

MAY

LOOSE LIPS

As the propaganda posters said in the Second World War, "loose lips sink ships." Though snitching is considered low behaviour amongst criminals, police officers like Barry Olds know well that desperate situations can make men like Theo Solomon loosen their lips, if one draws the right picture.

The police have many sophisticated levers and blandishments to make a man open his mouth on their behalf. But criminals like Blotter Boorman and his biker associates have one very simple, crude, and violent way to keep such mouths closed forever...

BEACH TOWERS APARTMENTS

Blotter had sent the two Mexican hookers Doug had sent over as party favours home for the night. Now, satiated with sex and tequila, he was calm. The rain was drumming on the windows outside, and he loved to watch it pelt the city from so many stories up, so he lit a spliff and stepped out onto the enclosed balcony to watch.

Blotter had always known wet places, first Seattle, and now here. Dry places felt alien to him, places like LA and Vegas, places where your snot dried out and your head ached. This spring rain, to him, was as comforting as the womb. He smoked his hash quietly and contemplated the raindrops, finding himself shifting from homicidal cokehead to harmless pothead in one easy step.

He had not, was not normally a violent person. But he was a lazy one, and that lack of motivation, together with the tenor of the times in the 60s and 70s, had let him drift into dealing drugs. It was the easiest way to make cash ever invented, by a long haul.

There was just one, small problem. People were always trying to fuck you. And that required violence, just to hold your place. And eventually, holding your place was never enough. You needed to move up or go under. That was the lesson Doug Harris, his father figure in this strange business, had spent years trying to teach him. You might not want to be a killer. But a killer you must be. You could push the button, or let the button push you, in Doug's memorable phrase.

The bikers had fucked up, and, stung by unaccustomed failure, they were going to let him handle things his way for a bit. But only for a bit.

Detective Grohmann, in a curious piece of kismet, had solved his Soulschnitzel problem for him. But other problems remained. Those problems were the sort of problems that kept people like him awake at night. Problems of loose lips.

First, there was Roach. Poor Roach. He desperately wanted to believe what Donnie kept telling him, that Roach was solid, or as Donnie said, "sound as a pound". He'd even run the problem past Doug, who'd been slightly more equivocal.

"Maybe he's bent. Maybe he's not. But can you afford to find out?"

The problem Blotter had was one of belief. He knew how cops and prosecutors operated. They didn't simply open the cell doors for someone as connected as Roach, caught at the scene of a multiple homicide. Things just didn't work that way. The only reason he could think of, for the man doing that?

To get Roach right back inside his organization. A live wire, giving a play-by-play. And there was no fucking way that was going to happen.

As for loose lips, that wasn't the end of it. In today's fiasco on Keefer St, in addition to losing a profitable storefront operation, he'd also lost a dealer, Theo Solomon. Theo, on his own, was not much of a loss. He was a refugee from the Sudan, dumb as cowshit, his only real talent as a dealer being his ability to outrun almost every cop on the Vancouver City Police.

Almost every cop, that is, except Rick Grohmann. Now, it turns out, the fucking idiot had sold a hotshot to a teenager, whose first stop the day he died had been Tusker's place. *Fucking wonderful.* Now, with a white Jewish kid dead, an *actual victim*, the cops were going to turn on the crocodile tears and go on a fucking rampage. It didn't matter that Blotter didn't know a fucking thing about it. Grohmann would hang it on him if it killed him.

He might credit Roach with being able to handle police interrogation, but he gave Theo Solomon zero chance. All it took was the cops waving around his Refugee Permit and suggesting he might be on the next plane back to Khartoum and Theo would sing like whatever kind of fucking bird lived in the Sudan.

That left Tusker, and his little darling wife. Blotter's instincts told him that she was the weak link, not Tusker. Eventually, she would feel the need to spill out her purse. Some nice, lady cop, like the kind he heard Grohmann was riding with now. Eventually, it was going to happen. Waiting for it was probably unwise.

This. This was how harmless, peace-loving dealers became killers. This fucking bullshit.

He flicked off the end of his spliff and launched it into the rain. Then, he turned and went inside. He picked up the brick phone, and dialled Donnie.

"You awake? Yeah, yeah, listen. Are you listening? Go over to the safehouse. Not that one, the other one. Yes. Now get everything ready. I'm clearing out and coming over there in thirty minutes. Yeah. Yeah. Whaddya mean, why? That fucking spearchucker is going to get us all fucked. Time to law low. Yeah, get some booze and some food. See you then."

Blotter began to pack and wondered how long it would be before he could come back.

He didn't love much. But he really loved this place.

**THE NEXT MORNING
312 MAIN ST
DRUG SECTION**

Barry Olds sat across from Theo Solomon and did a subtle mental inventory.

Based on his background, he could assume that Theo had, at best, a modest education. But Barry had long ago stopped making the reflexive assumption that that meant a lack of intelligence.

Yes, the man was hardly a polished operator. He was more a coiled creature of desperation. Like so many people in his position, Theo Solomon had needed to use every wile God gave him to get here in the first place, from whatever hell he'd come from. That was leaving out the wiles he'd needed to survive the very unfriendly streets of the Downtown East Side.

From the looks of his record, Canada was not exactly working out for him. Two convictions already, for assault and possession for the purpose of trafficking. The judges he had come before up till now had, or course, fallen for his sad story hook, line, and sinker. He'd done no more than a few days in jail, up till now.

But Canada Immigration was less impressed. Refugees could be held in detention pending their hearings, some of which took up till five years from date of claim. This gave Barry some very powerful leverage with Theo. And the fact that Theo already had an Immigration warrant for failing to maintain his residence of record allowed him to keep Theo for much longer than the usual drug suspect.

Sometimes, rarely, the law is a policeman's friend. This was one of those times.

"You look at my file there, I see. It's all lies." Theo was starting off from an unwise position of bravado. His long fingers were tipped with stained and crusted nails. His odour was ripe, his eyes, bloodshot. Barry idly wondered how on earth he'd ever convince an Immigration tribunal he was a good risk.

Mind you, they weren't necessarily the most sceptical bunch. "Are you suggesting my fellow law enforcement officers are liars? My my, that's not every respectful of your adopted country, is it Theo?"

"Well, I don't have to say anything. I know this."

"Oh yes, your rights. Very true. It's also very true that, if I call your Immigration case officer, Mr Samuelsson, and tell him that you are being most unhelpful, he may just find that bed in Immigration detention he's been looking for. Hmm, how long till your hearing do you think?" Barry rifled through the file. "Oh dear, this says you made a claim in June 1985. From the way things are going these days, that's at least three or four years in jail. Must be hard for a big guy like you, in such a tiny cell."

The room was not especially warm. But now Theo began to sweat. Great big beads stood out on his ebony skin. "Please. Please, Mr Police. I have the fear…you know, the fear of the small place?"

"Claustrophobia. Me too. It's a terrible feeling, isn't it?"

"Please."

Barry made a show of rifling through the file again, although he already knew everything he needed to know. "You know, Theo, I'm not an Immigration cop. I don't really want to send you back to Sudan. I bet it's very bad there, right?"

"The government kills the Christians, like me. Rape the women. Bomb us from the sky."

"Yes, I've heard." Barry nodded. "One hell of a situation to be sent back to. But here's my problem, Theo. You just keep selling heroin. Heroin is bad. Heroin kills people. People like Kary Bezoff." Barry held up the angelic, three years' earlier picture of the kid, who, in reality he knew was no angel when he died. "This kid died because of heroin you sold him, Theo. Very, very bad."

Theo looked away from the photo, too late. His eyes had registered shock and recognition. He was no good at this game. "I don't know this kid."

"That's not what three witnesses say."

"They lie."

"Hmm." Barry took an evidence envelope from his pocket. Inside were six dime bags with potent heroin Theo had on him when Rick Grohmann choked him unconscious the day before. "Recognize this?"

"No. You planted this."

"Ah, now that, Theo, is bullshit. You see, you're playing for the wrong audience."

"What do you mean?"

"I mean, you think I'm trying to make a case against you. A case a sympathetic judge is going to hear, like the judges you've already met in this country, a judge who says, 'Oh, poor Theo.' The only problem is, you're wrong. That's not what's going to happen at all."

The sweat had returned. Theo leaned forward. His left hand, resting on the desk, trembled. "What? What happens Mr Police?"

"What happens is, I just call my friend Mr Samuelsson. I tell him that you sold a Canadian, a promising young Canadian with his whole life in front of him, heroin that killed him, in an alley, like a fucking dog. And you know how we'll know that for sure?"

"How?"

Barry slapped the dope in front of Theo, who jumped out of his chair. "When we send this to the lab and compare it with the dope we took out of that dead boy's veins. That dead boy, being cut up on a slab, while his poor mother cried for Jesus to help her." He knew the kid was Jewish, but he figured Jesus wouldn't mind being used for effect. "That will be the same dope, won't it, Theo? The same dope you were too fucking stupid to cut properly, so you killed a seventeen-year-old kid, right?" Barry tried to search out Theo's eyes, but the man was boring a hole in the floor with his gaze now.

"So, tell me Theo, what do you think your odds of staying in Canada are once the Immigration tribunal hears that you're killing our kids? Wanna make a bet?"

"Stop it, please! Please, Mr Police! What do you want from me?"

Barry cleared the table. He took a legal pad and a pen from his briefcase and set them down precisely in front of Theo. "Complete cooperation. Names and details of the people you work for. In return, a new start in another city, and, Mr Samuelsson assures me, a much more favorable attitude towards your refugee claim. Or, you can be a tough guy, and see how that works when you get off the plane in Khartoum. Up to you."

Theo took a tissue from the table and wiped his eyes and nose. Then he picked up the pen and started writing.

MAPLE RIDGE
RANDY MCCLARTY'S FARM

Blotter stood in the open doorway of the barn, looking out towards the snow-capped mountains that fringed the flat farmlands of the Fraser Valley.

It was clear again today, the last day of May. Now, the warm days were coming, the days full of promise and profit, the days when Expo would well and truly pay off for a man in his position.

There were just a few "things," as the Sicilians called them, to be done. This thing today, was one of those things.

Randy McClarty looked at his watch. "Fuckers should be here by now. You sure that dipshit Donnie didn't fuck it up?"

"Sure. It's just a friendly ride home from jail. What's to fuck up?" But inside, he had doubts. Donnie could fuck up a wet dream. Only his reliable, and never questioned loyalty, such a hard thing to find, saved him.

Blotter did the calculations in his mind. The drive from Vancouver Pre-Trial to here, against traffic on the Number One, was maybe an hour-and-a-half.

One hour-and-a-half. Tied up, in the trunk of a car. Thinking the darkest of all possible dark thoughts. Hoping your end comes quickly, that there is no torture, no mutilation. For this is the most you can hope for.

How many times had he awoken, in a cold sweat, from just such a nightmare? If Randy McClarty was the type to discuss feelings, he'd have asked. But it was something people in this business kept to themselves.

Randy pointed to the long road entering his property. A black sedan barreled towards them. "Gotta be them."

"Yup." Blotter agreed. "Gotta be."

Suddenly, his coke-fuelled decisiveness had fled him, and he was there, in the moment, a man standing in a barn with a "friend" who would happily slit his throat if ordered, waiting to kill another "friend," a man who had never done anything but what he had asked of him.

He was a son of a bitch, and no mistake. But there was no going back now. To do anything but commit was to earn the label of "pussy," and then they would descend on you like hungry lions on an old, sad, wildebeest. *Commit.* The .357 in his hand felt like lead. His thumb rested on the hammer, ready to snap it back for a hair-trigger, single-action shot. Randy had pointedly handed it to him when he arrived, as if to say, *you can have my farm, and I'll do the cleanup. But the shot is yours.*

After all, it wasn't like he hadn't done it before, was it?

The Mercury pulled up in front of the barn doors. Donnie stepped out of the front passenger seat, a sick look on his face. Two Hangarounds he didn't know emerged from the car as well.

"How'd it go?" He managed to croak.

Donnie stammered. "Uh...smooth. Aye, he went along wi' it. Uh...boss?"

Blotter saw the turmoil in Donnie's face. "Take a walk, Donnie. I'll take care of it, okay?"

As Donnie walked away, the young, muscular Hangarounds began to work in silence, layering the hole in the ground with two layers of plastic sheeting, then stepping into rubber boots and donning rain slicks for the messy work to come. Blotter felt like heaving.

Randy pointed at Donnie, now a speck against the snow-capped mountains. "You sure you can trust him?"

"Donnie's an idiot. He's not smart enough to try and fuck me."

A banging came from the Mercury's trunk. "Hey! Hey! Blotter, is that you? Get me out of here! Please, there's been a mistake!

Please!"

Randy looked at Blotter. "We'll get him out. Let's do it fast." He handed Blotter a slicker to wear over the hip waders he already had on. "Here. No mess."

Blotter took the slicker wordlessly, slipping the .357 into the belly pocket on the hip waders and putting it on. His head was spinning now, and he desperately needed more coke. Randy and the Hangarounds opened the trunk and reefed a sweating and terrified Roach out of the trunk.

As they dragged Roach past him into the barn, Blotter noticed that he was bleeding profusely from a knock-out blow to the head. His gag had slipped off. His hands were purple from too-tight handcuffs.

Roach had stopped begging for mercy now, as the totality of the setup must've convinced him that mercy was not on the menu. The Hangarounds unceremoniously dumped him in the pit like a heavy sack, and he cried out in pain.

He's going to be looking at me, Blotter realized, and he accepted that this was just. Let it stay with me. He felt for the .357 and pulled it out, then walked to the edge of the pit.

"I never fucked you over." Roach said simply. "You're doing the wrong thing." His eyes were welling with tears, yet he kept whatever dignity a man could have in this situation.

"Maybe I am." Blotter acknowledged. "But in my shoes, what would you do?"

Roach looked at him, simply, and for the first time Blotter realized that the man had deep blue eyes. He wanted to get it over with now, more than anything, and his thumb snapped back the hammer. "We'll never know, I guess."

What happened next felt like it was done by someone else. There was a man in a pit, and another man, standing over him, shooting. When he came back, he looked down, and there were neat holes in Roach's face. His head rested in a halo of purplish blood. Randy took the revolver out of his hand.

"It's done. We'll do the rest."

"How are you...I mean, what do you..."

Randy shook his head. "Better you don't know, Blotter. Go home."

The Hangarounds were already tying up the plastic sheeting around Roach's body. One of them made pig snorts, and the other laughed. He looked down at the toe on his hip waders and saw a spatter of Roach's blood. *It was me, then.*

Blotter turned and walked outside, ditching the hip waders and slicker on the way. He lit a cigarette outside the barn and felt for his car keys.

Driving along the road to the mountains. The road Roach had come down, alive, not ten minutes before. Now, he was leaving, alive. Roach would be pig chow. He saw Donnie standing by the gravel drive and smoking. He pulled over, and the man got in, wordlessly. His breath smelled of puke.

They drove for a long time before Donnie spoke. "Would ye do that to me, ah mean, if it came to it, that is?"

Blotter flicked his butt out the window and let the cool air on his face resuscitate him. "Of course, I fucking would, Donnie. In this business, there are no guarantees."

"Ah need to get high, Blotter."

"Fine. Let's get high."

Feeling like it was him back there in that pit, Blotter drove away, knowing he would visit this place again; knowing it in his heart. But there would be only one more time. And that time, the appointment would be his.

The rest of this trip was downhill. And there were no brakes.

JUNE

DOMINO EFFECT

Some police officers, particularly females from communities where such work is not considered acceptable for women, fight a war on two fronts. The battle for acceptance never ends, whether from colleagues, or family...

OAK PARK

Bobbi awoke from a sun-drenched doze on the living room couch to find her mother staring at her. Care-worn eyes fixed on her daughter; her mother presented a pitiful sight. As if to underscore whatever traditionalist broadside she was about to deliver, today she was wearing *sari*.

"I'm not on the pyre yet, mother. Save your sadness." She sat up, with difficulty.

"And yet you are hurt again. You are killing me, if not yourself."

"Please! Enough, mother. Enough."

"Why is this necessary?"

"Because it is the job I chose."

"Why can you not do the simpler things, safer things, like work in the schools and teach the children about crossing the road? I always thought you would make a good teacher, Balwant."

Bobbi screwed up her face in frustration. "Because that's what all the male chauvinist pigs would love to see me do! Don't you understand? To see me take the easy way out! I have to prove I can do the tough stuff, too. I have to earn the badge, in their eyes."

"Oh, please do not call the men 'pigs,' you are sounding like the girls who like the other girls, Balwant."

Bobbi giggled. "Oh mother? Do you mean, 'lesbians?'"

"Oh, please do not say this."

Bobbi laughed out loud now. "Oh mother. Ow." She held her aching side. "Ow."

The phone rang. Her mother went to answer it, then brought it to her. "Someone from your work."

"Constable Sanghera, who is this?"

The voice was timorous and quiet. "Bobbi? This is Marianne. I think I might want to talk to you. But we have to be very careful."

Forgetting the pain, Bobbi sat up. "Yes, okay. Let's find a way."

**312 MAIN
DRUG SECTION**

Barry Olds entered the conference room with a swagger in his stride. Not often did he get to keep a room full of commissioned officers waiting. But today was no ordinary day.

For a guileless African refugee not credited with much in the way of brains, Theo Solomon had listened to and understood a tremendous amount of information. That information had covered thirteen legal-sized sheets and supplied information directly or tangentially implicating nine individuals and six properties in the trafficking of hard drugs.

Theo either did not know, or would not give, information on Blotter Boorman. But somewhere in there, there was someone who would. Now, as his son Tim would say, it was time to play Pac Man. He had arrest and search warrants enough to keep the whole section, as well as the Mounties, busy for weeks.

But Barry did not believe this case would take weeks. From

what he'd heard of Blotter's recent behaviour, he'd come unhinged as soon as his operation started suffering from the Domino Effect. First one, then another operation going dark. Trusted associates turning snitch.

He may not have had the arrest warrant yet. But Blotter would do something to bring him to his door. He knew it.

Inside the briefing room, a normally mouth-drying convention of people who could make or break his career. Selfridge, of course, and his boss, Inspector Heynemann. Heynemann's boss, Superintendent Froese. And the Deputy Chief of Operations, Angus Munro. A couple of Mountie bigwigs he didn't know were there too, plus Mitch Halperin from Crown. *All hands on deck.*

"Greetings, Sergeant." Munro was a cheery glad-hander who was better in the back room and sports field than he was on the street. But, unlike some, he was smart enough to recognize his limitations, and rarely got in the way of street cops. His round face was beaming this morning. "Am I to understand that the man who has turned our World's Fair into a lurid drug supermarket is about to go down?"

Barry decided to stay on his feet and play show-and-tell. "Perhaps, Chief. It's a start, anyway." He spread the warrants out on the desk for all to see. "Warrants for six addresses associated to the Boorman Organization, as well as nine individuals wanted for Conspiracy and Trafficking. Three of these were already in custody as a result of the other day's operation, and now they will not make bail. Six more are at large."

Froese was a miserable, balding old prick who'd come from Internal Affairs, and seemed to have a hard time viewing cops as colleagues instead of targets. "All based on the testimony of one witless negro dealer who has very much to lose? I'd say Judge Halloran needs to up his Metamucil dose."

Munro corrected him. "Nobody says 'negro' anymore, Ted. Remember that before your next press conference. Besides, what Halloran chooses to believe is Halloran's business. I'd say Sergeant Olds and his team have done well. Now, time to talk details. What do you envision as your operational plan, Barry?"

"Two warrants a day for the next three days. Between my squad and Nick Bartels', we should be able to handle them. Today, we'll scout them out for security and traffic. If we can use ERT for at least the tougher ones, I'd appreciate it, Chief."

"You've got whatever you need. And the people?"

"We're likely to scoop them when we hit the target addresses, as all six are associated to one or the other properties. Otherwise, we'll disseminate through the usual channels and hopefully Patrol, or GD will pick them up."

One of the Mounties raised a pen. "What's the radius on those warrants?"

"All Canada-wide."

Inspector Heynemann was much more a cops' cop than his boss Froese. He'd come out of ERT but hadn't left the jock physique and can-do attitude behind. "Just wondering, Barry, I don't see Boorman's name on anything here. Given his ties to the one-percenters, can we really count on people turning? Or how do you see it playing out?"

Barry pondered the question for a minute. He wondered if he should admit what was really on his mind. "The actions of a man tooting that much coke are hard to predict. Personally, sir, I predict a reaction, and not necessarily a rational one."

Heynemann frowned. "I was afraid you'd say that. How about you take ERT on every raid? We've already had shots fired on this file, I'd rather not…"

Froese interrupted. "ERT isn't yours to volunteer anymore, Mark."

Munro rolled his eyes. "Approved. ERT goes on each warrant. Well, Barry, you've got some planning to do. Let me know when you're ready."

"Will do, sir."

CITY CENTRE MOTOR HOTEL
MAIN ST AND 6TH AVE

The ringing phone awakened Rick Grohmann from a troubling dream. He'd been lying on his back, in a pit, a faceless gunman standing over him. Eventually, the gunman's face had resolved into Blotter's.

"Grohmann, what is it?"

It was Len Hope, a loser informant, usually of marginal usefulness. So useless he was actually registered at 312 Main. His only current selling point: he occasionally crossed paths with Donnie McCrae. "Hiya, Rick, how's tricks?"

"Give me info or don't waste my time, Len." He was still smarting from his battle with Theo. He popped two Tylenol and chased them with last night's scotch.

"Ah...okay. Has anyone seen Roach Lehmann?"

"In jail."

"Oh. I heard a rumour he was dead."

"Fuck off, Len." He slammed the receiver down. He was about to get up for breakfast when he decided to double-check.

"Pre-Trial Intake."

"This is Detective Grohmann from Drug Section. Is Robert Lehmann still being held there? The charges were ADW, Unauthorized Possession, Careless Use?"

"Hang on a sec. No, he was released yesterday."

"Any conditions or reporting?"

"Nah, says here it was a stay of proceedings."

"Thanks man." Rick hung up, feeling strange. Maybe Len was on to something...

The phone rang again, and he jumped. "Jesus, Len, what now?"

Bobbi Sanghera laughed. "Uh, wrong number?"

"Is that you, Bobbi? What's up?"

"Listen, I called the office, and they told me you were on the D/L too. I could use your help on something, and it looks like the rest of the office will be kicking down doors this week."

"Oh really? That big spearchucker decided to talk?"

"Yeah, apparently Barry convinced him he was going back to Sudan if he didn't play ball."

"Nice. What have you got going on?"

"Well...I think I might have convinced Marianne Taakoiennin to co-operate. But I'm nervous about going out there without cover."

"No shit." Rick looked around his dingy hotel room. *What the hell else are you doing these days?* "If you want cover, I'm your man."

JUNE

TAKING ONE FOR THE TEAM

In the mind of an already paranoid drug dealer, who has just eliminated one suspected police agent, the sight of his properties still being raided can only mean one thing: there is still someone talking.

But the vagaries of the cocaine-addicted mind mean that the determination of who this source is may be less than accurate. One thing is for certain: someone is going to die...

ALBERTA ST

Selfridge drove at patrol speed, as fast as he usually ever drove, at the tail end of a convoy of black ERT vans. Barry did a double-take at the presence of a CTV news camera truck on the curb. "Do you think the Chief is getting a bit carried away with the community engagement thing?"

"Ah, shit. Let's hope there's still somebody there."

"Well, at least I shaved this morning."

ERT unassed their vans in double-time, obviously sharing the same worries. Barry watched from behind their van, as the men in dark blue fatigues approached the front door single file, then rushed in as the ram man breached the door, screaming "Search warrant! City Police!"

"Are you getting this? Zoom in."

Barry turned to see the cameraman standing with a famously hot reporter, in full view of the suspects who stared out of the house's picture window. "Get the fuck down!" He screamed. "Get behind a tree or something, you idiots!" The second he said it, he knew that would be the lead on the six-o'clock news.

But the sight of two suspects jumping out the front window distracted him. "Paul, you see that?"

But Selfridge was already chasing a short dealer in a red t-shirt across the next lawn into the street. His friend, seeing red shirt's imminent capture in progress, reversed course, running straight into Barry's arms.

He was long and lanky, and he smelled of an old couch and Dorito dust. "Ow! Get the fuck off me, pig!"

"Settle down, shit for brains." Barry pinned him to the ground and handcuffed him with ease. "Hey, you're Jason Wells, right?"

"Fuck off!"

"I'll take that as a yes. You're under arrest, Jason." Now, the cameraman had his lens right over Barry's right ear. "Jesus, what did I tell you guys?"

"This is news." Donna Linden was tiny and exquisitely coiffed. Her high heels dug little divots of turf up everywhere she went. Her boldness at crime scenes was supposedly explained by her relationship with a married Superintendent.

"Suit yourself." Barry locked Jason Wells in the van, then found Selfridge limping back to the van with the handcuffed man in the red shirt. "Luis Sanchez?"

"Fuck off!" The goateed little man snarled.

"That's what the other guy said. Two for one. This day's looking up." The camera truck had attracted a crowd, and now, as ERT marched two more suspects out the front door, people milled around the van. Selfridge and Barry had to throw elbows to get Luiz secured inside.

Barry turned to Selfridge, who was still panting from the chase. "I should thank these clowns."

"For what?" Selfridge brushed twigs and grass off of his short-sleeved shirt.

"Letting me see you run. Worth a few days off his sentence, I'd say."

"Delightful, Sergeant. Let's get in there before those armoured goons make a mess of everything."

One of the men in the crowd was not looking at the cops and their quarry. He was looking at a familiar face, standing apart from the swarm. The watching man put two and two together and made a phone call.

WESTERN AND TERMINAL

Blotter Boorman was, as of yet, unaware of the wrecking ball Barry Olds was swinging in the direction of his short-lived empire. Sleeping off a coke binge once again, he had awakened to fresh coffee and croissants, courtesy of the live-in help, and the sight of the gleaming Expo Dome in the morning sunshine.

There were, he reflected, worse ways for a drug addict to wake up.

Was that what he was now? Even if he could regain the control he'd lost, could he keep himself from blowing it all? Take this "safe house," for instance. The other one, in Yaletown, was much nicer. And Yaletown was home to his favourite clubs.

This place? This place was a fuck pad run by the bikers on the top floor of a warehouse and retail building. Downstairs, they sold furniture. Up here, they put it to the test.

The "live-in help" was actually Larissa, if that was her real name, a Czech émigré and experienced madam, who insisted on looking after Blotter. She was getting on, but still hot in that dirty, truck-stop blonde sort of way. Too bad coke had put his dick out of commission for the duration. It had been days since he'd had a morning wood.

The fuck pad was okay, comfy beds and lots of running water, okay if you didn't dwell on how much jizz had been fired around the place. Best not to think about it.

The point is, it wasn't his first choice. Dealers at his level, guys like Doug Harris, were supposed to get *first choice.* He sipped his coffee and stared over at the geodesic football of the Expo Dome, dropped on the edge of the perpetual misery park that was the Downtown East Side. The adjacent Skytrain line meant the tourists could whip in, and whip out, never having to dwell on why a city with an open wound like Main and Hastings was blowing so much cash on a party.

Still, that weird-ass building meant cash, and lots of it. If he could keep his head until it all died down, until the politicians and media stopped giving a shit about what a dope-infested shithole their little City of Glass was, then, maybe, things could be fixed. He lit a smoke and dragged in deep.

The brick phone started ringing. At this time of the morning, it was unlikely to be anything good.

"Yes, who is this?"

"George Gazeris." There was street noise and chatter in the background. Blotter heard a police siren blooping, like the pigs did when it was time to clear a crowd.

"Who the fuck is that?"

"Come on, you took over two of my houses in QE."

"Oh yeah. The Greek guy." Gazeris was a quarrelsome prick with a big nose and a bigger ego. But he had great hash and smack connections, and no taste for trouble. "What's going on?"

"You don't know?"

"No. I'm laying low for a while."

"Yeah well, the thing is, you don't control those houses of mine no more. Neither one of 'em."

Blotter felt his head heating up, a coke rage coming on. Larissa, en route to refill his coffee cup, quickly diverted. "The fuck you mean?"

"I mean, I just came from one house, and I saw the cops kicking in the fucking door with the goddamned SWAT team. And that bitch Donna from the six-o'clock news, you know the little one with the big funbags, she was there with a goddamned camera crew. Now, I'm standing outside my other house, and damned if I ain't seeing the same fuckin thing. So? What happened to 'this is never gonna happen to us,' hah? What the fuck, Blotter? Somebody is fucking talking. So, you gonna kill him, or do I have to call in some *chastan* from Toronto? Because somebody needs to fucking die for this, Blotter. Somebody needs to fucking DIE!" Exhausted, Gazeris breathed heavily into the phone.

Blotter sat heavily on the back of a sofa. Somebody who was arrested the other day had talked. The old Chinese ladies? What the fuck did they know about QE? That dipshit Theo Solomon?

Possible. Theo had been whisked out of Vancouver Pre-Trial by Immigration, according to his sources. But the word his sources had heard was "deportation."

Why would they deport him if he was co-operating? Mind you, he was an idiot.

"You still there? What the fuck we gonna do, Blotter? You losing your shit over there, or what?"

"Watch your fucking mouth you hairy Greek fuck. I'm thinking."

"Well, if you're thinking about who fucked you over, I gotta real good idea."

Blotter lit another smoke off the embers of the last. He watched the little cloud of smoke envelop the Expo Dome. "Yeah? Who?"

"Harvey Fucking Sam. That fucking loser. Cops rolled up his operation, and never charged him. Now, I see him at both my fucking properties, watching what's going down, shit-eating fucking grin on his ugly chug face. He's right across the street, right now."

Blotter stood up. "Follow him. Follow him and call me when he stops somewhere."

"Hey, hey, this is your problem…"

"Wanna make 50 G, right now?"

"Now you're talking. He's moving. I'll call you back."

Larissa called to Blotter from the kitchen. "More coffee, Mr B?"

Blotter was already pulling on his Levis. "No thanks. Gotta go to work." He took the short-nosed .38 out of the dresser, checked the load, and grabbed two speedloaders with hollow points, stuffing them in his pockets. He picked up the keys for his loaner Trans-Am, then bounded down the stairs.

I am going to kill Harvey Sam, that rat bitch. And I am going to enjoy it.

HUDSON'S BAY CAFETERIA
WEST GEORGIA ST

Bobbi sat waiting for Marianne Taakoiennin in the mostly empty cafeteria and tried to keep her cool. The sight of Rick Grohmann hovering over a coffee eight tables over was reassuring.

Marianne had insisted on the meet, on a child's whim, wanting a roast beef lunch and a big slice of chocolate cake. Bobbi understood, if not the roast beef part, then the chocolate cake at least. How many times had she come here as a child?

She looked at her watch. 12:34. When she looked, up, Marianne was sitting opposite her with a full tray, sagging under the weight of food.

"You're not pregnant, are you?" Bobbi was startled.

Marianne smiled bashfully. "No, I just like to eat. Especially when I'm nervous."

"You don't need to be nervous. My partner is watching from a distance. He's a mean machine." Bobbi grinned.

"Oh." She looked unimpressed. "Okay." Marianne took a deep breath. "Let me eat a little. I'm famished."

Bobbi sipped her coffee and picked at her salad while Marianne ate like a death row prisoner. Finally sated, she dabbed at her lips with a napkin. "Good?"

"You have no idea, Bobbi. I don't get out much."

"Is that because of Tusker?"

Marianne swallowed. "He's always been controlling, but since... since what happened, he's crazy worried that Blotter's going to do something."

Bobbi nodded, trying to keep her excitement under control. She figured she might make a good detective someday if she could only master that. "Why would Blotter do something to you?" *Ask the question you already know the answer to and see what happens.* Barry had taught her that.

"I guess that's what you want to hear, right?"

"Marianne, he's coked out of his head now. Nobody is safe with him on the street." Bobbi paused for emphasis. "Least of all, you."

Marianne nodded in a businesslike way and drummed her fingers on the table. Bobbi noticed the nails were chewed right down to the nub. "I can tell you now. But giving a statement, or whatever...I don't know."

"Just between us is better than nothing, Marianne. But it's essentially hearsay as the courts are concerned. Look, I think you've got the idea that Blotter has this huge empire behind him; that you'll never be safe if you talk. But from what I hear, the bikers are already starting to hedge their bets. He's out of control, and they don't like out of control. You'll be safer if you go on the record."

"I don't know, Bobbi. It's scary." Her eyes welled with tears. Bobbi held her hand firmly. How did this fragile, innocent creature wind up in the middle of this shit?

Suddenly, Marianne sat bolt upright. She flipped a blonde bang out of her face and dabbed at her running blue mascara with a napkin. "They came to the house with guns. They wanted Tusker to sign a contract. How stupid is that?" She laughed bitterly. "He wouldn't go along, and I lost it. I screamed at them to get out. That's when...they grabbed me. They carried me into the bedroom, and their hands...went all over. They started to pull off my clothes, the two fat ones, when Blotter told them to stop."

Bobbi slid two mugshots across the table. "These two?"

"Yes. Fat, slimy fucks. They aren't going to..."

"One is dead. The other is missing. I'm guessing only Blotter knows where."

"I'll send some fucking flowers. They've got a nice place by the Skybridge." Marianne's composure dissolved in a mixture of laughter and tears. Bobbi gave the shit eye to two old ladies who stared as they passed by. "It's not so much me I'm worried about, Bobbi. It's Tusker. I know, I know what you think. Old guy, young girl, it must be money, right? But it's not. He cares for me, he really does. When I met him, I was living on the street.

Seventeen years old, turning tricks and using dope. He got me out of that life."

Not very far out, Bobbi thought. "We can protect you both."

"He has to decide, too. I can't do it for him."

Bobbi sighed. "If you wait too long...we may not be able to help."

"Uh, Bobbi?"

"What?"

"I've got a question."

"Yes?"

"Can I have another piece of chocolate cake?"

Bobbi laughed. "Sure. Pick me up one too." She handed Marianne a ten, and turned to Rick as she walked away, shrugging. Rick stared back at her, shaking his head.

You can't choose your witnesses. That was something else Barry Olds taught her.

KWOK'S NOODLE HOUSE
MAIN AND 33RD AVE

Blotter parked the Trans-Am in the alley behind the noodle house and waited for George Gazeris to emerge from the narrow walkway to the street.

His mood was a curious mixture of calm and vibration. He'd never liked Harvey Sam, an extension of his general dislike of Natives, perhaps, but in his case, it was something more. Harvey always seemed to drift through life on minimal effort, accomplishing a comfortable lifestyle without lifting a finger, doing his jolt in Kent without incident, never suffering the violence at the hands of competitors and the police that he had.

In short, it was envy that was going to pull the trigger today. Harvey Sam didn't have a quarter of the money or a tenth of the charm of Blotter Boorman. But he had twice the luck. Until now.

Gazeris skipped down the walkway, and emerged, eyes wide, staring at the Trans-Am. "Shit, Blotter, this ride…"

Blotter tossed him the keys. "Keep it running. I'll be fast. He still in there?"

"Yeah. Having some noodles with a hooker I know. Brenda James. She's a nice girl, Blotter…"

"Fuck her. She shouldn't have gone for noodles with Harvey Sam. What table?"

Gazeris stared up at the sun and mopped his curly unibrow with a handkerchief. "Sure is hot."

"Which fucking table?"

"Second from the door, Blotter."

Blotter dipped his toot spoon into a vial of coke and snorted. "Ahhh…have some."

Gazeris waved his hands. "Oh, no, it's okay…"

"Take a fucking hit! If I come out here, and you're gone, you're dead, understand me?"

Gazeris snorted a hit in obvious misery. "Jesus…fuck…not used to that…"

Blotter laughed and slipped into the walkway. He stepped past pissed-off cats and over milk crates. When he reached the street, he paused as a marked police car drove by, then emerged and walked straight to the ratty white awning that marked the noodle house.

Blotter was wearing a raincoat with a cut-out pocket, the .38 concealed, but in his hand. The feelings of conflict and guilt that were there for Roach were absent now. All he felt was a giddy anticipation. He paused in front of the glass storefront.

Perfect. It was still early for the lunch rush. An old Chinaman stood behind the counter, wearing a headscarf and a dirty apron. Harvey sat facing the door, his head tucked into a bowl of noodles, with a long-haired, skinny woman in hooker wear facing him.

Blotter opened the door, casually. A chime sounded, and as the door closed behind him, Harvey looked up. A sardonic smile spread on his face. "Blotter. Bad day for business, hah?"

Blotter raised the .38 and pointed it at his skull. "Not as bad as your day's gonna be."

Harvey's mouth went wide. He dropped his chopsticks. The girl's head began to turn, and the old Chinaman began to shout, but Blotter wasn't hearing it. He pressed the trigger, and a picture on the wall exploded. He pressed it again, tracking Harvey as his head began to move left, and this time, he caught him.

Harvey's head jerked back as a hole opened in his cheek, then a round entered his mouth and painted the wallpaper in purple abomination. The girl, Brenda, had turned now, and to Blotter's surprise she leapt up from the chair, swinging her purse, hitting his outstretched arm.

Blotter pulled her close by the front of her bra and put the revolver to her heart. He pulled the trigger twice, and she slid to the ground.

The old Chinaman wasn't yelling now. His back was pressed to the wall, and he watched Blotter with silent, pleading eyes. Blotter raised the gun and slipped his finger inside the trigger guard.

Something about the man's passive, pleading stare made him lower the gun, and walk out the door. He walked back, unhurried, down the walkway. When he got to the Trans-Am, he registered the scene only slowly.

There was the car. There was George. But George was lying on his back, his mouth and eyes open, staring at the sky. He knelt next to the body and felt no pulse.

A fucking heart attack? No wonder he didn't want to do coke. You've got to be kidding.

Blotter looked down at his raincoat. Brenda's blood covered the chest. A taxi pulled into the alley, reversing quickly when he pointed the revolver.

He folded up the raincoat and tossed it on the ground next to George. He wiped the grip of the revolver as best he could and set it on the ground next to the body. Then he got into the Trans-Am, reversed out of the alley, and turned onto East 33rd just as the first sirens began to sound.

He began to laugh hysterically as he passed cop cars, screaming to the scene he'd just left.

Good old George. Taking one for the team.

JUNE

ESCAPE AND EVASION

Police vehicular pursuit is an inherently dangerous and controversial activity, even more so when the quarry is a motivated, drug-fuelled individual like Blotter Boorman...

GRANVILLE SKYTRAIN STATION

Marianne hadn't objected when Bobbi suggested she ride the Skytrain back to Broadway Station with her. Bobbi kept her distance in the crowded car, but Marianne being Marianne, she couldn't resist flashing a smile in her direction every so often.

Bobbi fought the urge to doze after eating more than she was used to. She hid her face behind a *Vancouver Sun* and watched Marianne carefully. *How did a kid like that wind up in a shit scene like this one?*

Well, Marianne had told her, hadn't she? How she'd wound up on the streets, selling her ass at the age of seventeen, was something Bobbi cared not to reflect on.

Her earbud crackled with Rick Grohmann's deep voice. "On the

Viaduct now. Should be at Main St in five minutes." As they rode underground, he drove overhead, ready to tail Marianne back home.

Of course, Bobbi reflected, the real danger to Marianne knew her address. And could get Tusker to open the door. Marianne would not be safe until she was out of there. The intercom chimed the next station. "The next station is Stadium." The crowd in her car thinned out by a third, and now Bobbi could see a thin man in a grey overcoat, all knees and elbows, red Doc Marten's boots, and an unseasonable wool watch cap, standing just past where Marianne was sitting.

He had his back turned to her, but for some reason Bobbi's gaze lingered on him. There was something there…

The train had emerged from the warren of tunnels under the city, and now surmounted the elevated track that gave it its name. The cars bucked and swayed as they passed the inflatable dome of BC Place, coming even with the crowded entrance to the Plaza of Nations.

"Main, turning onto Kingsway now." Rick announced.

"Next station is Main Street." The intercom chimed. The train slowed, then came to a screeching stop in front of a jammed platform. Marianne smiled at her again, and Bobbi smiled back, just as the man in the grey overcoat turned and made eye-contact.

Bad teeth, fisheyes, chicken neck. No wonder he was wearing the watch cap. *Donnie Fucking McCrae.*

He smiled rottenly at her, taken aback as she was, before the jam of pressing people entering the car obscured him. Bobbi fought her way to the exit on her end, catching a glimpse of Marianne, still seated, and Donnie melting into the crowd on the platform.

She tried shouting into the lapel mike and got only feedback.

Now, she reefed the hefty portable out of her backpack and shouted for Rick. "Rick, turn around and come back. Donnie McCrae just got off at Main Street!"

"Copy that!" Bobbi could hear the engine roaring and the siren blipping as Rick turned the LTD around. "You stick with her!"

"10-4." Now, obvious police radio in hand, she felt the gazes of everyone in the car on her. Marianne was staring straight ahead. Bobbi squeezed into a corner just in time to hear a bulletin override their talk-around channel.

"Station all cars, station all cars, pursuit in progress vicinity of Queen Elizabeth Park. Suspect vehicle is black Pontiac Trans-Am, white male driver in early forties. Suspect in triple-homicide at Kwok's Noodle House. Be advised subject armed and dangerous. Patrol in contact with suspect, last known location northbound on Midlothian at Dinmont. Units not involved, avoid area."

Bobbi fought the wave of worry that came over her and fought to keep Marianne in sight.

WEST 29TH AND CAMBIE ST

Now, with four police cars on his tail, Blotter Boorman was regretting not having a less conspicuous ride. It had only taken three blocks' travel for the first marked car to make him, and like flies on shit, they'd all converged.

But, he thought as he swerved around a bus and drove a Honda Civic into a stand of trees, it *was* a lovely day for a car chase. And now, he was going to give these pigs something to think about.

In his early, early days in Vancouver, Blotter had boosted cars before moving into the far more sedate realm of dealing drugs. This frequently resulted in pursuits, and he was proud of his record: In twenty-one pursuits, he'd only been caught twice.

How? He was never afraid to take chances that a cop with a pension and two kids to feed wouldn't. Now, as he approached the busy North-South boulevard of Cambie, he did just that.

As he cranked the wheel hard left into the oncoming lane, the four cars chasing him overshot, one of them smoking a bread truck and driving it into the side of a house. Now, he corrected the spinning wheel, dodging four cars and one truck, seeing angry faces, wide open mouths, veering sedans.

Blotter made a quick calculation: West 30th into the park, take the loop road, then go all-out asshole. Hearing sirens running parallel to him on Cambie, but seeing nothing in the rear view, he reefed the wheel hard left, flattened onto the stub of West 30th, then fishtailed wildly as he made the narrow turn on to the ring road.

"Yee hah, motherfuckers!" Blotter screamed out of the open windows, as pedestrians stared in stupefaction at the roaring intruder. He peered out the windshield, seeing the sign he was looking for, the gently sloping path behind it, the geodesic dome of the Bloedel Conservatory rising from the flowerbeds.

In the rear view, three cop cars remained, and now a fourth swerved on the ring road, clipping a city truck before righting itself and joining its fellows.

Blotter smiled to himself. *How many day's suspension would a cop get for doing this?* He gunned the engine, mounted the curb with a slam, and now he was gunning it along a pedestrian trail that led all the way to the top of the hill. He laughed hysterically as picnickers and rubberneckers threw themselves out of his way, and bicyclists lost control and plummeted down the steep, grassy slopes.

In the past, he'd always heard banjo music in his head, but this time it was "Yakety Sax" from *The Benny Hill Show* for some reason, maybe the comic panic amongst the sun-worshipping squares. He plowed a cyclist off of his ten-speed at the top of the trail, then did a fearsome donut in the parking lot of the Conservatory.

Siren sounds, getting closer, suggested that his pursuers were taking the long way up. *Where to go?*

Blotter wheeled the car around, waving at staring tourists, then mounted another trail and drove straight down the hill, past the crags and grottos of the Quarry Garden, headed for a clearing below. From the sounds of the sirens, the cops had reached the Conservatory, but following him would take a cop like Rick Grohmann. And there weren't enough cops like that to worry about.

Blotter peeled off the path and pointed his car straight down the hill. He opened the door, then gunned the engine and let the handbrake go. The Trans-Am picked up momentum at a fearsome rate, but Blotter mustered coke courage, and dropped out of the driver's side, rolling as he hit, feeling only the pain of a smashed pinky as the huge door recoiled on his outstretched hand.

Up at the crest of the hill, eight astonished cops watched with a hundred tourists as a man rolled down the hill behind the speeding car, which kept accelerating. The man and the car disappeared from view, only the car re-emerging from the woods.

NAT BAILEY STADIUM

At the foot of Queen Elizabeth Hill, the Vancouver Canadians AAA farm club were doing infield drills when the players heard a roaring sound. Some of them looked up in time to see a black, four-wheeled meteor hurtle out of a stand of trees, skip right across two lanes of traffic, and head straight for the outfield wall.

The car smashed through the wall, shedding two wheels, and

dug a wide divot into the turf, before coming to rest just short of first base, on the foul line.

"Jesus H Christ." exclaimed the Assistant Manager in a Texas drawl, "That's the most exciting thing I've ever seen in this fucking park."

QUEEN ELIZABETH PARK

Blotter Boorman wrapped his purple and red pinky finger in a ripped piece of his outer shirt, which he now discarded to make identification more difficult. Fifty metres down the hill, he emerged from the woods with a nonchalant strut.

He spied a city bus coming down Midlothian and jogged to the stop in time to catch it. Looking back as he boarded at the hole in the Canadians' outfield wall, he laughed out loud.

Boorman, it's been fifteen years since you stole a car. But man, you've still got it.

JUNE

THREE MONKEYS

In traditional lore, the Three Monkeys will hear no evil, see no evil, and speak no evil. In the case of Regina v Neil Boorman, there are three monkeys who will speak no evil, and unless a breakthrough occurs, the brazen murders at Kwok's Noodle House cannot be pinned on Blotter Boorman...

TERMINAL AVENUE

Rick Grohmann blipped the siren as he u-turned in messy traffic, scanning the streets for Donnie McCrae's trademark high-as-a-kite bop. On the north side of Terminal, the sidewalks were jammed with Expo visitors, moving in herds from the overpriced parking garages that every businessman in the area had erected overnight to fleece their kind.

If Donnie was there, they were fucked.

He gave up on scanning the north side, and drove instead at patrol speed, slow, down Terminal, hoping for a glimpse of that can't-miss-Mohawk.

It took him only a minute to mark an out-of-season knit watch cap on a skinny fucker with that trademark, be-bopping, *I'm getting high* walk. As if sensing the eyes on him, the cap wearer turned and looked at him.

Ooh, hello Donnie. Rick mounted the curb with a blast of the air horn, while Donnie stood and stared, his face scrunching into a wince as the LTD stopped just short of his shins.

They'd stopped in front of a row of warehouses, with only scattered rummies and cart-pushers for company. None of the tourists were stopping to look. Rick got out of the car, slamming the door.

"Central, show 2339 10-6 at Terminal and Western with one 10-85 subject." Rick flipped the portable in mid-air and grinned at Donnie.

"10-4, 2339, do you require car to cover?"

"Negative." Donnie looked uncertain of whether to run or stay. "If you need to run, run. If you don't, don't. But show me your fucking hands before I ventilate you, asshole."

Donnie put up his trembling hands, flashing a horrible grin. "Oh yeah, that's right, copper. I heard you killed poor wee Soulschnitzel. You ever kill any white men, then?"

"All of sudden you're Martin Luther King, is that it Donnie? Actually, I killed him because he pointed a rifle at me. Which, even though you're technically a white man, I'd kill you for too. How is Roach, by the way? I never got his thank-you card."

There was just the merest twitch in Donnie's face. "I've not seen him about."

Rick smiled coldly. "Should I be sending flowers?" He walked up to Donnie. "I mean, is Blotter starting to re-organize his workforce? Oh, dear me. Well, you know how to keep yourself alive, Donnie."

"Fuck you. As if I'd suck yer cock just to stay alive, you great fucking animal."

"Ooh, now that hurts. Up against the wall, asshole."

"What for? What are ye detaining me for? I want to..."

Rick drove a fist into Donnie's solar plexus. The wiry man dropped to his knees and exhaled slowly. In the warehouse behind him, a woman watching from an upper-story window quickly ducked out of view. "What's that? You going around thinking you're a fucking human being again, Donnie, instead of a recycled tampon from the Glasgow sewers?"

"That's...that's fucking brutality! In broad fucking daylight, you giant whalloper! You're a right fucking rocket, you are!"

Rick picked up Donnie by both arms and propped him against the wall of the warehouse. "I said, up against it, you Irn-Bru swilling monkey." He ripped Donnie's overstuffed wallet out of his breast pocket and tossed it on the hood of his car. He turned out the man's pockets, and frisked him tight around his nutsack, to no avail.

"You see? Ye fuckin' boak? Ah'm clean, and I'm gonna file a fuckin' report on you for that, pig."

By now, Rick was rifling through Donnie's wallet. He pulled out a glassine envelope with sticky white powder in it and held it up for Donnie to see. "What's this, citizen?"

"Ah...ah, I kin explain..."

Rick whipped him around again and handcuffed him. "You can explain to the judge. You're under arrest for possession of a narcotic, Donnie."

KWOK'S NOODLE HOUSE

Olds and Selfridge had arrived at the scene of the slaughter on Main Street to find Phil LeBretton already taking notes over George Gazeris' prone form. Patrol units had the alley blocked on both sides, and LeBretton's supervisor Mickey Morely was quizzing an agitated Sikh cabbie a few doors down.

LeBretton looked up from Gazeris' body. "Recognize him?"

"Yeah." Barry offered. "George Gazeris. We just hit his properties."

"Seems like too big of a coincidence." Selfridge peered over his glasses at the corpse. "Wait a second, I thought this was a shooting?"

LeBretton smiled. "Two out of three, yes. Gazeris? Not a mark on him. If I had to guess, I'd say it was a heart attack."

Barry Olds laughed. "I hope we had something to do with it." At the other end of the alley, the first camera truck had arrived. "Didn't take them long."

"Yeah, and the chief won't be far behind." LeBretton shook his head. "If you don't want to be on the news, I'd suggest you split."

Barry ignored the suggestion. "Any witnesses, Phil?"

"Just one. Mr Kwok, the proprietor. He's having a little memory trouble, if you get my drift."

"Mind if give it a try?"

"Have at her, Barry. Just don't sick Grohmann on him."

Selfridge demurred. "I'd better call Heynemann."

Barry walked down the narrow walkway to the front of the building. In the walkway, a crime scene photographer was taking a shot of a tiny drop of blood on a milk crate. Barry gingerly stepped around him, and emerged onto the street. It was hot, and getting hotter, and a crowd now pressed against four harried cops trying to keep them on the other side of the yellow tape. Cameras emerged from the crowd and tracked him as he walked to the entrance.

Major Crimes had already posted big white screens in front of the shop windows to prevent ghoul shots of the crime scene. A hulking Corporal standing outside the noodle house waved him in.

Past the screens, the door was propped open. An Ident man was busily powdering every surface for prints. Just inside the restaurant, a toppled chair sat next to an ownerless high heel. Blood spatter covered the wall and the table.

And one former drug dealer sat, head snapped back, with two holes in his face, and black blood oozing slowly out of his mouth, as death took over and slowed him to a crawl.

"Hey Sarge."

Marvin Yau was a hard-working detective, LeBretton's protégé since his stint at Sex Offence Squad, but hardly his equal in the fashion department. Where Phil LeBretton's dress since could best be described as "James Bond," Marvin Yau's was more "Herb Tarleck."

"So, Marvin, natural causes, or what?"

"In their line of business, sure. This guy here is Harvey Sam."

"Thought I recognized him." Barry peered at the corpse. "He's uglier now, though."

"Yeah, you guys put him out of business awhile ago. Heard he had a beef with Blotter Boorman."

"Half the dealers in the city could say that. Who was he with?" Barry indicated the toppled chair.

"Girl by the name of Brenda James, according to ID. CNI for a few soliciting and possession busts. She still had a pulse when Patrol showed up, so they did a scoop-and-run to Women's Hospital. DOA."

"Where's the witness?"

"In the back, but I wouldn't waste your time."

"He speak English?"

"That's not the problem. A continuing desire to stay alive has fused his mouth-brain connection."

"Lot of that going around. Mind if I take a crack?"

"Go for it, Sarge. His *guailo* name is Charlie."

Man Wing "Charlie" Kwok was typical in appearance for an Asian cook, in Barry's experience. Slight, bony, balding, arms covered in burn scars from decades of battling hot woks and hotter oils. He sat on a milk crate in the brown-walled kitchen, chain-smoking. Kwok looked up as he walked in, then down again.

"It's Charlie, right? I'm Sergeant Olds with Drug Section." Barry put out a hand. Kwok looked at it and ignored it.

"No drugs here. We never sell drugs."

"Nobody said you did, Charlie. But the dead man out there did. And I bet the man who killed him did too. If you tell me what you saw, I can protect you until he's off the street."

Kwok made a grimace. "Hah. You cops always say this. But always people wind up dead. This neighbourhood used to be good. Now, it's shit. What you cops do? Nothing? I had eyes closed, whole time."

"That girl who was shot, Brenda, right? You know her?"

Kwok looked up and paused for a moment. "Yeah. Nice girl. Have a shit life, but nice girl. Used to give little candies and toys to my daughters. She not deserve it. Maybe other guy, okay, he sell drugs. But she was nice person."

"So? She was nice, but not nice enough for you to tell the police who killed her, right? That means nothing then, right Charlie?"

"Listen, cop. I know what you are trying to do. No tricks. I can say nothing if I want to."

"I bet you won't sleep tonight, Charlie. I bet you won't sleep tomorrow, or the next night after that. Maybe never, if you don't tell me who killed Brenda."

"How can I know?" Kwok yelled and stood suddenly. "Just another white guy! I can't tell! Just leave me alone!"

"You okay back here?" Marvin held back the beaded curtain with a gloved hand.

"Yeah, yeah." Barry took out a business card, and slipped it into Kwok's hand. "I was just leaving, anyway."

In the alley, LeBretton flagged him down. "Cabbie's description sure sounds a lot like Blotter Boorman. Charlie give you anything?"

"No. Maybe I planted a seed. Sure as fuck sounds like Boorman."

"Out of his mind on coke, from the sounds of it. Apparently slipped Patrol by going the wrong way on Cambie, driving up QE Hill, then letting his car roll down the hill while he jumps out. Car winds up plowing through the outfield fence at Nat Bailey."

"Holy shit. This is getting out of hand. Anything on the car?"

"Body shop loaner. Biker business."

Barry spat. "Fucking dead end. And what about George?"

"Working theory?" LeBretton paused. "George is pissed about you guys raiding his dope houses. Blotter's obsessed with a snitch in his outfit, which maybe is why nobody's seen Roach Lehmann this week. George tells Blotter the snitch is Harvey Sam, who Blotter's always hated anyway."

"And George is dead, why?"

"White powder in the nostrils. Hot shot?" LeBretton smiled. "Poetic justice if it is. Blotter sees the body back here after doing the deed, decides to drop the gun and the overcoat in a clumsy attempt to divert us, and takes off in the Trans-Am. Voila."

"That's why you're a homicide dick, and I'm not." Barry noticed Selfridge waving at him from their car. "Gotta run, Phil. Keep me in the loop."

"You got it."

THORNTON PARK

Rick Grohmann was freaking out the usual assortment of dopers and lowlifes who tended to accumulate in front of the train station. He drove lazy circles around the park, slowing every so often to ensure the passersby got a good look at Donnie, who cringed in the back seat, handcuffed and unable to cover his face.

"Have they not got anything better for ye to do? Jesus Christ!"

"Nope. I work on my own pretty much."

"Tha' explains the cologne."

"That's a good one, Donnie." Rick slammed on the brakes, forcing Donnie's nose into the plexiglass partition. "Black dog."

"Yer a fucking psycho, you know that? I thought they had testing for coppers, you know, ta see if yer a fucking nutter! How the fuck did ye get this job?"

Rick grinned in the rear-view mirror as they sat in the parking lot. "Good looks?"

"Aren't ye supposed to book me, or wha'ever?" Donnie's nose now dripped a steady stream of blood.

"Nah. I figured I'd bring you home to mow my lawn."

"Wha?"

"Sure. Handcuff you to my Toro. Tell my neighbours it's a work release program."

"Seriously, though, wha' the fuck? Wha' are we doing?"

"Waiting for Blotter to show up."

"Ah told ye, ah've no idea where tha fuck he is. Ah told ye!"

"So, what were you doing down here then?"

"Out for a stroll."

"Fuck that." Rick scoffed. "Nobody strolls around here. And since we can't find Blotter at his address of record, even his homo PO is ready to breach him. So, where is he?"

"You think you can get me to snitch for a fucking possession beef? Yer out of yer fucking mind."

Rick turned to Donnie. "No, Donnie, that's not what I think. What I think is, if Blotter is around here, and he sees you and me spending all this quality time together, he's going to come to entirely the wrong conclusion. And your life will become shorter than a baby raper's in general population, Donnie."

Donnie began to spit blood. "You fucking bastard! Let me out a here, you fucking psycho! Let me out a here!"

Rick calmly rolled up the back windows and slid the silent partner shut. The noise was attracting stares.

One of the stares came from a man with a grievously wounded pinky finger, working his way down Terminal through the crowds. That man watched from behind a pillar for a long time, until the cop released his prisoner and drove away.

BROADWAY STATION

When the doors opened at Broadway Station, Bobbi had hurried to catch up to Marianne in the crowd. The girl was making a serious effort to avoid her, but Bobbi caught an elbow and slowed her down on the escalator.

"Are you crazy?" Marianne hissed at her. "And what was that back there? You're not very good at going undercover."

"That was Donnie McCrae, one of Blotter's guys. He just happens to be on the same train as us? Marianne, it's now or never!" Bobbi whispered urgently.

"Then it's never!" Marianne had slipped out of her grasp and disappeared into a waiting cab. Bobbi had been left, standing like a stood-up prom date, thinking she'd blown it completely.

"Bobbi, you there?" Her radio hissed.

She pulled out the portable, no longer giving a shit who saw her. "Yeah. Pick me up at Broadway."

When Rick Grohmann arrived, he had news. Bobbi had just gotten into the LTD when he dropped it. "Blotter wasted two people at a noodle house on South Main. They can't get a positive ID, star witness has a case of amnesia, but they think they've got enough to call him a person of interest. Olds wants us back at the office for a conference."

Bobbi turned to him as he aggressively bulled his way through the traffic. "But then we've got to go back to Marianne and Tusker. This might be our last chance."

"No." Rick was firm. "Olds was definite about that. No more freewheeling."

"You're one to talk. You catch up with Donnie?"

Rick nodded, a rueful smile on his face. "Yeah. Out for a stroll, he said."

"Bullshit. He made us."

"Yeah, well maybe Blotter made him."

"How do you mean?"

"There's no reason to be in that neighbourhood if you're someone like Donnie, and you're not looking to score. My bet is, Blotter is somewhere around there. So, I let everyone see us together."

"So maybe Blotter thinks Donnie is the rat, not Marianne? Evil."

"Yeah. Desperate measures, I guess."

"But that area is all flophouses and warehouses." Bobbi considered.

"Great place to put a safe house, then. Who's gonna look?"

"One thing's for sure. It's almost over."

"Yeah." Rick nodded. "I get that feeling, too. We might have three monkeys who won't speak evil. But we've got one coked-out bad guy who'll make our job easier. Only question is, how many people have to die before we get him?"

Bobbi stared out the window at the unsuspecting city and wondered the same thing.

JUNE

PERSON OF INTEREST

In criminal investigations, when the evidence against the prime suspect is insufficient to justify an arrest warrant, police will often release information anyway on what they call the "person of interest." The purpose of this is often threefold: to warn the public, to determine the subject's whereabouts, and to force the subject's hand so that he does something to justify an arrest warrant...

TERMINAL AND WESTERN

Donnie had taken every precaution to avoid being tailed, even hailing a cab and getting the driver to bring him in from Kingsway and drop him three blocks south of the warehouse.

He thought he was being smart.

When he unlocked the rear door and hurried up the stairs, breathing roughly through the tissues stuffed in his still-bleeding nose, the sight of Larissa waiting at the top was a reassurance.

"Oh, Donnie, I saw you down there with that policeman, he was being very cruel to you. Are you hurt?" She wore a very distracting tight black dress, with a plunging neckline that awakened some inconvenient urges in Donnie.

"Ssssh, Larissa. Dunnae tell Blotter abou' the polis. He'll come to tha wrong conclusion, love."

Suddenly, Blotter emerged from the bathroom, a towel around his waist. "What wrong conclusion? You keeping secrets, Donnie?"

Donnie backed up, feeling the railing of the stairs in the small of his back. He watched Blotter stop at the bar for another line and a glass of scotch. Larissa made herself scarce. "Ah, that psycho cop, Grohmann, he was fucking wi' me, Blotter. I did'nae want you to get the wrong idea..."

"What wrong idea was that?" Blotter advanced on him. "That while I was taking care of one snitch, you were setting up to be his replacement? You playing me, Donnie?"

"No, no, no...ah've got some news for you though..."

"Great." Blotter gave him a wide, toothy grin. "And I've got news for you, too." Blotter swung the scotch glass in his right hand, hard against his cheekbone. Donnie saw black, slouched against the railing, and began to tumble down the stairs. He heard Larissa screaming as he rolled end-over-end.

Donnie came to rest in the doorway, on cold lino. He opened his eyes to see Blotter, towel slipped off, surging down the stairs like a rabid chimp, cock and balls swinging. Donnie backed up towards the door, but Blotter landed square on his chest and began to pummel him.

"Had a nice ride in the policeman's car, did you? Did he let you play with the siren? Did he touch you in your special place, eh Donnie?" The blows landed on his head, in his face, on his ears.

"Stop it! Stop it for fuck's sake! I know who the real snitch is! I saw them!"

Like someone had hit his off switch, Blotter sagged. Slowly, he stood. "You...you saw them?"

"Aye!" Donnie struggled to sit up. He coughed blood onto the lino. "Aye, I did, for fuck's sake. I saw that darkie cop, the girl who rides with Grohmann, she was on the Skytrain. With Marianne Taakoiennin."

Blotter sat on the stairs. "You did?"

"Yeah. An' after she spots me, she lets her fucking partner ha' a bit a fun wi' me. He told me he was trying ta make you think

I was a snitch, Blotter. They're trying to protect Marianne and Tusker, man. There's your real problem, mate."

"Oh." Suddenly, the enraged chimp had become the chastened schoolboy. "Sorry I hit you in the face." Upstairs, the phone started ringing. Larissa called down the stairs.

"Blotter? Is Randy, for you."

"Yeah, okay." Donnie watched as a naked Blotter trudged up the stairs in a daze, his hand dripping blood.

He wanted to run, but he could not. Where could he run to? Cops closing in, now the bikers calling...where could he turn?

Instead of running, he got up off the floor and started picking glass out of his cheek. He pulled himself up the stairs, and Larissa met him with a wet bar towel, pressing it to his face. It felt so good.

"Scotch, Donnie?"

"Aye, angel, aye." He sat at the bar and let the scotch warm and calm him. Then Blotter sat beside him.

Blotter chewed a fingernail and lit a smoke. He sipped at the scotch Larissa brought him in silence. Finally, Donnie let his curiosity get the better of him. "What did Randy want?"

"A meet. Out at the farm." His eyes looked hollow and unfocused.

"Jesus, Blotter...they're going to kill us."

"Not if we kill them first." Donnie noticed that Larissa's green eyes went wide at that, but she said nothing. They drank in silence until the pizzas showed up.

312 MAIN ST
THAT EVENING

An impromptu group of men and women from Major Crimes, Drug Section, and the Strike Force sat around the conference table or stood against the walls. A closed-circuit monitor showed the press conference by Inspector Heynemann and Staff Sergeant Selfridge, who were joined at the end by the Chief.

When it was over, a ripple of commentary spread around the room. Barry Olds stood up and brought the room to order. "Yes, yes. Lots of opinions. I've got mine, too. But right now, we have no perfect solutions. We've got no prints at the scene tying Boorman to the crime, the gun is a ballistic ghost, and the only eyewitness who got a good enough look at Boorman isn't sure he wants to play ball. But we have to do something."

"Person of Interest?" Mickey Morely scoffed. "That might work with some fish, but Blotter knows when he's being bluffed. He knows how to keep shtum. Don't forget, this wouldn't be the first time we've had him in the box on this case."

"It doesn't matter." Rick Grohmann tapped a pen on the table. "From what I hear, and from the looks of that chase this morning, coke will do the job for us. He's already blown his stack. From here on, it's either an OD or a hollow point that ends it. Period."

"Looking for another notch on your belt there, Clint?" LeBretton chided him.

Rick shrugged. "It is what it is. Now, Bobbi and I have been working another angle…"

Barry nodded. "Marianne Taakoiennin. But wasn't that blown by Donnie McCrae?"

Bobbi spoke up. "All the more reason to try one more time. I'd hate to see them on the body count."

Barry nodded. "Try again tomorrow. Push a little harder. In the meantime, everyone go home and get some sleep. Strike Force will keep an eye on the situation during the wee hours. We meet here at 0830 and begin shaking our snitches for anything on Blotter. His mug has gone out to all Patrol teams. In the morning, if he hasn't done a Belushi…"

"God willing." Connolly genuflected. "Where's Silverbag Smith when you need her?"

"If he hasn't, we start over. Although I agree with Rick, we have to have a Plan B." Barry concluded. "It's been a long day. Goodnight."

JUNE

LAST SUNRISE

The culmination of a long and torturous case like this one can produce desperate and unpredictable behaviour, in cops and criminals alike...

CITY CENTRE MOTOR HOTEL

Rick Grohmann awakened to the persistent sound of the phone ringing. He blinked twice and looked at his watch. 0635. Reluctantly, he picked up.

"Grohmann? It's Bill Davies. I wake you?"

"Jesus, Davies, of course you fucking woke me. And how the hell did you get this number?' Bill Davies was a reporter, sometimes a useful source. But, like most reporters, using them as informants was always tricky. They were playing you at the same time you were playing them.

"Well, I figured I ought to give you a heads up. Mike Inoburi is doing a story on you in tomorrow's *Province*. And it won't be pretty."

Rick sat on the edge of the bed. He pulled back the blinds. It was raining steadily. A perfect match for his mood. "What's it about? Let me guess...a tennis pro who can't keep his dick out of other men's wives?"

"Yeah, more like the cop who almost beat him to death for it. And two departments who covered for him because they want him on Blotter Boorman's ass."

Rick shook his head. "You looking for comment? Here's your comment. Fuck Mike Inoburi, fuck Lawrence Dyck, and fuck the *Province* too."

"You're welcome."

"Fuck off." Rick slammed the phone down and stared out at the rain. He lit a smoke and pondered what might be his last day on the force.

If it's my last day on the force, it's Blotter's last day on earth. Fuck everything else.

BURNABY
MORLEY ST

Barry Olds padded as quietly as he could to the kitchen, hoping not to wake his family.

Outside, the rain drummed steadily on the windows. Vancouver did that to you, he concluded. Took away the sun suddenly, just to remind you where you were.

But he didn't mind. He was a rainforest kid at heart. This was all he knew. He stopped in the kitchen door, finding Tim already awake and hunched over the books.

"You're up early."

"So are you, Dad. Finals. If I don't buck up, it's bad news. What's your excuse?" Tim smiled. He had the piercing eyes and untamed red hair of his mother, but the solid physique was all Barry. He was talking more and more about being a cop. Part of him was proud, and part of him wanted to slap it out of the boy.

"My excuse is Blotter Boorman." Barry picked up the coffee pot and poured himself a mug. "You want more?"

"Nah. More than one gives me the jitters." Tim demurred. "The TV said that guy is nuts."

"For once, the TV is right."

"Be careful out there." There was genuine worry in his son's eyes.

"Oh, I always am."

"No, you're not, dad." Tim stared at him earnestly. "Don't go in the door first today. I know what you're like."

Barry patted his son on the shoulder. "I promise, I'll be careful." His son wrapped an arm around him and would not let him go.

OAK PARK

Bobbi Sanghera almost made a clean getaway too; except she was ambushed in the living room by her father.

Jaswant Singh Sanghera was a veteran of the Second World War. He wore his turban straight and proud, over top of a stern face and an impressive moustache and beard. He was sitting in his favourite armchair, watching the morning news. "You are going out to catch this crazy man today, Balwant?"

Bobbi sagged, fearing another pointless argument about her future. "Yes, father. He's very dangerous. We need to get him off the street."

Her father extricated himself from the armchair painfully. Arthritis, and a forty-year-old war wound were taking their toll. But he stood in front of her now, parade-ground straight. "Please embrace me, daughter."

She wrapped her arms around him, surprised, smelling sandalwood and leather, father smells.

He released her, finally. "I wanted to tell you, Bobbi." He smiled down at her. "We are very proud of you. Please be careful."

"I promise, daddy." She wrapped herself around him again, not knowing when she would get the chance again.

MAPLE RIDGE

The low-pressure system now lashing Vancouver with rain had not yet reached so far inland. Donnie piloted the Buick LeSabre along Randy McClarty's gravel road, raising a cloud of dust he was sure could be seen for miles. Sun bathed his face and reflected off the snow-capped peaks of the mountains that framed the prairie.

A good day to die? In Donnie McCrae's world, there was no such thing. He touched the bandage over his glassed cheek and winced. Every day in this world was a day to die.

"Mmmph....mmmm!" Donnie looked in the rear view at Larissa, handcuffed and gagged, after Blotter's orders. A full, sleepless night of coke had convinced his boss that poor, harmless, heart-of-gold Larissa was a spy.

"Relax, gorgeous. We'll just let you off here with your boys. He'll probably sleep through the whole thing." Donnie jabbed a thumb in Blotter's direction. "Let you off, and turn around."

"Mmmm. Hmmmm!" She did not sound convinced to Donnie. Donnie had not convinced himself. Secretly, he was praying that Blotter's long snooze turned into an OD. It would solve so many problems.

"Stop here. Make it look like car trouble." Suddenly, Blotter was awake and sitting upright. Donnie almost drove off the road.

"Jesus! Blotter!"

"Just fucking do it, Donnie."

Donnie sighed deeply and stopped the car. He popped the hood and got out, pantomiming pathetically that he had engine trouble.

Blotter, his view of the road now obscured, opened the passenger door and peered down the road at the barn where they'd killed Roach. He had no doubt that this morning, a similar arrangement awaited him and Donnie.

Hence the bag between his feet. In the criminal world, a summons was almost always a bad thing. If it was a proposal, something positive…well, then they usually came to you, didn't they?

There was a ringing in his ears and throbbing in his head that was not entirely unpleasant. Coke was a strange thing. It had kept him awake all night. Larissa and Donnie had joined in, and he'd been treated to the zoo-like spectacle of watching the mohawked Scotsman rail the curvy Czech incessantly. He had to give it to Donnie: the lad could fuck.

As if hearing his thoughts, Larissa moaned. "Mmmm! Hmmm!"

Blotter looked back at her. If she'd been better at this game, she'd have known that, for her, it was already over. After all, she wasn't even blindfolded. "Relax, baby. It's almost over."

Something in her face showed that she got the double entendre in his words. Silently, she began to weep.

Blotter looked away, at the mountains, seeing the sunlight reflect off white peaks, seeing the beauty that was always all around him, but that he never took time to reflect on. Death focused the mind.

He had an end game. A tenuous one at that, but he had one. He was no kamikaze.

"They're coming. Ah see them, Blotter. Ah, fuck, it's a van, man. There could be a dozen in there, for fuck's sakes…"

Calmly, Blotter stepped out of the car and watched the approaching van, an old Ford, enveloped in road dust. Behind it, the solid black wall of a rain front.

"Christ man, let's gi' out of here!" Donnie was doing an agitated little dance.

"Shut the fuck up, Donnie." Blotter stooped to pick up the bag from the floorboards. He unzipped it and produced a Browning Hi-Power, which he checked the action on, then slid across the seat at Donnie. "Keep it hidden." He pulled the AK out of the bag for himself, racking a round, tapping the long magazine to make sure it was tight and locked. He put a second mag in the small of his back.

"Jesus Christ, Blotter, do you know how to use that fucking thing?"

Blotter smiled at Donnie. "No, but I've seen it on TV."

Donnie smiled back nervously. Fifty metres away, the van slowed and stopped. Blotter slid cautiously back to the rear door and opened it. He pulled Larissa out. "Out. Walk to the van now."

She nodded, looking at the AK lying on the seat with wide, red-rimmed eyes, then taking her first stumbling steps to freedom. At the van, Ricky McClarty had stepped out of the driver's seat. Nobody else was visible.

"Car trouble?" He yelled at them. "You expect me to believe that?"

Blotter yelled back. "That big old van, and just little old you in it? You expect me to believe that?"

Larissa looked back at Blotter, then at the van. She began to quicken her pace.

"Listen man, we just wanna talk." Randy held his hands up in supplication. "Things are getting outta hand. Like yesterday, for instance. Not cool, Blotter, not cool."

"Oh yeah?" Blotter yelled back. "You know what's not cool? Inviting me and Donnie out here and prepping a big hole in the fucking ground to waste us in."

"Bullshit, Blotter! You're fucking paranoid! Doing too much blow, man! Let us get you clean, man. There's a guy on the Island we sent all out members to…"

"Fuck you, Randy. If you didn't invite us out here to kill us, then why are the big-assed tire treads on the pickup those two Hangarounds use right fucking here! Those guys who got rid of Roach, right? They're fucking here, aren't they?"

Larissa stumbled in the gravel, then got up, casting a worried look back at Blotter. She turned, trying to yell a warning at Randy. "Mmmph! Hmmm!"

Randy's right hand went to the small of his back. A head popped up inside the van. Blotter snapped up the AK and fired on full auto.

Randy fell first, stitched across the chest, the .45 he was going for flying into the air. The head in the vehicle ducked down. Then, Larissa, running now, comically almost, then tragically, the bullets knocking her off her feet, her body rolling into a ditch.

He shot dry, quickly. As he reached down for another magazine, the side door of the van opened.

The two Hangarounds stepped out, one with a 12-gauge, the other with a MAC-10, alternating bass thumps and a horrible ripping sound. Fighting to reload the AK, his small motor skills suddenly gone to shit, Blotter watched in fascination as the 9mm rounds from the MAC pimpled the hood but did not go through.

A scream from Donnie distracted him as the 12-gauge exploded the side mirror, and his partner went down, clutching his right hip. To his surprise, Donnie came up again, firing the Hi-Power wildly.

A third man, one he did not know, but a man wearing a biker vest and sporting a crazy beard had emerged from the van, wielding his own AK. He was just bringing it to bear when Blotter heard a solid "snap," telling him the magazine was seated. He snapped back the bolt, raised the weapon, and opened up again, catching the bearded man in the face before he could fire a shot.

Now, stupidly standing in the middle of the road, the two Hangarounds stared at each other in shock. They had both shot dry at the worst possible moment. The one on the right produced a long magazine for the MAC, slammed it home, then worked the bolt. There was some sort of problem, though.

The Hangaround with the shotgun seemed to have forgotten how to reload it. Or perhaps, he hadn't brought any reloads. Comically, he hefted the shotgun like a club, then reconsidered, dropped it, and began to run.

The running man got five metres before Blotter's AK ripped his back open. The man with the MAC-10 dropped his weapon and put up his hands. Blotter watched as Donnie limped up to him, trailing blood on the gravel, the Browning shaking in his hand.

Now, they were level with the van. It was empty. Smoke and steam poured from the radiator. "Cover him." Blotter ordered Donnie, who nodded. He stepped around the van, finding nothing. Then he walked up to Randy, who was lying on his back, his copious belly soaked in blood, a choking rattle coming from his throat.

Blotter stood over his old associate. Randy's dark eyes searched out his. He raised a hand.

Blotter set the selector to "single shot" and put a bullet in his face. He walked back to Donnie.

The Hangaround had closed his eyes and was mumbling a

prayer. Blotter nodded at Donnie. "Do it."

Donnie fired two shots into the Hangaround's head, and he dropped onto his back. "You okay?" Blotter asked.

Donnie glared at him. "No. I am very fucking far from okay, Blotter. Why'd ye kill her? Huh? Why her? What did she ever do to ye? Am I next, then?" He held open the pistol, its locked-open action showing it was empty. "Look, I'm out! Ye can do it now, ye fucking psycho!"

But Blotter simply slung the rifle over his shoulder and walked back to the car. He opened the trunk and tossed the AK inside. "More of them will come. Get back here Donnie."

Donnie was crying uncontrollably. But, as always, he did as he was told. As they backed away and turned around, leaving five dead people on the road, the rain began to fall.

Blotter tossed a towel to Donnie. "Soak up the blood, Donnie. It doesn't look that bad." He checked the gas gauge. *Enough fuel to do one more job.* Then, it was clean out, and move on. He lit a smoke off the dashboard lighter, aimed for the mountains, and stepped on the gas.

JUNE

10-30

"10-30" is police radio code for an "armed and dangerous" subject. The police officers pursuing Blotter Boorman have no idea what has just transpired in Maple Ridge, and so cannot know just how accurate that designation is...

312 MAIN ST

Barry Olds had just marshalled his troops for battle, now he sat in the conference room, watching them head out onto the road.

He hoped he hadn't understated the dangers. He'd emphasized the need for body armour and shotguns, and he'd gotten a commitment from Munro to have ERT at his beck and call all day. Unless something happened. Which was always the problem with relying on ERT. Murphy's Law meant something *always* happened.

But he felt he'd done his best. The warrants for the remaining properties given up by Theo Solomon were all in play today, an accelerated schedule approved by the Chief. If Blotter Boorman were watching, if he wasn't dead of an OD or a suicide somewhere, this might bring him out to play.

Recent events had shown that the man was not pursuing a strategy of subtlety and restraint. "Wrecking Ball" was more like it.

"Sergeant?" The young clerk steno who'd just started entered the room meekly. She was tiny and dark-haired, and looked like she was sixteen. Barry tried to think of her name and failed.

"Yes?"

"There's a man outside who says he saw something he needs to tell you about. He has your business card."

"Thanks, I'll be right out." He was hoping it was who he thought it was. Barry hadn't thought his speech was all that convincing, but then again, Selfridge was always telling him that convincing people was one of his strong suits. He got up and walked out to the elevator lobby.

There, Charlie Kwok sat, dressed in a suit that must've predated The Beatles. Hell, he'd even brought a hat. The old man stood slowly.

"Sergeant Olds. I thought about what you said. I could not sleep, all night, thinking of Brenda. I will help you."

Barry Olds smiled and shook his hand.

EAST 20TH

Rick Grohmann pulled the LTD under the cover of a broad oak and watched the house down the street. The rain was pounding down now, unhooking branches and dropping them all around the car. "Cats and dogs." He observed.

Bobbi looked at her watch. "Rick, we need to be on that warrant. Seriously, it's timed for 1000 hours."

He lit a smoke off the dashboard lighter, forcing a grimacing Bobbi to roll down the window and get pelted by rain. "I know. I also know ERT is doing the entry. Which means we've got some time. I just want to keep an eye on Marianne, that's all."

Bobbi sighed. Her sometime partner was a complicated beast. One moment, a self-contained army, answering to nobody, pursuing his own, hermetically sealed agenda. The next, showing at least a shadow of the caring protector.

It was something she'd seen in more than a few male cops. The cynic and the saviour, sharing the same headspace. "You know, Rick, she's an adult. She's going to make up her own mind. We can't do it for her."

Rick took a long drag. "She's a child, Bobbi. The kind of fucked-up child this town produces by the bus full. She wouldn't know her own best interest if it crept up and bit her in the ass. And that fucker Tusker is trying to stay on Blotter's good side. He doesn't know that Blotter doesn't have a good side."

"Well, it's almost over. Blotter's got nowhere to run. And the bikers can't be too happy with him."

Rick nodded. "True. But look at the way he's acting. Cornered, doing so much blow he's gotta have a hole in his septum by now. That means he is righteously dangerous. And I just know this is going to be his next stop."

Bobbi squirmed in her body armour. "Damn, this shit is uncomfortable."

Rick laughed. "Does your mother know you talk like that?"

"I try not to bring it home."

The radio squawked. "2339, what's your twenty?" It was Sergeant Bartels, trying to locate them. Rick picked up the mike.

"2339 is en route. ETA five minutes."

"Well, light a fire under it, will ya?"

312 MAIN ST

Barry watched through the one-way glass with Phil LeBretton, as Marvin Yau presented Mr Kwok with a photo lineup.

LeBretton was dressed especially snappily today, Barry thought. "Are you rich or something?"

"No." He adjusted his cufflinks. Barry could count on the fingers of one hand the people he knew who even owned a pair. "But my wife is."

"Ah. Either that, or I figured you were bent."

"You kidding? If I were bent, I'd be on Vice. Murderers are all poor."

In the interview room, Kwok had just stabbed a finger at a face on the photo lineup. "Number 2. That's Blotter. Time to get a warrant."

"You're already set?"

"Yeah, Halperin said all things considered we were good to go once we got a positive ID. Two counts First-Degree Murder, and it's bye-bye Blotter."

"See you on the road?"

"I wish. Three autopsies today, and I can only pawn one off on Marv. Happy hunting."

TERMINAL AND WESTERN

Blotter was relieved to see the ugly face of Gregg O'Brien when he pulled in behind the warehouse. O'Brien was a former boxer, a Cape Breton Islander whose accent was so thick he found Donnie more intelligible. But what made O'Brien invaluable in criminal circles was, in addition to his skills in delivering violence, his skills in cleaning up after it.

Gregg O'Brien was a decent cut doctor, and since they could hardly go to a hospital, the solid, potato-faced man hunkering under the awning from the rain was their next best bet. "Donnie, wake up. We're here. Gregg's gonna take that buckshot out of you."

"Aye...oh fuck, it hurts."

"Shut your whining. Mama's gonna make you shortening bread, you pussy."

"Aye." Donnie was well toasted on Dilaudid now, and whatever pain he was feeling must've been in his mind. With Gregg's help, they got him in the front door, then slowly up the steep stairs.

While Gregg looked at the wound, Blotter poured them all drinks. Gregg took his with gratitude. Donnie noticed. "Oi, am I havin' a pisstank operating on me then?"

Gregg smirked. "You're free ta take yer business elsewhere, bye. Ah'm the only game in town, ya rig."

As Gregg gingerly explored the wound, he engaged in an incomprehensible dialogue with Donnie. He picked up something about Gregg getting his balls kicked in by Rick Grohmann at the Gandy Dancer. Blotter wandered into the bar and turned on the TV. For a fleeting moment, he wondered where Larissa was. He noticed her purse on the bar. *Oh yeah. Probably ought to get rid of that.*

On the TV, they were interrupting their regular programming. Blotter watched, numbly, as he drank his scotch.

Vancouver Police have issued a warrant for 39-year old Neil Boorman, of Vancouver. Boorman is wanted for the murder of two people at an East Side noodle house yesterday. Police say he should be considered "armed and dangerous." If you see him, do not approach, but call the police immediately.

They had an old mugshot of him, from his last time inside. He hated that picture.

So, Murder One then. Twenty-five to life. It was clearly time to exit the stage. But how?

Hadn't he been telling himself he had an exit strategy? Did he really think that bullshit with George was going to fool any halfway decent copper?

Jesus, this fucking coke is doing a number on me. Blotter fought to remember what to do next. There was money in here, that was important. And guns. Had to get those.

And then what? And why the fuck was he here? As if the bikers wouldn't figure out where he was. This was *their* fucking crib, after all.

Gregg. He'd leave Gregg here while he tied up his loose ends. Gregg was smart enough to convince the bikers he'd flown the coop. From the next room, a yelp from Donnie announced that the surgery had begun.

Surgery. Good term. Blotter was going to do some surgery. But first, he was going to take his medicine. He opened the round marble container on the desk, took out a coke spoon and a credit card, and began to lay down lines.

312 MAIN ST

Hours of tension, release, then tension again. Rick Grohmann had taken off his soaking wet gear, lit a cigarette, and sat down to write the letter he'd been putting off all day.

The raids had been a predictable routine of storm and noise by ERT, followed by methodical search and cataloguing by Drug Section. It was monotonous work, Rick's least favourite part of the job. While he tested, weighed, and bagged Blotter's dope, Blotter was out there somewhere, either causing or plotting more mayhem. That bugged him.

What bugged him more was the fact that he'd only have a few more hours as a cop left to do anything about it. Once the *Province* story broke, he was dead meat. For all his bravado, Rick Grohmann knew that he, like any other cop, was entirely disposable if he was embarrassing the department.

And, with the eyes of the world on Vancouver, embarrassment would not be tolerated. He knew the Chief Constable well enough to know that. What was that old saying? One "Oh Shit" cancels a hundred "Atta Boys?"

Something like that.

While the squad room swirled around him, other officers recounting the raids, or just hammering away at reports, Rick started to type his farewell.

To the Chief Constable
Vancouver Police Department

Dear Sir:

As a result of the unfortunate incident detailed in the Province story this morning, I believe it should be apparent that I can no longer serve as an officer in this department. I regret the embarrassment and scorn my actions have brought on this fine organization. For this, I sincerely apologize.

I have enjoyed every moment serving this great department and city. My greatest regret is that I can no longer do so. As my last service to the Police Department, I tender my resignation, effective immediately.

Yours,

Richard Grohmann
Detective # 847

When he was done, he sat and stared at the letter for a long while. Then, he realized that there were tears in his eyes. He stood, suddenly, feeling the room sway a little, and quickly walked out, needing to be sick.

Bobbi Sanghera returned at that moment from the Jail, where she'd finished booking a female prisoner. She found Connolly leafing through a thesaurus. "What's another word for hidden, Bobbi? Olds says I should 'diversify my vocabulary,' whatever that means."

She sat at Rick's desk, peering at the letter. "It means, use different words sometimes. For hidden, try 'concealed,' or 'sequestered.'"

"Huh. 'Sequestered.' I like that one." He resumed typing.

"You seen Grohmann?"

"Yeah, he just went out. Don't know where. I tried asking him a question, but he was tuned out, you know." Connolly punctuated his answer with a loud snap of chewing gum.

Bobbi read the letter, her temples thumping, the room going quiet suddenly. Without thinking, she snatched it out of the typewriter and went into the hall.

"Thanks for the word power, Bobbi!" Connolly called after her.

She found Rick coming out of the men's room, looking wan and pale. "What the fuck is this?" She held the letter out to him.

He leaned against the wall, dabbing his head with a damp paper towel. "It's personal."

"No, no it fucking isn't. You're my partner. You should tell me I'm going out there with a short-timer. Especially now."

"I didn't think you cared."

"Of course, I do. Is this about your ex?"

"Yeah. I beat the shit out of the guy who was screwing her. He filed a report, but the Mounties killed it. Now the media's got a hold of it."

"So, you're just throwing in the towel?"

"Yes. I have my reasons. Can we talk about this somewhere else?"

"You wanna go 99?"

Rick nodded wearily. "Yeah. Then one last check on Marianne. If I'm only around for a few more hours…"

Bobbi cut him off. "Don't commit to that just yet." She held up the letter again. "In the meantime, this goes in my pocket."

Rick managed a tired smile. "Yes, ma'am."

TERMINAL AND WESTERN

Lou Reed droned on the stereo as Blotter sat on the couch, watching Gregg help himself to another line, and Donnie swaying dreamily on the floor to the music.

Just a perfect day
Feed animals in the park
Then later, a movie too
And then home

Oh, it's such a perfect day
I'm glad I spent it with you
Oh, such a perfect day
You just keep me hanging on
You just keep me hanging on

To nobody in particular, Blotter spoke aloud. "I never got this song until I became a junkie."

"You're not a junkie, Blotter." Gregg responded. "Yer' a cokehead, bye. Dat's different."

Blotter started to laugh. "Right." He looked at Donnie, who'd stopped complaining about the pain. Now, his face was a mask of bliss. "Donnie!"

"Aye?"

"Get it together now. We've got a job to do. One more, then we split, okay?"

Donnie nodded, but kept doing his weird little dance. "Where we going, then?"

"The Maritimes, bye!" Gregg announced. "Fuck this town, we'll be the kings of Cape Breton!"

"Aye." Donnie smiled.

"Gregg, give him a rail, will ya? I need mean Donnie. Not happy Donnie."

"Aye." Donnie agreed. "Mean Donnie."

BINO'S RESTAURANT
KINGSWAY

Bino's was a 24-hour favourite of cops, a local chain with a police discount, and the kind of fatty, salty fare that killed more cops by far than guns and knives. Bobbi and Rick took a table at the back, nodding at a cluster of Patrol types on their 99 on the way in.

Outside, the rain had finally stopped. The sun was long gone, the clouds moved on, and the wet pavements glistened in the moonlight. "Full moon." Rick looked out the window. "Figures a shit magnet like me should go out on a full moon. Anything can happen."

"You still believe in that?" Bobbi scoffed.

"Never seen anything to contradict it."

"You given any thought to what you might do if you quit?"

"Fuck if I know. PI maybe? Maybe go back to the Forces, if they'll have me. Anyway, I got money saved. I figure I'll do some travelling, blow it all before Clarissa can get it."

"Good idea. You sure you two are done?"

Rick sighed. "I saw a shrink a couple of weeks ago. *Don't* tell a fucking soul, right? Anyway, I figured maybe she and I were kind of…uh, abnormal, I guess is the word." He looked over the table with the cops. "I get off on her being a slut, and she gets off on being punished for it."

Bobbi swallowed. She had no idea what to say.

"Anyway, the shrink said we were 'co-dependent,' I think was the term. Basically, a fucked-up team. Not healthy."

"I guess not. Look, Rick, I know it's going to be hard. But you're a good cop. You should fight."

"Thanks. But the Chief will make me walk the plank, Bobbi."

"Maybe you should be a pirate, then." Bobbi smiled.

Rick laughed until the food arrived, saving him from further self-disclosure. As they ate, they missed a Buick LeSabre driving past, headed for a little house on East 20th.

JUNE

10-33

"10-33" means "officer needs assistance" in police radio code. In practice, this code is not used lightly, but is only screamed into the radio in the most desperate of situations. It will be hard afterward for any of the officers involved in this 10-33 to imagine a more desperate situation...

312 MAIN ST

Barry Olds looked at his watch, downing the last of a cold and bitter cup of coffee from a mug that read *Pig and Proud.* It was almost 2300 hours, and he still wasn't finished.

The worst part was that Blotter Boorman was still out there. Riding high on coke, no doubt, and armed to the teeth. He'd had to field five phone calls from white shirts, all the way up to Munro, asking him the same question.

"Is he still out there? Well, what are you doing about it?"

Yes, he is. And what I'm doing is paperwork. No, it's the system. I didn't invent it.

He was halfway to falling asleep at his desk, a forgotten cigarette burning in an over-stuffed ashtray, to the sound of Connolly and Dupuis, his only company, pecking away at their typewriters. A ringing phone made him sit up with a start.

"Sergeant Olds."

"Bill Prescott, Maple Ridge GIS. You're the guy listed as the contact on Boorman, right?"

Thanks a lot, Phil. "Yeah, you got something?"

"Couple of our guys went out to a vehicle fire on the property of a known one-percenter, Randy McClarty. When they got there,

there was a vehicle with a couple of obvious scumbags watching them, who took off when they got close. Anyway, the vehicle was shot to shit, and it was a fucking massacre. He's a KA on your warrant for Boorman, so I thought I'd give you a call."

Barry sat up straight. "A massacre? How bad?"

"Five dead, including McClarty, and another patch holder called Lou Vought, a Nomad. Couple of Hangarounds, and a chick."

"Jesus Christ." Connolly and Dupuis had stopped typing and were staring at him now. "A chick?"

"Yeah." Prescott paused. "That's the thing that doesn't fit. She was gagged and her hands were bound, but no signs of sexual assault or anything. Weird. No ID, but we printed her. PIRS shows a couple of suspected prostitution entries associated to a warehouse on Terminal Avenue. Name of Zuzanna Czepicky, if I'm saying that right."

Terminal Avenue. Where Grohmann had boosted Donnie McCrae last week.

"Olds? You there."

"Yeah, yeah. Gimme a second." Barry scribbled furiously and motioned Connolly over. He put a hand over the receiver. "Call the radio room. Get ERT to meet us at Terminal and Western. Grab body armour, shotguns, and a ram, and meet me in the parkade. Go!"

Connolly, eyes wide, went back to his desk and started dialling. "Hey, Olds." Prescott continued.

"Yeah?"

"Be fucking careful. From the looks of the shell casings, one of these scrotes had an AK."

KINGSWAY

Rick Grohmann drove with intent, under rotoscoping streetlights, his last shreds of determination overcoming his profound fatigue.

"They won't be up, Rick." Bobbi dozed in the passenger seat; her little frame curled up like a resting cat. "Now is not the time for an interview."

"Call it a welfare check, then." He lit a smoke off the dashboard lighter. One more to add to the overflowing ashtray. Bobbi rolled down the window in disgust.

"Welfare check. Fine." They pulled off of Kingsway and turned onto the tree-lined street. Ahead, they could see the house. "Shit. Rick?"

"What?"

"The screen door. It's open."

"Fuck!" As they pulled to the curb, the inside of the house lit up with flashes. Four shots, in quick succession, followed by a terrifying scream. Then, one last shot.

Rick was on the radio as Bobbi bailed out of the passenger seat, her .38 already in her hand. "Central, 2339 show us 10-6 at 866 East 20th Avenue, shots fired this location, 10-33."

"10-4 2339, all units in the vicinity 866 East 20th respond Code Three, officers need assistance, shots fired this location."

"Bobbi, hold up, goddamnit!" Rick yelled as he retrieved the shotgun from the trunk. But his partner was already in through the front door, .38 aimed in a combat crouch.

Bobbi walked into a scene of horror. Tusker Taakoiennin sat on his couch, in front of his table, exsanguinated, a massive hole in his neck, and another in his forehead. Marianne was in the entrance hall, crawling on her belly through a thick pool of her own blood, dressed only in her underwear. "Rick!" Bobbi screamed. "Rick!"

From the darkness of the kitchen, Blotter Boorman emerged, wearing black leather gloves and a cattleman's coat, a .357 in a two-handed grip. Bobbi snapped up the .38, but Blotter got off the first shot.

Bobbi saw the flash, then felt the hammer blow to her chest, which send her skidding through Marianne's blood and slamming against the front door jamb. She looked up as Rick Grohmann stepped over her, firing the 12-gauge from the hip at Blotter.

There was a revving engine, a screech of tires, and a series of curses from her partner. Another shotgun blast. Bobbi rolled over and saw Marianne, who struggled to lift her head from the pool of gore. Her left ear was shot off, and black blood bubbled from her lips.

Bobbi reached out for her, stroking her blood-matted hair. "Lay still, Marianne. Lay still."

"Oh…Bobbi…oh, I'm sorry. I'm so sorry." Her head dropped onto the floor, her eyes staring straight through Bobbi.

Rick was yelling into his portable. "Central, 2339, shots fired, officer shot, roll BCAS times three, Code Three! Suspect vehicle brown Buick LeSabre, partial BC plate Alpha Charlie Sierra, two occupants. One is Blotter Boorman. A and D, Central."

"10-4, 2339, BCAS en route. All units, officer shot 866 East 20th Avenue. Suspects in Brown Buick LeSabre. All units, 10-33 in progress, clear the air unless urgent."

The airwaves were now crowded with Patrol units responding, and the night air filled with the sound of sirens. Bobbi reached for the doorknob and pulled herself up, her breaths coming in stabs.

"Bobbi, stay still. Bobbi, goddamnit, stay down."

"Fuck that!" She spat. "Let's go."

"Go? Go where?"

Bobbi touched the hole that the bullet had made in the outside of her vest. A warped piece of lead fell to the floor. "What was... what was Donnie doing at Main and Terminal? Why was he there?"

"Guesswork, Bobbi. You need a fucking doctor, now!"

Bobbi looked down at the body of Marianne Taakoiennin. "No... I need Blotter Boorman. In the fucking morgue."

"Well." Rick put a steadying arm around her. "Let's go then."

TERMINAL AND WESTERN

Behind the warehouse the PIRS system listed as Zuzanna Czepicky's last known address, there was a park for semi-trailers. Barry Olds, riding with Connolly and Dupuis, nosed his LTD in behind a trailer, shut off the ignition, and waited.

"Dupuis, you're light on your feet. Go get a little closer on foot. See if there's any signs of life."

"Light in the loafers, more like." Connolly joked. Dupuis ignored him.

"Got it." Dupuis opened the right rear door and scampered down the line of trailers, pausing behind a cedar bush and staring at the warehouse. After a few minutes, he returned, and gingerly opened the door. "Lights on. No signs of movement. One vehicle parked out back. I got a plate."

"Call it in."

"Central, 2550, run wants and warrants on BC Golf Echo Zulu two niner niner."

"Stand-by." A minute passed. "2550, your plate comes back to a 1975 Ford Pinto wagon, red in colour, registered to a Coleman, Vicki Patricia. Plates and val tag reported stolen as of last month."

Dupuis shook his head. "It's a black Honda Civic." In the background, the radio started to go crazy with urgent calls. "Full moon." Dupuis observed.

"Just our luck. Was that a barricaded gunman in Shaughnessy?" Barry asked.

"Of all places. Even the rich are howling at the moon tonight." Connolly observed.

"Central, this is Sergeant Olds. Any word on my ERT request?"

"That's a negative at this time, Sergeant. ERT is en-route to Shaughnessy."

"10-4." Then, the radio exploded with another gun run, and this time, Barry heard Rick Grohmann's voice on the radio.

"Holy shit." Connolly whispered. "Is he with Sanghera?"

"2339 from 2550, respond." Barry got on the air again.

"2339, go ahead." Bobbi sounded breathless. A siren wailed in the background.

"If you're able, attend 242 Terminal Ave. Code Three."

"We're en-route." Then, a minute later, she was on the air again. "Central from 2339, show us in pursuit, suspect vehicle Brown Buick LeSabre, BC Plate Alpha Charlie Sierra four six eight!"

"2339, be aware, suspects may have an AK-47!"

"10-4."

Barry turned to Connolly and Dupuis. "Check your actions. Put another one up the spout."

EAST 12TH AVENUE

"Central, 2339, now passing Carolina Street, still westbound on East 12th. Speed eighty-five." Bobbi called the chase as they hit another speedbump, the mike almost flying out of her hand. "Where the hell is Patrol?"

"Speed eighty-five?" Rick grinned at her. "You're such a fucking liar. You might make a good cop yet."

Bobbi held on to the dash as they swerved around a petrified driver. "If I said you were doing one-ten, they might ruin all our fun."

"These fuckers are dead meat." He said it with deadly intent, and Bobbi believed him. Up ahead, the LeSabre did a hard right, and turned onto Prince Edward.

"Central, suspect vehicle now northbound on Prince Edward, crossing East 11th."

"He's going for that warehouse, Bobbi. We fucking got him!"

"I hope you're right."

TERMINAL AND WESTERN

Some chases take forever and go nowhere. Others are over in the blink of an eye.

Barry Olds was just about to raise the mike to his mouth and call for Patrol units to attend the scene, subtlety be damned, when a Brown Pontiac LeSabre flew into the parking lot, trailing sparks.

"Shit, that's them. Deploy, and wait. Wait for Grohmann to show."

"Right." Connolly and Dupuis answered in unison, scrambling out of the car to take up positions behind the trailer nearest the building. Olds opened the trunk, slung a 12-gauge over his back, and hefted the battering ram.

As he crept forward, he heard a dog start barking. Two men emerged from the LeSabre, which had parked at an angle behind the warehouse. One man was reedy and fast-moving, his long head topped with a mohawk. The other was more substantial, dirty blond hair, wearing a cattleman's jacket and hefting an AK. *Jesus Christ, the Mounties were right.*

Barry Olds was still digesting the implications of that sort of firepower when an LTD with a screeching siren and a glowing fireball on the dash slammed to a stop behind the LeSabre. Sanghera and Grohmann piled out and went straight for the back door.

What the fuck are they doing? In the warehouse, a head appeared in a window, and in that moment, Barry Olds knew any surprise he had was gone for good. He turned to Dupuis and Connolly. "Hug the wall and get to the front door. Cover the exit onto the street!"

As the two detectives hustled for the side of the warehouse, their shotguns at port arms, Barry hefted the battering ram, and ran across the open lot for the rear door.

When he reached the door, he found Grohmann hugging the wall, shotgun at the ready, and Bobbi Sanghera on the portable, calling for more units. Her raid jacket was slick with blood.

"You okay?"

"It's not mine. He killed the Taakoiennins, Sarge."

Barry nodded. "That's some firepower. ERT is tied up, you know."

"Now or never." Rick insisted.

"I'd argue with you if we didn't already have our balls on the chopping block. This position sucks."

Rick smiled at him. "Well, then. Let's dance."

Shots from the street settled the issue. "Shots fired; shots fired!" Connolly screamed into his portable. Barry hefted the ram and readied to swing.

"Get behind me." Rick nodded at Bobbi. "If it goes to shit, fall back and wait for ERT."

"But..." The objection died on her lips. From the street, the AK had joined in now, and Connolly got on the air again. "10-33! Officer shot!"

Without pausing, Barry swung the ram. The door was metal and didn't give at the first hit. He swung again, breaking the door at the jamb, then caving it with a final kick.

The ram fell to the pavement with a clatter. Rick shouldered his way through, then started taking the steep stairwell two at a time, with Barry close behind, his shotgun aimed high.

Behind the backs of two big men, Bobbi could see little. Feeling inadequate with nothing but a snub-nosed .38 to bear, she plugged on regardless, her breath coming in short stabs, feeling like she was on the Academy obstacle course all over again.

There was a smell, a firing range smell mixed with an iron tang of blood. That, in the years to come, would be the thing she remembered first.

Because what happened next happened so fast, she could never really make sense of it.

Rick was hugging the right side of the stairwell, two-thirds of the way to the top now, and nobody had fired. The shots from the front had slacked off too, and now Bobbi thought, *here comes the AK.*

Barry was on the left, close to the railing, his shotgun at waist height now. Between the two men, Bobbi could finally see the top of the stairwell. The room above was dark, lit only by the blueish light of a TV with it's sound off.

There was a flash, a deafening bang in the echoing stairwell, then another. Rick Grohmann clutched at his neck, his 12-gauge going off, high, showering them all with plaster dust. Barry fired back, one-handed, the 12-gauge bucking in his hand, the gunman at the top retreating.

Barry looked back for a second at Rick, who was halfway down the stairs, reaching for his shotgun. Bobbi leapt over him, trying to keep a steady eye on the top of the stairs. Then, she saw him.

"Sarge!" She must've screamed it, or perhaps only thought it. But, outlined in blue shadow, there was Blotter Boorman, and the AK. She fired, one-handed, then got a proper grip and fired again.

But it was too late. The light and the sound were overwhelming now, like strobes in a disco.

Barry danced like a puppet on the strings of a mad owner. He flew past her, and in that moment, she knew he was dead.

But there was no sign of Blotter. And Rick was on his feet now, his face a mask of animal rage and pain, the shotgun in his two hands. He surged past her, just as the unmistakable mohawk of Donnie McCrae emerged at the top of the stairs.

She fired and fired again until she heard nothing but clicks. Rick fired too, the blast deafening, the ejected shell hitting her in the forehead, causing a moment's panic. *Am I hit? If I were hit there, would I still be thinking?*

Donnie McCrae disappeared in a cloud of gore and plaster dust.

Rick reached the top of the stairs and crouched for cover, feeding shells into the shotgun with a speed and dexterity she'd never seen. "Call it in! And reload!" He yelled.

Bobbi went to her knees and snapped open the cylinder on her .38, feeling in her pocket for a speed loader. She fumbled it at first, then lined up the rounds properly and snapped the cylinder home. Then, heart racing, she looked back at Barry.

He lay, facedown, at the bottom of the stairs, in a spreading pool of blood. Ragged holes dotted the back of his raid jacket, proof positive of the AK's deadly power.

Now, from the front of the house, the hollow ripping sound of the AK came again. *I didn't kill him. I fucked up.*

"Get on the fucking air! Olds is dead! Call it in, Bobbi, we're getting fucking murdered here!"

She reached down for her portable, only to find it smashed in by a bullet. Bobbi let it drop just as two Patrol officers reached the foot of the stairs. They pointed their guns at her. "VPD! VPD! Suspect's gone out the front, he's got an AK!"

Bobbi looked back at where Rick had been. He had gone into the darkened room. *Not without me, you don't.* She charged up the stairs, past the shredded body of Donnie McCrae, past the ghostly light of the TV and the purse of a dead woman, sitting on a coffee table striped with lines of coke. She got to the front entrance stairs, looked down, and saw Rick stepping over a dead body in the entranceway. *Dear God, Connolly or Dupuis?*

She pelted down the stairs, stumbling and almost turning an ankle. The front door glass was shot out, and to her relief it covered the body not of one of her fellow officers, but a man she did not know.

Bobbi stopped for a moment. She looked down at the dead man, who had cauliflower ears and a pirate's red beard. She willed her breathing still and deep. "Combat breathing," they'd called it in the Academy.

Now, she was ready to go. She sprinted into the street. Down Terminal to the east, Patrol units approached, sirens screaming, red and blue lights reflecting off the pavement. To her right, Connolly and Colleen Strzok were loading a limp and pale Dupuis into a PC.

The pavement was littered with spent shells and casings. She ran, now seeing two men in the distance, heading for the glowing orb of the Expo Dome.

JUNE

GUILTY AS CHARGED

Most police officers never have to take a human life. But when a criminal like Blotter Boorman decides to kill one of their own, most, including Rick Grohmann and Bobbi Sanghera, are entirely prepared to return the favour...

THE EXPO DOME

Two men ran at a loping pace now, conserving what energy they had left for the confrontation both knew was coming.

Blotter Boorman knew it was over. There was no exit strategy now, no road trip to Cape Breton. What the fuck was he going to do, swim to Japan? Worse still, he was leaking from the scalp and the left arm, with God knows how much cop lead in him. His coke high was gone now, replaced only with a bottomless weariness, and a murderous determination not to surrender. He was sure the cop behind him would be more than happy to oblige.

For Rick Grohmann, the chase was literally running down the clock. He had a curious, fleeting sense of himself as Cinderella, the giant orb ahead as the pumpkin carriage, the clock approaching midnight.

If he'd have had the air to spare, he'd have laughed.

Rick Grohmann's only exit strategy was to end Blotter Boorman. Beyond that, his future was a blank. He was leaking, too, the superficial wound in his neck bleeding more than he would've thought possible, sticky blood now coating the inside of his t-shirt all the way to his tailbone.

Briefly, as Blotter staggered across Main Street, and a cabbie screeched on his brakes to avoid hitting him, he considered simply shooting the motherfucker in the back. *Why not?*

It would be nice and legal. He'd murdered a policeman, as well as two civilians, probably more. And he was hefting a cannon that would keep half the ERT pinned down all night.

But that was not the way, Rick Grohmann thought. He had something to say. He wanted to give the man a chance to die with his boots on. But die, he must.

Now, Blotter disappeared around the curve of the Dome building, beyond which there was only a promenade and a railing. And the cold black water of False Creek. He slowed his pace, coming across the blood trail Boorman had left.

Rick stopped and thought. Around that corner, was death. Probably why Blotter had lured him here. Better to wait for backup. He turned and signalled to Bobbi. *Over here.*

She stopped, her breaths coming in ragged heaves. "Where? Where is he…"

He put a finger to his lips. "Around the corner. See the trail?"

She nodded. "Ambush."

"Right." He hefted the shotgun and checked the action, then made a decision. "He's expecting me to follow. So, I will. You go the other way. If I go down, you kill him, understood?"

"Rick, no…"

He put a hand on her shoulder. "Somebody has to do it. Since I outrank you, it oughta be me."

"Or, we could just wait for backup."

"No. I need this. You need this, too."

She nodded emphatically. "He killed Barry. And Marianne. Fuck him. See you on the other side."

"Okay, partner." Rick smiled sadly as she ran into the darkness, then held his shotgun ready and walked slowly around the curve of the building.

Down at the Plaza of Nations, the partiers were still going strong. On Main and Terminal, a knot of Patrol units had assembled, no doubt calling for them on the radio, no doubt telling them to wait for ERT.

Like the man said, *I wasn't even in their fucking army anymore.* He looked down to where the blood trail ran out, in the alcove for a fire exit. Hesitating a moment, he stepped around, sweeping with his barrel, seeing nothing but a bloody towel and a spent AK magazine.

Rick Grohmann was catching his breath when the shooting started. Now, he ran, heedless, headed for the sounds, convinced he'd gotten his partner killed.

Then, he stopped short. Under the lights of the dome, Blotter Boorman stood in the open, cursing and fighting to clear a jammed AK. There was no sign of Bobbi, but from around the corner there was the sound of spent brass hitting concrete.

"Technical difficulties, Blotter?" Rick raised the shotgun and took aim. "Too fucking bad."

Rick was pressing the trigger when Blotter spun rapidly, and the AK sprang to life. Rick felt a hot stab in his thigh, saw his shotgun blast hit home, the AK flying out of Blotter's arms.

Now, calm, for a moment. Rick was on his knees, reaching for his .38, the 12-gauge lying between him and Blotter. Blotter leaned on the railing, looking at the shotgun, a steady pump of blood coming from his left arm.

Blotter was closer. He staggered over to the shotgun as Rick struggled to free his revolver, and he was two steps away when Bobbi Sanghera shot him in the back.

Blotter stopped, a look of astonishment on his face, like he wanted to say something and now never would. He fell face first over the shotgun and died.

Bobbi rushed from the shadows and came to Rick's side. "You're hit bad."

"No...oh, yeah." He looked down at the wound in his thigh. "Fuck, that's my femoral."

After that, he remembered nothing else, except how cold Vancouver could be when you were close to the water.

For an Edmonton boy, it was a revelation.

EPILOGUE
THE FRONT PAGE

In a television show, the end of the June 1986 shootout at Terminal and Western would be just that. The end. But for officers involved in such events in real life, there is no real end. The repercussions of such a night will follow them for the rest of their lives. Some will respond better than others. In police work, there are precious few happy endings...

VANCOUVER GENERAL HOSPITAL

Rick Grohmann was toying with the machine that was supposed to give him all the morphine he wanted, when he wanted it. "Hey, nurse? Nurse?" He rattled the cage of the pissed-off, menopausal witch they'd inflicted on him. "This thing is broken."

The nurse, whose name he thought was Phyllis, or something else unattractive, turned in a slow burn move. Her hairy upper lip twitched. "Cowboy, if that thing actually gave you all the morphine you wanted, everybody would leave this hospital an addict."

"With this kind of service, it's a wonder anyone leaves this hospital at all."

The lip twitched again. "Pardon me, Detective?"

"Uh…nothing. I guess I can suck it up."

"Of course." Phyllis gave him a phony smile. "After all, you are a hero policeman."

Rick shrugged glumly. "That's me." Rick thought he'd met his match last night. Turns out, it was today. Phyllis left the room, and he heard a familiar voice.

"Excuse me, nurse, is this where Detective Grohmann is?"

"Are you his partner?"

"Yes, ma'am."

"You should get a medal."

She entered, carrying a ridiculous bouquet and a box of chocolates, wearing a summer dress. Rick did a double take. "You're a girl."

"Sometimes." She shrugged. A newspaper landed in his lap. "Thought you might want to read the front page of the *Province*."

"Not sure I do." Reluctantly, he unfolded the paper. A picture of the bloody scene of the shootout was topped by a screaming headline:

VETERAN COP, THREE SUSPECTS DIE IN EXPO SHOOTOUT

Two other cops wounded; expected to live

Rick broke down and sobbed. "I guess…I guess he really did take one for me. In more ways than one."

Bobbi sat on the bed and put her arm around him. "More than that, Rick. You're a hero. That's all they can talk about in there. You know the media, you can either be a brutal cop or a hero cop. Not both. Guess Lawrence Dyck will have to get his free publicity elsewhere."

He composed himself and held her hand. "I'm not the hero. You are. You saved my life, Bobbi. Thank you."

She set the box of chocolates in front of him. "Better eat these now. If you pass out, Connolly will sneak in and steal them all."

"Fat bastard. Guess he's a hero too, huh? Connolly." Rick shook his head.

"Yeah, he is." Bobbi grudgingly agreed. "You know what the crazy thing is?"

"What?"

"According to the Mounties, a biker hit squad showed up five minutes after we got there, then turned tail and left." She shook her head. "If we'd been a little slower…"

Rick felt himself on the verge of tears again. He saw Clarissa lingering in the doorway. "Ah, fuck this job. Next time, I'll let the bikers do the dirty work." He let his voice drop to a whisper. "I've got a visitor."

She looked back at the doorway and took the hint. "Okay. I gotta get going. See you around?"

"Sure. You never know."

"No." Bobbi's eyes had a faraway look, and he could tell she'd been crying too. "You never do." She was almost out the door when he called to her.

"Constable Sanghera?"

"Yeah?"

"You immigrants make pretty damn good cops. No offense."

She smiled. "I told you. I was born in Surrey." She waved and disappeared. When his wife came in, Rick Grohmann made small talk, and tried to be nice.

But his mind was somewhere else. He wondered when that morphine would kick in again.

From the nurse's station, a faint tune made its way to his ears, while outside his window, drizzle fell on Expo City.

Help me to decide
Help me make the most
Of freedom and of pleasure
Nothing ever lasts forever
Everybody wants to rule the world

BARRY OLDS *was buried with full honours in one of the largest funerals in the Department's history. Staff Sergeant Selfridge played the pipes, and when he played "Danny Boy", there wasn't a dry eye in the house. Two schools and a scholarship are named after him. His son, Tim, was sworn in as a VPD officer in 1993.*

RICK GROHMANN *was promoted to Sergeant in 1989, but alcoholism, marital issues, and chronic Post-Traumatic Stress Disorder took a toll on his career, and he retired on a medical pension in 1998. He committed suicide in 2000.*

BOBBI SANGHERA *resigned from the Vancouver Police Department in 1991 and began a new life as a secondary school teacher. She is married with two children and lives in Abbotsford.*

OTHER WORKS BY THE AUTHOR

FICTION

THE WILL BRYANT THRILLERS:

SOUTHERN CROSS

BACK IN SLOWLY

THE WOLF OF PENHA

ONLY THE DEAD

SPECTRUM

OTHER WORKS:

GOODTIME CHARLIE

WHEN YER NUMBER'S UP

BOMBER'S MOON

SLOWLY, THE WORLD BURNS, WHILE I HELP TO FAN THE FLAMES

THE TROIKA OF OSIP TEITELBAUM

THE STALE MIRACLE

NON-FICTION

ACTS AND OFFENCES: OPINION, 2017-2020

A LIFE ON THE LINE

COMING SOON

AN UNEARTHLY GLOW: CRITICAL MAN, AND OTHER NUCLEAR LULLABIES

Made in the USA
Monee, IL
12 March 2021